Unclaimed Acre
a novel

Bryce Gibson

Copyright© 2014 by Bryce Gibson

All rights reserved. No part of this book may be reproduced in any form without the author's written consent.

This is a work of fiction. All characters, places, names, and events either are a product of the author's imagination or are used fictitiously.

Cover Design by Humblenations.com

ISBN-13: 978-14997119925
ISBN-10: 1499719922

Visit the author online at BryceGibsonWriter.com

"The heart has its reasons which reason knows nothing of."
- Blaise Pascal

"Love is a fire. But whether it is going to warm your heart or burn down your house, you can never tell."
- Joan Crawford

prologue

WHEN LEVI Stanley first regained consciousness he had no idea where he was.

In fact, there were only a few things that he knew for certain.

One, the building that he was in was dark.

Two, underneath the smell of old timber there was another. It was one of grimy auto parts. It was the kind of odor that sticks to the hands and the clothes of mechanics.

And three, his head pulsated with agony.

As his vision adjusted to the darkness he began to look around at his surroundings and realized that he was lying on the slats of a hardwood floor. From what he could tell through the resonating pain that shot from his cranium and throughout the entirety of the rest of his body, the confinement seemed to be that of a single room structure. He could see that on the other side of the windows, the sky was pitch-black. There was the occasional flash of distant lightning. The lightning was the first thing that caused him to begin to remember.

Hadn't there been severe storm warnings for the area?

Levi twisted his head to the side and winced with agony. Even though he tried, he wasn't able to stand. His wrists and ankles had been tied. The length of old binding twine itched where it touched his skin.

Was he in some type of convention center?

He looked up at the ceiling and saw that there was a simple x shaped wooden chandelier that held a single, flickering candle on each of its four arms. The lighting fixture was hung by a much thicker piece of rope than what tied his wrists and ankles. The light was something that he vaguely recognized, but from when?

Even though the sight of the old light fixture stirred on the fringes of familiarity, it wasn't Levi's current location that was brought to mind. Somewhere in his memory, a long time ago, the light was somehow associated with the small town where he grew up. That was it, the realization. He was in Devlin. Then bit by bit other pieces of *before* began to slam to the surface.

The last thing that he remembered before blacking out was being in his family's house. He had come back to sell the property. He could recall someone being in the house with him. Two people actually, one had been his assailant. The person had arrived unannounced. Levi could remember being surprised and terrified of the sudden entrance. It had only been a moment before he was attacked. He had not been able to see the face. All he could remember was seeing a dark clad figure approach him just before he was thwacked on the side of his head.

The impact had left a lasting impression. Even though he couldn't reach his hand up to feel the injury, he could tell that a huge knot had come up where the instrument had made contact with him. He could feel the blood and the heat radiating from the spot as it throbbed with his every pulse. Had it been a piece of wood that he had been struck with? It seemed more solid, a metal pipe maybe?

The increasing wind caused tree limbs to scratch at the outside of the structure. Levi wondered how far away from another person he was. He wondered if there were any houses nearby. He thought about screaming for help. His eyes scanned around the room. It seemed that he was indeed alone.

Where the hell am I? Levi thought about his surroundings and then it hit him. He had been there before. It was only a few short miles from where he grew up. Of course the last time that he had been there it had been on Halloween night many years earlier. He had been in high school at the time. He was in Mercer Creek Baptist Church. It was an abandoned building that had been rumored to be haunted for as long as he could remember. It was the place that all the kids dared one another to venture to late at night.

But who had brought him there now? And why?

At the opposite end of the building, one of the two doors swung open and a silhouetted figure stood in the entranceway. Levi could feel the other's glare on him. He could sense the hatred from across the width. He knew that it was the same person who had already knocked him unconscious and was now coming back to finish the intentions. Levi closed his eyes and wished for help. When he reopened his eyelids the figure was already standing over him.

part one
ghost story

I

Two days earlier, Thursday...

FROM WITHIN the dark of the bedroom there was a cry, a whimper. Levi woke and there was a new sound, that of thick claws scratching against the wooden door. Out of context, being woken by the sound of claws against wood could be sinister, something of nightmares, but within the safe realm of reality it was a strangely comforting sound. Craven, Levi's five year old basset hound was asking to be let out. Levi looked at the clock that sat on the bedside table and flung the sheets and comforter aside before stepping out of bed. It was time to get up anyway. Light from the just rising sun was beginning to creep through the slats of the window blinds. Levi put on yesterday's pair of jeans, placed an old trucker cap over his disheveled brown hair, and stepped into his sneakers before opening the door.

"Morning, love," Levi's roommate Paige was walking toward him down the small condo's narrow hallway. She had a freshly brewed, steaming cup of coffee in her hand and was already dressed for work in a pair of black slacks and a blouse that was an identical shade. A white towel was wrapped around her head, drying her recently washed hair. She smelled of over-fragrant bath soap. Levi thought that it smelled of flowers, maybe a hint of rose petals. But then there was an undercurrent of cotton candy. On their own, each of the two fragrances was enticing, but when put together into one scent it just caused Levi to be confused. Paige stopped and sipped at her coffee. "When will you be back?"

"I'll have to stay the night, maybe two, just to get things in order. I'm supposed to meet with the real estate agent later today." Levi kneeled down, clasping a brown, leather leash onto Craven's collar. The dog patiently sat at Levi's side until the familiar sound of the leash's metal clip could be heard and then Craven jumped to his feet.

Paige nodded and sipped more coffee. "Will you call me when you get there?"

"Will do," Levi said. He already had his back turned to Paige and was walking down the hallway toward the living room, approaching the front door.

"And Levi," Paige called from the other room. "Call me when you're on your way home, OK? Maybe we could do something when you get back? Go out to dinner, maybe?"

"I'll let you know. See you later." Levi and Craven stepped into the common hallway of the building. None of the other residents were out yet. As he and Craven walked toward the end of the hallway where the steps were located, Levi could hear muffled sounds from behind some of the closed doors. The morning news, laughter, the closing of kitchen cabinets all intermingled together into the daily cacophony of the world waking up.

Outside, the day was already hot even though the first day of summer had only been a couple of weeks earlier and the sun had just peeked over the horizon of the city's tallest buildings. In fact, the past few days had been some of the hottest in Atlanta's history. The weatherman on the local news had reported on the previous night's broadcast that people should take extreme precautions against the unusually early heat wave; stay indoors as much as possible and drink plenty of fluids the man had said.

Even though a large city park was easily within walking distance, Levi led Craven to the apartment's community green space. Craven preferred the wider open space of the park to what the apartment had to offer. And Levi liked it better too. He liked to take Craven there so that he could watch the picnickers, joggers and other dogs, but that day there wasn't enough time to make the walk.

Levi sat on a raised concrete wall as Craven walked along the sidewalk as far as the leash would let him travel. The dog sniffed at a bed of red geraniums before stepping off the concrete and onto the soft turf of green grass. Car horns blared on the nearby streets as people tried to get to work. Everywhere that Levi looked people in work clothes were beginning to emerge from behind closed doors and around corners. The city was coming alive around him. Everybody seemed to be so busy with their lives. Just two weeks earlier Levi had been one of those people.

"Levi, I'm going to have to let you go," Scott Rankin had

said as he slid the termination notice across the width of the mahogany desk. "Because of downsizing," he began to explain in his next statement.

That day, sitting in his supervisor's large office that overlooked the cityscape, Levi had been devastated. It seemed that everything was being taken away from him. He had worked so hard to make a name for himself in the city and then with one piece of paper it had been brought to a crashing halt. Levi had been fortunate enough to have Paige as a friend. She also worked at the office and was willing to offer her condo's spare bedroom until Levi was able to get back on his feet. Since then he had spent countless hours on the internet job searching and sending his resume out to various companies, but nothing ever materialized. Even the interview that he had gone on the previous week, one that he was sure he had nailed, had gone unanswered. And now with his bank account teetering on the edge of nothing there was only one option that he could think of.

Even though the return to Devlin would be brief, he was only going to settle things, to sell the house that had been in his family for generations, just the idea of stepping foot within the town limits sent Levi's nerves racing. So many things from his past were starting to creep back into his memory. It's not that any of it was ever really gone or forgotten; it was just that until recently, within the past couple of years, it had all simply been placed away in a safe spot of his consciousness, rarely to be thought about. Then little, unexpected things began to creep back in, haunting him, spinning his mind back in time.

Then it hadn't been long before the dreams started.

It had been in the midst of a dream when Levi walked down the center of a long dirt road. He was flanked on either side by the tall pines and oak trees that stood across the sides of the stagnant water filled ditch banks. The night air was pleasant, not yet crisp but no longer hot. There was no light except for the moon and that of the self made lantern that Levi carried within his right hand. The lantern had been constructed from a large, bright yellow summer squash. The squash's end had been sliced off and the fleshy pale insides and nearly white seeds had been scooped out, leaving only a hollow shell. Inside was a single flickering tea light. Levi carried the lantern by the long, crooked, handle shaped neck, letting the orange candle flame illuminate the ground where he stepped.

Further down the road a tall figure of a man appeared and began to approach Levi. As Levi got closer it became clear that it was his grandfather that stood before him. Within a moment, Levi and Maxwell were face to face. Being that Levi had never known or even seen Maxwell in person, the man that stood in front of him was the spitting image of the lone photo that he had ever seen of him. The man was younger than Levi, probably only twenty years old. He wore a light colored shirt and suspenders. His hair was neatly parted and shined with pomade. Levi could smell the aftershave and cologne coming from him. The scents were so pronounced that they overtook that of the nearby pond. The moonlight cast a white pallor over the other man's flesh, yet the candle light from Levi's lantern gave him the occasional flicker of warmth. Maxwell's hand reached out to Levi. Held within his grasp was a book. Levi recognized the offering immediately as being the copy of an old almanac that had been in his family for generations. Levi reached his free hand out to the tome. As his fingers wrapped around the book, his grandfather's hand did not let go. Instead, Maxwell placed his other hand on top of Levi's. There was movement behind Maxwell, a rustle of leaves. When Levi looked, he saw the figure of a blonde woman. Her back was turned and she was walking away from where he stood. Her white dress dragged through the dust and dirt. With her left hand she motioned for Levi to follow, but when he tried to walk his feet wouldn't budge.

That was when Levi had woken up to the sound of Craven scratching at the door.

Levi looked at his watch and sighed upon the realization that even with the time that he had he would still be in a rush to grab a shower, pack an overnight bag, and get on the road in time to meet the realtor at the scheduled time. He knew that he would be stuck in rush hour traffic, that the I-85 would be gridlocked before he would even be able to get out of the city. Levi had lived in Atlanta long enough though to know that he had to allow enough leeway time for travel. He stood from the concrete seat. "OK, buddy. Let's go."

Craven obeyed and scampered alongside Levi as they went back inside. The apartment was empty. Paige had already left for work. Levi picked up his cell phone that he had left sitting on the kitchen counter and saw that he had a new text message. It was from Paige. It was a reminder. Paige was not the kind of person that would ever succumb to the silliness of the typical texting lingo like using the number *4* instead of the actual word *for,* and so in a correctly spelled and punctuated sentence she had typed:

> Levi, please be careful. Remember what I said about how it is sometimes hard for people to let things go. Call me!

☐

SEVERAL HOURS later, Levi's dented blue car had already passed by fields of ripe peaches, fluffy white cotton and acres of the produce that was Devlin's claim to fame, bright yellow summer squash. The time was already later in the morning but many of the orange flowers on the vines were still standing open. Levi, like most people from the town, knew that there was only a narrow window of time in the morning hours where the blossoms were open and pollination could occur. Bees and other insects would move from the male pistons and transfer pollen to the female flowers. There were some gardeners that woke at sunrise to pollinate the plants in their backyard beds by hand. Some used a soft bristled paint brush while others used the found feathers of red birds or wrens to move the pollen from one flower to another. The fields though were too big for such a delicate task and the farmers had to rely on nature to take its course. And it looked like things were turning out just fine. Scattered among the healthy green and orange were countless ripe squash waiting to be picked by the wavy line of workers who were making their way across the fields from left to right, snipping the vegetables off with rusty clippers and tossing them into woven baskets.

Levi's car was now emerging from a dense copse of trees. The gnarled, outreaching limbs of the pecan trees that stood on each side of the asphalt had formed a cover over a short stretch of the road. The car rolled into an intersection and braked at the stop sign. Diagonally from where Levi sat there was an old gas station. Other than the store, the intersection was surrounded by farmland and woods. At the stop sign Levi turned the car left onto the road that would eventually lead him directly to his destination. He didn't travel far before the low fuel light came on. His mind was so worked up that the sudden dinging was an alarming sound that caused Levi's heart to skip a beat. Craven was sitting in the passenger seat and tilted his head and looked at the dashboard, searching for the source of the sound.

    Levi had known for a while that the gas tank was running near empty, but he had been so caught up in both his thoughts and the country music within the car that he had let it slip his mind that he needed to refuel. He couldn't remember how far it was to the next station, and wasn't even sure if the *next* one was even still there, so he pulled the car over to the side of the road, checked for any oncoming traffic from each direction, and did a u-turn back to the gas station that was at the just passed intersection. The store was old and seamed to have a permanent coat of grease and grime on every surface. In the parking lot there was a weathered, leathery faced man who was sitting on the tailgate of his rusted pickup. Baskets of peaches and squash were lined precariously along the makeshift wooden platforms that he had constructed in the bed of the truck. The man sat patiently waiting for the produce to be purchased. After pulling up to the pump Levi turned off the engine and stepped out of the car. The hot July humidity crashed into him. The pavement smelled of heat and gasoline. He reached to the door and cranked the window down to just a narrow crack at the top so that Craven would be able to get a circulation of air within the car. To Levi's dismay, the gas pump had a handwritten paper attached to it stating *CREDIT NOT WORKING PAY INSIDE*. Levi sighed and turned back to the car. He leaned down to the slit at the top of the window and whispered to the dog, telling Craven that he would be right back.

    After paying for the gas and returning to the car, Levi placed the nozzle into the gas tank. As the tank filled, Levi looked around at his surroundings. Fields and trees stood on all four sides. Far in the distance there were several large farm houses. The gas station was not near any other major highways or interstate. It seemed to exist solely for the purpose of the locals. It was a place for picking up a late night jug of milk, live bait for fishing, or for the teenagers of Devlin to buy beer and condoms. Like the other three sides, directly across the street from the gas station there used to be farmland, but now it was a picture of neglect. A rusting, once green combine that was used to harvest grains sat at the edge of the trees. Poke weeds that were nearly half as tall as the hulking piece of farming equipment shot up all around its settled mass. Levi could vividly remember when it used to be an abundant field of wheat that grew where the trees and weeds now stood. It seemed like only yesterday. How had the land gone through so much change without him noticing? He tried to remember what family owned the land and wondered when and why they had given up and let their livelihood slip into its current state.

The outdated, rotating meter on the gas tank began to slow down, indicating that he was nearly reaching his prepayment of twenty dollars. After the pump clicked off, Levi replaced the nozzle and got back into the car.

"See. I told you I'd be right back," he told Craven.

The dog answered by tilting his head to the side and perking his ears.

"Soon this will all be taken care of and we'll be back at home before you know it."

Not long after resuming the drive, the speed limit signs showed that the maximum speed was getting lower, indicating that they were getting nearer to the beginning of the town limits. Levi drove past a fast food restaurant and a car dealership. The road led him underneath the old train trellis and before he knew it he was rounding the curve and the main part of the town was opening up before him. A *WELCOME TO DEVLIN* sign was on the right side of the road; it was simple black lettering on a white background. A scattering of yellow squash had been painted across the bottom.

A white picket fence ran alongside the street and sidewalk. Ancient, large plantation houses stood a short distance from the road. Along the same street there was a bank and several businesses. It was weird to think that at the time that the houses had been built the land around each of them had been plowed and cultivated instead of serving as plots for brick buildings that would serve as the base for various businesses many years later.

Within the old buildings that stood around the square there was a diverse assortment of them that were still in operation. There was a diner, several antique stores, a hardware store, a veterinarian, and a finally, an old library that was situated on one corner. Sadly, a handful of buildings were vacant. The center of the grassy square held a gazebo. American flags were standing upright from each of the power poles that stood around the square. A yellow banner was stretched across the road. *SQUASH FESTIVAL - FIRST SATURDAY IN JULY* was spelled out in green letters that were bordered in black. Levi was surprised to see that the annual festival was still held in the town even after so many years.

Directly in front of Levi was the brick courthouse that stood on the corner of the town square. Like many of the buildings, the courthouse was a monument to the history of the town. The traffic light in front of the courthouse turned red and Levi pressed down on the brake pedal, bringing the car to a screeching and grinding stop. It was mid morning and there were very few people milling around the square. Levi presumed that most of the adults of the town would already be at work by that time of the morning and the kids had probably yet to emerge from the confines of their homes.

From Levi's left, a red pickup truck crept through the intersection. He could see that both the passenger and the driver were studying him. Even though he didn't recognize either the man *or* the woman, each of them seemed to be about his age. He wondered for a moment if they recognized *him*. After the truck passed, Levi turned right. It was only a short distance before he turned the car to the right again, onto the road that would lead him to the reason that he was there, 3 Cucurbit Street.

☐

THE HOUSE was the third on the right side of the narrow, unlined road. It was nestled in between two larger homes that had been built much later than the construction of the Stanley house. At one time, a long time before, the land surrounding the house was in Levi's family and was used for planting rows of squash that stretched nearly as far as the eye could see. In fact, it was where the still flourishing squash industry of Devlin began. Over the course of the past century, due to increased in-town construction, the farms had been pushed outward, into the more rural areas where they were now located. Levi's family hadn't owned any farmland in decades, only the small lot that the house stood on. And all around town where there was once farmland, there were now homes that were in close proximity to one another just like those on each side of the Stanley house. Judging by the looks of the two neighboring houses' exteriors, each of them was happily occupied. In stark contrast to the recently mowed lawns and tidy flower beds of the homes that it was sandwiched in between, the white picket fence that stretched around the small yard of the Stanley house was not in the best of shape. Thick, abundant vines of ivy were weaving their way in and out of the peeling boards that were scattered with green patches of growing moss and lichen.

Levi pulled into the driveway that led up to the side of the house and parked the car. The gravel of the driveway had weeds shooting up in countless places. Levi hesitated before opening the car door and when he finally did so the heat and humidity of the air crashed onto him again, just as it had when he had stepped from the car at the gas station. Almost immediately upon standing from the interior of the car, mosquitoes attacked his bare arms. He swatted the insects away, only for them to return a split second later. Levi took note to himself that he would need to find some bug repellent and then thought how foolish and naïve it had been of him not to bring any.

Had he really forgotten so many realities of a small town South Carolina summer that the sure threat of mosquitoes had eluded him? And that year promised to be worse than usual. The past couple of weeks had brought a historic amount of rain to the area and all of the standing water had created a mosquito breeding ground.

He attached the leash to Craven's collar and let the dog jump out of the driver's side of the car. He watched as Craven raised his snout and sniffed the air. It made Levi happy to see the dog enjoying the cleaner atmosphere than what he was accustomed to. Levi followed suit and instinctively did the same. The air *did* smell different than it had in Atlanta. It smelled cleaner. It smelled familiar.

In the distance there was the sprink, sprink, sprink of irrigation. Like every summer of childhood that Levi could remember the smell of the pond that the water was being siphoned from permeated the air. Aside from the smell of pond water there was another, it was one of rot. All along the county roads in the summer months, squash and other produce would often roll out of the baskets and tumble from the trucks and tractors that were transporting them. The vegetables would splat onto the asphalt where they would eventually begin to decompose under the hot sun, filling the air with a pungent smell of decay. Levi closed his eyes and as he inhaled the air once again he was briefly taken back in time. He could have been five years old, or ten, or eighteen, or any where in between. Even though it was a smell of fishy water and rotting vegetables, it nonetheless smelled undefiled. The stink of the city that he had become familiar with had not invaded the town of Devlin and filled the air with the foul odor of metal construction and vehicle exhaust. And then Levi was surprised at the sudden, uncontrollable thought that came to him next.

For a brief second he thought that the air of Devlin smelled like home.

But it *wasn't* home anymore, he reminded himself. It used to be, but never would be again.

A moment later he popped open the trunk and removed his carry bag. It was a small bag, just big enough for a couple changes of clothes and some essential toiletries. He threw the bag's strap over his shoulder and picked up his laptop. Several rubber bands held a clipped together stack of papers to the top of the closed computer. After slamming the trunk, Levi turned to look at the tall, single story house for the first time in two years. The weathered, aging white of the siding, the overgrown lawn, the unused driveway, it all seemed to be falling apart where it stood. The place looked haunted, so much so that it could just as easily be the set of a horror movie that he had somehow wandered onto instead of the house where he had grown up. He wondered if the kids along the street had come to be afraid of the house, if it was on its way to becoming its own legend similar to that of Anna Moore, the ghost that haunted the grounds around Mercer Creek Church. He wondered what kind of stories the kids had concocted surrounding the seemingly perpetual vacancy of the place. He wondered if they thought that his mother's ghost was stuck there, hovering about the porch and yard during starry moonlit nights.

Levi was apprehensive about facing the memories that lingered around the property. Ghosts of the past were everywhere. Of course they weren't the same type of ghosts that Levi imagined the kids of the town would be afraid of. Theirs were flights of fancy, just crazy, cock and bull stories they made up to scare one another. But Levi's ghosts were real, more real than those of a ten year old boy anyway. It wasn't hovering spirits that he thought about. What haunted the house were wisps of memory and experience. He would later come to see that they were everywhere he looked, in every room, and each square inch of the property. Some of the memories were so vivid that they seemed like only yesterday, while others were blurry and were now fading into a dim haze that made it hard to know what had been real, made up, or only imagined. It was as if everything that he had ever done, seen, or experienced was imbedded within the structure of the house itself. It was in the trees, in the grass and even the dirt of the yard.

For the past couple of years his own past had been haunting him. It had followed him from Devlin and back to Atlanta. Even when he tried not to think about any of it, the past would creep up on him like a wraith and try to wrap him in its clutches. It tugged at him in torment. Sometimes it would linger about the bedroom while he was trying to sleep, keeping him awake, hovering over him. In those moments even if he tried to think about something else, anything else, the awareness of the ghosts was still there. He knew that no matter how hard he tried he would never be rid of them. His eighteen years in Devlin would always be with him. In Atlanta, he was over two hundred miles from the town, but the knowledge of the house continued to nag at him nonetheless. Sometimes it was as if the house itself seemed to call out to him over the distance. Lying in bed with his eyes closed he could picture it, standing dark and empty for the first time in decades. He knew that far away the house was there, wanting him back. It was tumultuous, being that far away from something and not being able to rid it from your thoughts. And other times, like just the night before, the ghosts would even invade his dreams, sometimes placing him on a dirt road with only a lantern carved from a squash to light his way.

He thought that selling the house and property would be killing two birds with one stone. Not only would it give him money to get back on his feet, but it would also be a way of exorcising his demons, so to speak. Selling would sever the final tie that he had to Devlin. And that was, what he thought at the time, exactly what he needed to do. Hopefully soon the house would be sold and it would all be history. Maybe then he could put the past away and move on to the next part of his life, never looking back.

Levi and Craven finally began to follow the sunken stone pavers that led from the driveway to the side of the house where the slatted gate was connected to the fence by two rusted hinges. Levi lifted the latch and pushed the gate inward. It barely budged. The hinges screeched. He pushed again, harder this time, and the gate went a little further, ripping and pulling the thick weeds and vines that in their unharmed growth had weaved in and out of the bottom boards.

The front yard was even worse than what Levi had imagined. It had only been just over two years since anyone had lived in the house, but the neglect had taken its toll. Thick weeds were everywhere, nearly overtaking the grass. The huge oak tree in the corner had young saplings shooting up from the ground all around its base. Because of the shade from the tree, a lushly green lawn had never been able to grow in the yard. Instead, wild yellow dandelions and purple petunias had always grown freely each spring and summer, but when his mother had been alive she had always kept them snipped back to a manageable area, allowing space for basil to grow. Basil was an herb that she had always loved. Jill Stanley had never been great at gardening, but like most people that tried, basil was something that she seemed to be able to grow without fail. She used the fresh picked leaves in recipes ranging from salads to marinades for grilled steak. This was the first time that Levi had ever known that basil plants were not growing bush size in the yard. This year though, as opposed to the absent basil, the dandelions and petunias seemed to be almost rampant, spreading halfway across the lawn. The stepping stones were barely visible because of the overgrowth, but Levi knew the path so well that he barely had to look down at where he was walking.

When Levi ascended the wooden steps that led to the front porch, the one on top creaked under the weight of his foot. It was a sound that he had never noticed before and wondered again if the house was slowly but surely coming down. He looked at his feet and noticed that the deep green paint of both the porch floor and the steps was chipping and peeling up in various spots. The white walls and railings were in the same state of upset. At the end of the porch was the white swing that had been hanging there for the past couple of decades by its two, now rusting chains. Even from the distance that Levi stood, he could see that pollen and dust were thick across both the swing's seat and its back. Sitting on the porch, just where Levi had once left it, there was a hanging basket that held a plant that was now nothing more than a brittle image of death. Levi could remember like it was yesterday when he had taken the basket down and placed it there. By that point the plant had already gone days without water, and since there would no longer be anybody there to care for it, Levi had removed it from where it hung and placed it on the porch floor. And it had remained there ever since.

That day had been the last time that he had stepped foot on the property.

He had been in town for his mother's funeral.

Levi placed the key into the latch and turned the old, crystal door knob. He pushed the door inward. Craven hesitated at the threshold, staring intently into the dark house. Without budging, the dog perked his ears and let out a short, low growl before turning around with his tail tucked between his legs and running back down the steps and into the yard. From the porch Levi watched as Craven wandered the yard, circled around and eventually hiked his leg to pee on a thick patch of dandelions.

Levi wondered what had caused the strange reaction from Craven.

It must've been the uneasiness of going into a new, unknown place.

Or was it possible that Craven could have somehow sensed the same, haunting memories as Levi?

And there was yet another possibility. Could it have been something else, an actual ghost?

Levi quickly dismissed the idea and turned back to face the open entranceway and felt his own sense of trepidation. Finally he stepped in, leaving the door open for Craven to enter once he decided that he was done exploring the unfamiliar yard.

The inside of the house was dark. All of the long, lacy white curtains and wooden slat blinds were pulled closed. The musty smells of dust and void lingered, but underneath those smells, there was another. Like outside, it was one of deep familiarity. Even though what little remained of the house's contents were all packed up and the house was nearly empty, it still smelled like he remembered. He placed his clothes bag onto the floor. There was a wooden dining chair next to the door. He sat the laptop and stack of papers on the seat of the chair.

It was difficult to walk any further, too many memories, but he pushed forward anyway. Just as he knew it would, the hardwood floor creaked underneath his feet at all the same spots that it always had. Each creak pulled him further into the past.

Here was his mother reading a book.

There was his father, with his feet propped up, watching TV.

Levi checked the light switch to make sure that the power had been restored as he had requested through the power company several days earlier. It was a relief to see that it had been. It was good to know that *something* in his life was going right. He pushed the curtains to the side and opened the blinds in an effort to let in some of the summer sunlight. Other than the chair by the door, the only seating that remained in the room was a large, cozy, beige couch and a red formal chair. A dark wood coffee table stretched across the length of the couch's front. Several paperback novels were stacked neatly on its surface. Levi's eyes quickly scanned the selection. They were all romance novels. For the most part, aside from a thick layer of dust and noticeable cobwebs, the house was just like it had been when he had last left it.

Levi walked down the hallway that led to the rest of the house. The walls were bare. All the family photos that once lined those very walls were now packed up and stowed away in a box somewhere. Which box in particular, or where it was located, Levi could not be sure.

If you were to walk further down the hallway you would pass by the black and white tiled bathroom and wind up at the back of the house, in the kitchen. At the time of the house's construction the kitchen had not been there. In those older times, food would have been cooked on wood stoves within the front room. Later, when kitchens became common to most households, the room was added on at the back of the house, lending the peculiar layout when being compared to more modern homes.

From the spot where Levi stood in the hallway, to his left there was his old bedroom and on the right, directly across the hall from his own, was another bedroom. This was the room that his parents had once shared and then later had belonged solely to his mother.

Levi began to step toward his room and out of instinct, without realizing he had done so, he stepped over the wooden threshold that was stretched across the width of the door. Like so many boards of the house's old floor, that particular one had squeaked for as long as Levi could remember and it had long ago become habit to step over it.

After stepping inside the room, Levi's body was, without any kind of warning, suddenly overcome with heat. It crashed over him, flushing his skin. It was like stepping into an oven. What he felt was akin to the sensuous burn of passion, that of first love.

☐

The month of May, eighteen years earlier...

"WELL WHAT do you want to watch?" Levi asked Claire Carlson as they stood in front of the horror section at Movie Town, a locally owned video rental store. They were both bummed that the movie that they had wanted to watch was already checked out. It was thirty minutes till closing time and other than the two of them, along with the outrageously thin sales clerk, there were only a few other people browsing the shelves of the store. The sales clerk was behind the counter. His feet were propped on a table and his face was glued to the TV screen that sat on top of a metal filing cabinet. An obnoxiously loud action movie played on the TV. The explosions and gunfire were the only sounds in the store aside from low customer conversation.

From beside Levi, Claire gasped with surprise and quickly grabbed one of the empty cardboard VHS boxes from the shelf. It was the movie that they had been in search of. The movie was a sequel and should have been shelved within the new releases where they had looked originally. Someone must have been considering checking it out, but upon deciding against it had placed the box in the wrong place within the store. "They have it," Claire stated proudly at her find and handed the box to Levi.

Even though he knew that it was the movie that they would be checking out, Levi read the summary and studied the several boxed-in pictures that were printed on the back. He liked to savor the entire experience of new horror movies, starting with the box art. According to what had been printed on the back of the box, the movie promised to be as nerve shattering and blood soaked as the first.

"Awesome," Levi said with a smile and quickly scanned the backlist titles and picked up the box for the first movie.

After taking the empty boxes to the register, the clerk paused the movie that he was watching, picked up the boxes, and using the hand written numbers on the side of each, retrieved the movies from the rows of cramped shelving behind the counter.

Levi and Claire walked back to his house. It was only a street over from where the store was located on the town square. The sun was just setting and quickly disappearing over the horizon. It was late in May, a Friday night. There were only three days of school left. Monday, Tuesday, and Wednesday, all days full of exams. The next school year Levi and Claire would be in college.

Levi's mother was sitting on the porch swing. If his father had still been alive, he would have been sitting there with her, his arm thrown around her shoulders.

"Hey," Claire said to Jill as she and Levi stepped past her and began to go into the house.

"Diesel's not coming over tonight?" Jill asked, surprised that it was only the two of them. Usually the three friends watched movies together.

Levi's hand was on the doorknob. The door was already halfway open. He paused, waiting on Claire's answer.

Claire shrugged her shoulders. "I haven't talked to him."

Levi felt a wave of relief wash over him at the fact that Claire hadn't invited Diesel.

"Is everything OK?" Jill asked. She looked from Claire to Levi.

Based on the look of concern that was spread across his mother's face, it was obvious to Levi that she thought it odd that Diesel hadn't been around much lately. For their entire lives the three kids had been nearly inseparable. Just up until the past couple of weeks, that had never changed. And it was the first movie night where Diesel had been absent in who knew when.

Did she suspect something? Levi wondered.

Was it possible that his mother could tell that something was going on? That something wasn't right? That Levi and Claire were harboring a big secret?

"I haven't talked to him either." Levi shrugged and looked at Claire. She was quiet.

Jill didn't press the inquiry any further and so Levi and Claire went inside the house. By the time that the video cassette was in the VCR, night had already fallen. The steady hum of cicadas could be heard through the old glass windows. After returning from the kitchen with a fresh bag of popcorn, Levi noticed that his mother had now come in from the porch and was sitting in the living room, on the couch with Claire. Claire's shoes were off and her feet were pulled up onto the seat of the couch. Her hands were wrapped around her knees. The VCR was paused. The tape was just at the beginning. The movie studio's red logo was a silently static blur across the screen. It was the only light in the room. An eerily still quietness had descended upon the room as Levi entered. Claire looked at Levi and smiled. Levi looked from her to his mother. They were quiet and looking at him.

What conversation had he walked in on? What had Claire and his mom been discussing during his absence?

Diesel?

"Did I miss something?" Levi asked as he shoved a handful of hot, buttery popcorn into his mouth. "Or should I leave again so y'all can finish talking behind my back?"

Claire rolled her eyes and laughed. "We weren't talking behind your back, Levi. We were just discussing the fall."

The fall, Levi dreaded it. He had yet to make a final decision, but it had to be done in the next couple of weeks. One time he had thought that he would go away to school, but recently he had been considering staying home and commuting to the local college. That way he could be closer to Claire.

Letting the topic go, Levi walked further into the room and fell onto the couch between Claire and Jill, shoving another handful of popcorn in his mouth. He picked up the remote.

"What are y'all watching?" Jill asked.

"*Cemetery of Blood* part one *and* two," Claire answered excitedly.

Jill groaned with disgust. She hated the gory horror movies that Levi and his friends liked to watch. "Haven't you already seen that?" She wondered how many times one person could watch the same movie before becoming just sick of it.

"Part two just came out and we need to watch the first one again before we see it," Levi answered.

Jill was already standing from the couch. "Watch it again for the in depth plot devices and subtle, yet brilliant acting?"

Levi and Claire laughed.

"I'm going to go for a walk. Be back soon."

Jill left through the front door, leaving Levi and Claire alone.

Levi resumed the movie. The spooky, intense music of the opening credits filled the house. Throughout the entire running time of the movie, Levi could barely concentrate on the story. His mind was wandering.

It was also the anticipation of *later*. Levi had finally built up enough courage to act on the recent intensity that he had been feeling toward Claire. He and Claire had been flirting with one another for a while, and now, finally, it was going to happen. The idea of being with her filled him with an excited eagerness. His teenage hormones were raging. He was finally crossing over the line that separated the two of them from being friends and into something more. He couldn't pinpoint the exact time or day when he realized that he liked Claire that way. It just seemed like an awakening, a spark; all of a sudden it had become clear to him. And ever since that realization, whenever he was around her, the spark seemed to ignite into flame. There had only been one thing standing in the way, Diesel, her boyfriend.

Jill was gone for the entirety of the first movie and returned from her walk at the beginning of the second. When she entered the room, a teenage girl was screaming in blood soaked agony as a creature ripped slashes across her flesh. Jill paused in the living room and watched the scene that ended with the girl's head being ripped from her body. She shook her head in aversion.

She just didn't get it, Levi thought.

Jill said good night and went to bed. Levi only slightly turned the volume down on the TV.

As the second movie neared its open ended conclusion, Levi's heart was hammering in his chest with nervous anticipation with what was coming next. His body felt feverish with heat. After the movie had been rewound and the TV had been turned off, Levi and Claire went to his room.

This fact alone wasn't one that would be considered unusual by any means. They had gone into his room late at night many times before, but until that night the reason for going into the room had been different. Before then it had been to look at magazines or listen to music. That night he made *extra* sure to step over the old, squeaky piece of wood across the threshold of the door.

What they were doing needed to be secret.

It had to be.

If they accidentally woke his mother then it would surely only be a matter of time before she figured out what they were up to.

And that was the big secret.

That was one that could not, no way, get out.

☐

IT SURPRISED Levi to realize that even after all the years that had passed since that night, the habit of stepping over the wooden threshold still held an air of adolescent mischief.

Levi had read somewhere one time that there is a kind of haunting that is referred to as being residual. A so-called residual haunting is nothing more than energy that is left behind by big, emotional events. In the theory, the energy generated from heightened emotions is absorbed into furniture and walls and can still be felt within the room many years later.

Maybe that was what he was experiencing; the heat was from that long ago night when he had been eighteen and had snuck into the room with Claire. On that night, Levi's entire body had been so flushed and overcome with the burn of desire that at the time he could have sworn that it would be possible that the four walls and the window frame of the room would later be visibly charred.

He wondered if others that walked into the room could feel the same thing or if it was only because he had been there, had experienced those emotions first hand that caused him to feel the heat.

Thinking this, Levi quickly dismissed the idea of a haunting and attributed the heat that he was feeling to memory. In fact, the memory was so vivid that he could easily see the scene unfold once again in front of him just as if it was happening at that very moment.

Near where he stood, an awkwardly teenage version of himself was kissing Claire for the first time. Her blonde curls were tied back with a red ribbon and her hands were gently resting on each side of the young man's waist. The teenage version of Levi slowly raised his hand and clumsily slipped it underneath the soft cotton of Claire's shirt.

Levi remembered the spark that he had felt that night, the buzz of anticipation. It was the spark of first love. Those little touches and kisses had seemed to have set him on fire.

Like he had done in the living room, Levi tested the light switch. Once again, to his relief, the lights in this room also worked and came on with a quick, bright yellow glow, sending the memory of the two love-struck teenagers away into nothing.

And the heat began to lift from Levi's body.

Like the rest of the house the walls of the room were bare. The black and white *Frankenstein* movie poster that had once been tacked onto the plaster wall was no longer there. There was nothing sitting on the old, antique dresser, no knick knacks, or photos, or teenage things that he had left behind. Everything that Levi had wanted to keep he had already taken with him. Off in the corner, on the floor, there was a cardboard box with its top flaps splayed open. Without looking Levi knew what was inside, he had placed the menagerie of items there himself to take with him later: a large conch shell, an almanac, a postcard of a sideshow mermaid, a framed, sepia toned photo of his grandfather, and a discolored pack of squash seeds.

He kneeled down onto the floor by the box and reached inside. The first thing that he pulled out was the old almanac that had belonged to his grandfather. It was the same book that had been popping up in his dreams as of late. The book was for the year of 1935. Each page was dated and predicted the weather patterns; planting, watering, and harvesting times of various crops were written out on the pages for future reference. Levi gently traced his fingers over the brittle cover and then fanned through the pages. Levi smiled. Deep within in the crease, there was a small piece of paper that had always remained there. It looked like the ripped corner from the page of another book. It was stained with a splotch of darkness. Family lore insisted that it was a teardrop.

A moment later Levi stood from the floor and walked back into the living room. He laid the almanac onto the coffee table next to one of his mother's paperback novels. The cover of the book featured an illustration of a handsome, unveiled beekeeper that has his arms wrapped tightly around a beautiful woman. A swarm of bees hovered around a set of framed hives that stood in the sunlit background.

Levi walked through the open front door and discovered that Craven was nowhere to be seen. It was only for a brief moment that Levi panicked before he spotted the dog's perky ears among the weeds and wild flowers.

Craven was lying on the ground, happily panting beneath the enormous oak tree that stood in the corner of the yard. A mosquito buzzed past and Craven snapped his jaw at the insect, narrowly missing. Levi remembered that the only dog that he had ever had as a child also seemed to like that particular spot of the yard. He recalled how Bowser, that had been the small Terrier's name, used to cry until he was let out of the house and then do nothing more than lay underneath the tree, sometimes flipping onto his back and rubbing his head vicariously against the grass. Years later, Bowser had even been buried there.

Letting Craven enjoy the yard, Levi returned to the porch and hesitantly approached the swing. Once, even just months earlier, he didn't think that he would ever have enough courage to sit there again after what had happened.

Two years earlier, the news of his mother's death had spread quickly throughout Devlin, just the way things tend to do in small towns. The way that the story went was that Jill had been in the yard pulling weeds that morning until a sudden, unexpected thundercloud had come up. Taking a break, she sat down in the porch swing to read. It was later in the afternoon, after the storm had passed, that Calvin Harris arrived to remove a few dead limbs from the oak tree in the front yard. By that point the man had been coming to the house and helping out for a while. It was Calvin that had found her. A paperback romance book was lying fanned out across the boards of the porch. A half drank cup of sweet tea was on the windowsill. The ice cubes hadn't even completely melted by the time that the ambulance arrived. Jill was pronounced dead and the cause of her sudden, largely unexpected passing was determined to be a stroke.

Ever since then, with the little time that he had spent in Devlin, Levi hadn't gone near the swing. In fact, he had avoided it at all costs and now when he finally thought that he might give it a shot, it just looked too dirty to sit on. Levi scanned the porch and noticed a plastic bucket that was shoved in the corner against the house. Underneath the gardening gloves and rusty clippers he found what he was looking for, an old red rag. Levi reached his hand into the bucket, being careful of spiders, and pulled the rag free. He shook the rag out and began dusting the old, wooden slats of the swing when he noticed something odd. The side that was closest to the house was not coated in dirt and pollen the same way as the other. Levi stood on the porch staring at the swing, confused about what he was seeing. No one had been living in the house for two years but it was obvious that very recently someone had been sitting in the swing.

Just as Levi had been able to envision his younger self minutes earlier, he could now see his mother sitting in the swing before him. The vision was as plain as day. She was reading a book. Her legs were kicked up onto the seat. Her shoes were off and lying where they had dropped onto the porch floor. A cold glass of sweet tea was sitting within reach on the nearby windowsill.

Jill Stanley looked at her son and smiled.

"LEVI?" A woman's deeply southern twang of a voice came from the other side of the fence.

The sudden calling of his name startled Levi and tore his attention away from the swing. One moment he had been deep in thought about who could have possibly been sitting in the swing and the next he was having a strikingly vivid recollection of his mother.

And then the abruptness of the woman's voice had sent his heart racing.

From where Levi stood on the porch he could see a bobbing head full of teased black hair as the woman that had called his name stood on her tip toes to peek over into the yard. On the inside of the fence Craven was standing on his back legs, stretching his front paws toward the woman as far up the fence slats that they would go.

"Levi?" The woman asked again as she peered over the fence. Her eyes darted around the property and then she was looking directly at him.

"That's me," Levi called out to her and tossed the red rag that he had been holding back into the bucket from where he had found it.

"I'm Kathy Anderson," the lady announced from where she still stood on the other side of the yard. She smiled with a mouthful of perfectly white teeth. She looked at the watch on her wrist. "Sorry, but I'm a little early."

"Oh, that's fine," Levi said and began stepping from the porch. Kathy was the realtor that he was scheduled to be meeting with. "The gate's unlocked." He pointed to where the gate was located at the side of the house.

Kathy was already walking around the perimeter of the fence. Levi met her at the gate as she was attempting to push it inward. Just like Levi had experienced earlier, because of the thick weeds around the gate area she was failing miserably at opening it even far enough for her thin body to slip through.

"Gosh," Kathy said as she was looking down at the ground. "Now you have got some weeds growing 'round here."

"Yeah." Levi chuckled and grasped onto the metal handle that was on his side. He pulled the gate inward at the same time that Kathy pushed. "Nothing a little weed killer won't fix though."

After getting the gate open just wide enough to where she

could finally make it through by turning sideways, Kathy caught sight of Craven who was now rushing toward her in an enthusiastic, tail wagging greeting. Kathy quickly closed the gate behind her, careful not to let the dog out. She was dressed in perfectly ironed charcoal gray pants and matching jacket. In one hand she held a file folder that had several sheets of paper shooting out from the inside. She reached her free hand out to Levi. "Kathy Anderson," she introduced herself once again with a smile.

"Nice to meet you," Levi told her as he placed his hand in hers. "Levi Stanley," he said.

Craven was jumping up again, but this time it was on Kathy instead of the fence. The dog stood on his hind legs, reached his front feet out and planted them on Kathy's hip. Levi winced at what he was seeing. He hoped that Craven's paws were clean. Kathy didn't look like the type that would be OK with filthy paw prints on her obviously expensive clothes.

"I didn't think bassets were so energetic," Kathy said with a smile (she smiled a lot) in response to Craven's abundant energy.

"Craven, get down boy" Levi told the dog and looked back at Kathy. "I'm sorry. He's a little hyper I guess."

Craven removed his feet from the woman and she was brushing the dirt from her pair of slacks.

"No. No. It's OK. I have a couple of them myself. Not bassets, but spaniels. I know how they can be."

Levi already had his hand gripped around Craven's collar in an effort at keeping the canine from jumping onto the realtor a second time. He kneeled down and pulled the dog closer to his crouched body. Craven panted from both the humidity and the excitement of meeting someone new.

"It's a beautiful place." She looked back at Levi. "I've always thought that, you know?"

"Thanks." Levi presumed that if she *really* thought that it was as beautiful as she said then she must've considered him to be crazy for wanting to sell and be rid of it.

"I was so sorry about what happened to your mother. I hadn't been living in town all that long at the time, but I had gotten to know her a little bit. She was a wonderful lady."

Levi nodded in agreement. "Yeah, it's been tough but somehow you manage to get through it."

"Oh believe me, I know all about that. I lost both my parents in one swoop. They were in a car accident years ago out on Highway 22. It took a long time for it to get better, but it does." She nodded assuredly at Levi.

After the brief exchange, an awkward silence settled on the scene.

"Well I guess you probably need to see the inside," Levi said, breaking the quiet.

Levi led Kathy into the house. Craven scampered alongside them. Once again the dog hesitated at the door, but this time it was only a brief hesitation before he stepped into the house along with Levi and Kathy. Levi closed the door behind them.

"Oh, wow," Kathy said as she entered the living room for the first time. "Old houses like this come with so much history." She looked around at her surroundings. "Is the fireplace functional?" Kathy was staring at the old, built in fireplace.

"You know, we used to use it back when I was a kid, but I don't think that it's been lit up in a long, long time." Levi recalled how on windy nights the draft would cause the cast iron cover to rattle. Thinking back on it, it had probably been nearly three decades since there had been a crackling fire built in the house. In fact, the cover that had a tree imprinted on the front had been in place pretty much as long as he could remember. He couldn't recall the last time that it had even been removed. The fireplace itself was probably filled with old ash and soot, maybe even a bird nest or two.

Kathy continued to tour the house, pointing out the things already in place that potential buyers liked. The built in shelves that flanked the windows in the living room, the beautiful claw footed bathtub, the classic hardwood floors, all of these were things that Kathy assured Levi people would be excited about.

And then there were other things that Levi would need to consider. The lack of a third bedroom that could potentially be used as a personal office or nursery, the kitchen being located at the back of the house, the outdated orange kitchen appliances, all were just a few of the things that she recommended to him to think about changing.

"Any upgrades or renovations that you can do only add value to your home. Keep that in mind." The two of them had returned to the living room where they stood facing one another. "And I know I just got done telling you how people love the old tubs like the one you've got, but then on the other hand the drawback is that in a house this size where there is only one bathroom, and even though the tub has a shower head and wrap around curtain, there is not a traditional step in shower." Kathy paused as if reading Levi's expression. "And it's not good to have only one bathroom either." She scrunched her nose. "People don't like that."

Levi was dumbfounded at all the major changes she was suggesting. As he was pondering everything that she had just said, Kathy walked away and began snapping pictures of each room, focusing on the positives that she had seen. Levi knew that he didn't have the amount of money to make the kind of renovations that the realtor was suggesting. The things that she was proposing were way out of the scope he felt capable of. She was talking about adding rooms to the house, relocating the existing kitchen, renovating the current bathroom to include a shower. In his current financial situation all of it felt, and it was, preposterous.

But Kathy was the realtor. She was the one that knew what sold houses, not him. The truth of the matter was that there was no way that the renovations were a possibility, so all Levi could do was only hope that she was wrong. Or wish for a miracle.

Once Kathy returned to the living room the two of them went into the front yard where she continued to make suggestions.

"The yard and porch will need to be spruced up. Potential buyers love to see instant curb appeal. You know, just little things, nothing major. Paint the porch. Mow the lawn. Trim the bushes. Plant some flowers in the ground and in pots, just normal, everyday stuff." She shrugged her shoulders as if all of that could be done by the waving of a magic wand.

Levi wondered what the lady's own house looked like.

Kathy's eyes scanned the yard and settled on the tree in the corner. "Have you considered having the tree removed? I mean it's a beautiful old tree, but it allows very little sunlight into the yard. The size of that tree is way out of proportion for this yard. I mean, the branches barely let any sunlight through." She looked around the area of the ground where she stood in her high heels. The wild flowers and weeds reached up to her calves. "I'm surprised that anything at all grows out here. People nowadays want a lawn and garden, the whole nine yards."

"No. I've never even thought about it."

"Well, that's all it is, just something to think about. In the meantime I'll get the place listed and we'll see what happens."

Kathy smiled enthusiastically.

The realtor continued to snap a few more pictures from the outside. She went to her car and returned carrying an *ANDERSON REALTY - FOR SALE* sign that she staked into the ground at the street corner. Levi watched and was impressed that she could push the stake so forcefully into the ground with the shoes that she was wearing.

After the sign was up, Kathy returned to the yard. She opened the folder that she was holding and removed the top sheets of paper. She studied the stapled together pages to make sure that what she was handing to Levi was the correct form. Levi signed his name to the paperwork.

"After you clean up the yard and the inside, let's just leave everything the way it is. Don't make any changes just yet." She touched Levi's arm in a calming gesture as she said this. It must've been obvious that he was distressed over what all he had heard. "We'll let some people see it and that way we'll get some sort of feedback as to what people think." She placed the paperwork back into the folder. "I'll let you know as soon as anybody is interested in seeing the inside. And in the meantime you should consider having an open house. Just to get people inside, get them interested, get some gossip flying so to speak."

Kathy and Levi shook hands and Kathy began walking toward the gate.

It was only a couple of hours after Kathy left that Levi found the listing for the house on the internet. It was located on the homepage of the Anderson Realty website.

*Beautiful mid 19TH century home * convenient location * beautiful front yard* was the description that accompanied the house's carefully framed photo.

II

A LONG time ago, before tractors or fuel burning farming equipment were ever invented, the size of an acre was considered to be the amount of land that a yoke of oxen could plow in one day's time.

For some, those that are not so familiar to the working endurance of an ox, an acre may be easier to envision as being slightly smaller than a football field.

So picture this, a football field of any high school in any small town. Take away roughly one third of the area and then what is left is about the size of land that we are talking about. Now make the goal posts and bleachers full of cheering parents and teenagers disappear. The light posts, cheerleaders, marching band, all gone. In their place put trees, pine and oak. It shouldn't be a thick wood, but more of a scattering of trees here and there. Just enough to make the area of land feel somewhat secluded. If the vision that you have in your mind still resembles the neatly mowed turf of a playing field, then scratch that image and instead picture years of weed and brush growth. Finally, a dirt path, only a few feet wide, should lead into the land.

To get to the start of the path, Levi had to walk down the road a piece, past the neighboring house, a tall wooden structure that had flowing white curtains in each window. The boards on each of its four sides were gray with age. Aside from a few neat flower beds against the house, the yard was a stretch of green. Levi remembered the eccentric old man that had lived all alone in the house for so many years. The man's name was Mallard. What stood out the most to Levi about the man was the way that the he would always be dressed in a black suit and tie no matter the time of day or year. Levi recalled how the man even mowed his yard wearing the same attire. When Mallard cut the grass around his house the entire block was filled with the smell of the wild onion that grew in abundance on his property. Levi recalled how the man had always had a thing for taxidermy animals. One Halloween night when Levi had been in elementary school, he had hesitantly walked up the steps of the house trick or treating. As Mallard stood in the open doorway and placed candy into Levi's plastic pumpkin, Levi had peered in through the door at the animals that lined the walls and the shelves in the room beyond. That night, the lifeless animals had added an extra dash of spookiness to the night. Now, as Levi walked past, he wondered who currently lived in the house. Surely Mallard was no longer alive, he reasoned.

In between that house and the next there was an alleyway that led to other homes. Levi turned to the left and followed that narrow, gravel alley. Craven scampered along at Levi's side. A blue leash was clipped onto the dog's collar and led to Levi's right hand where it was held firmly in his grasp. Rancid, still water was in the ditch banks at each side. Craven ran over to the right side of the alley, closer to the ditch bank, and inspected the water and overgrowth that surrounded it. To Levi the water looked like a perfect breeding ground for mosquitoes. And just as Levi thought it, he saw several of the insects buzz around Craven's face. Levi knew that mosquitoes were not only a threat to humans, a way of contracting West Nile, malaria, or other diseases, but one bite could cause deadly heartworms in canines. And not only were there mosquitoes around the ditch, but being born and raised in the South, Levi was also fully aware of the other possible threats of the area. Since Craven had only lived in the city, the dog wasn't accustomed to the menace of snakes and the other dangers that were scattered around Devlin. Levi gently tugged on the leash, guiding Craven away from the curiosity.

Aside from the ditches, the alley was flanked on each side by the two house's back yards. On his left, the back yard of Mallard's house was enclosed by a chain link fence. Similar to the front, very little was done to the yard's landscape. It was a simple green lawn. A wooden picnic table with a faded black umbrella stood alone amid the grass. The only pop of color would've come from the far corner, a lone camellia that had been covered with bright pink flowers late in the winter. Another plant, a wisteria vine, had grown from the ground near the small tree's base and wrapped itself around the limbs. The grape like clusters of purple flowers had hung low from the camellia branches in the spring but the plant was now a woodsy vine without bloom. As opposed to what he was seeing within the chainlike fence, the back yard of the house on the right was not fenced in. Instead, the yard was a picturesque garden of flowering plants. Yellow roses and orange and red lantana grew in well tended beds. It was the showy, proud type of yard that wanted to be seen, not contained. There was however a white picket fence at the back that stretched along the length of the yard. The fence wasn't there so much as a marker for the end of the property, but as a way to block the untamed piece of land that lay beyond.

  This is where the path began, right after the clean white picket fence. Levi stood facing the entranceway. There was another house and another fence to his left, but what he had come to see was in between those two properties. The area of land belonged to no one. For as long as he could remember, it had simply been a piece of land that Mercer Creek ran through. The creek was only a few feet wide and Levi wasn't even sure if it was technically a creek, stream, or brook, but he had always known it to be called a creek and so to him, it was a creek. The old folks of Devlin said that the narrow creek once ran all the way through town and ended at the large pond that stood between Mercer Creek Baptist Church and Hollyhock Road. It was interesting to look at old, hand drawn maps of Devlin and see the line of the creek as it snaked its way across the surface of the paper. It ran through areas that were once dense woods and farmland but were now full of houses and yards of green grass. Now, the creek seemed to be nothing more than another ditch with water standing it. Most of the time the creek was dry, but there were those occasions where, just like that day, because of the recent amount of rain a few inches of water stood in the bottom.

  Now, for just a brief moment, let's go back to the football field analogy. The acre of land that was in the middle of Devlin was not the blocky square of land that you had probably originally pictured. An acre is just a square footage, a measurement. The land that makes up an acre could be any shape, as long as the land surface meets 43,560 square feet. In this case, the acre was long and narrow. The width was about the size of three cars parked side by side. The land wasn't big enough to build on and had never been cultivated. It had always simply just been there.

  Levi stood before the dirt foot path that led deeper into the land. Thick vines and briars grew out of control on either side but there were no weeds growing on the pathway itself. This fact led

Levi to believe that other people still went strolling through the property from time to time. When Levi and his friends had been little they had always thought of the land as being theirs even though it had been unclaimed. It was a place for them to go and get away. It was a place of solace. He, Claire, and Diesel had spent many summer days playing there when they had been kids.

    Levi carefully pushed the thorny vines aside with his right hand and stepped into the woodsy growth. It was the first time that Levi had stepped foot on the land since the year he graduated high school. Tall weeds covered the ground on each side of the path. As he walked a few feet further, it turned out that the vines and weeds had been thickest at the start. With each step that he walked, the thinner the overgrowth became. The area of land felt tighter and smaller than he remembered. The fact that it was little more than a line of trees that ran between two home properties was more evident as an adult. When he had been little and moving about the narrow strip of land it had felt like he was miles away from any type of civilization. Now it was impossible to feel that way. Despite the trees and vines that were growing everywhere that he looked, the fences on either side of him were almost always visible each step of the way.

    After walking nearly two thirds of the way across the stretched acre, Levi came to a small clearing. Yellow dandelions scattered the ground. Several blackbirds fluttered from tree branches that reached across the magnificently blue sky. If he would have kept walking he would have come out the other side and ended up on the piece of land where Diesel had grown up. Levi peered through the trees and could see the barn-red metal siding of the shop that stood behind the house. It was a building where Diesel's father had spent countless hours working on cars. It was where Diesel himself had learned, under his father's tutelage, the workings of and mechanics of vehicles. From the distance Levi could see an abandoned car that sat lifelessly atop four cement blocks at the building's side.

    Levi remembered one day, long before, when he had unexpectedly wound up at the exact same spot where he stood now. He had been seven years old. It had been a warm spring day and he had spent the better part of the morning at home playing in the front yard. His parents had been inside at the time. Unbeknownst to Levi, the side gate was not closed all the way and with no warning his dog had managed to slip through. After escaping, the small terrier had darted down the road as if he knew exactly where he was going and had somewhere to be.

As soon as he realized it, without hesitation, Levi had frantically jumped to his feet and bolted after him, yelling the dog's name every few steps of the way. Bowser, the dog, never even looked back at his young master whose arms and legs were pumping frantically trying to keep up. Instead, Bowser turned and ran down the path that led to the clearing. That day the briars and bramble had slowed Levi so much that he momentarily lost sight of the dog. As he pushed through the overgrowth, his heart hammered in his chest with the worry that something bad would happen to his beloved pet before he could catch up with him. When he finally came to the clearing he saw that Bowser was safe. Levi was overcome with relief that the dog was OK.

It wasn't the first time that Levi had been there. He had been on walks with his parents through the strip of land before, but it *was* the first time that he had been there on his own. And it was the first time that he had ever seen anybody else on the land.

In front of him, Bowser was standing on his back legs and happily panting with a boy and girl who were sitting cross legged on the ground. Through the break in tree cover the sun shone down on them. The girl had blonde curls and was giggling at the jubilation of the young dog. Levi recognized the other two kids immediately. He went to school and church with them but had never really spoken to either of them before that day.

Their names were Diesel and Claire. He knew that Diesel lived nearby and that Claire's stepfather was co-owner of the auto shop with Diesel's father. Levi approached. A scattering of small glass jars that were each only about an inch tall lay on the grassy ground between them. He saw a larger, canning sized jar that held several frantic bugs within the glass. Mosquitoes. Levi's first thought upon spotting the trapped insects was one of trouble and torture, but quickly dismissed what he was seeing as science.

"Culicidae," Levi said.

Diesel, who was wearing a camouflage cap that day, looked up at him from underneath the cap's curved bill. "What?"

"Culicidae. It's the family of insects that mosquitoes belong to."

"How do you know?" Claire spoke up.

"My parents," Levi shrugged. "They know everything there is to know about bugs."

Levi watched as Diesel picked up one of the bottles and held it between his thumb and index finger. The bottle was full of shimmering blue liquid and was closed with a small, round cork at the top. The sunlight caused the liquid to sparkle. Levi's eyes scanned the ground and saw a half empty bottle of mouthwash. He knew what the other boy was doing.

Glycerin had long been used to preserve insects and the since the mouthwash had a small amount of the liquid as one of its ingredients it must've been Diesel's only knowledge of and access to what he thought he needed. Levi then noticed that Claire wore one of the tiny bottles around her neck. The bottle was tied onto a thin black twine and was full of green liquid, presumably spearmint mouthwash.

Even though Levi had been around framed and pinned insects his entire life, his parents were both etymologists, what Diesel was doing seemed cruel. What the other boy was doing wasn't using the proper materials and technique. It seemed barbaric. That and the fact that the mouthwash was so thin that the insects would probably only float on the top instead of appear to be suspended in mid air the way that the thick glycerin would allow.

What goes around comes around, Levi thought.

Sooner or later, karma will get you, he had always been told.

But underneath the sense of wrongness, there was another layer to what he had seen that day. The small, shimmering jars were beautiful. They were *so* beautiful in fact that Diesel had made a necklace out of one of them and given it to Claire who proudly wore it around her neck.

Levi picked up Bowser and turned to head back home, back down the overgrown path, but turned to face the other two kids one more time.

"My name's Levi," he said before turning back around and walking away.

That was when the friendship between the three of them had begun.

Pretty soon Levi had shown them the right way to preserve bugs, using the correct equipment and actual glycerin instead of the brightly colored mouthwash that Diesel had been using.

After learning from Levi, Diesel made a new necklace for

Claire. Like the first, it held a mosquito. This one was encased in crystal clear instead of bright green. Claire wore it around her neck, on the same black twine as the original, for several years later.

Now, as an adult, Levi thought about that day when he had discovered the two of them there. Should he have taken his initial reaction of what Diesel was doing with the insects as a sign of what was to come years later? Was it a sign of Diesel's meanness? Or had the act of bottling the insects been only an example of a child's innocent curiosity?

Where Levi and Craven stood in the clearing there was a pecan tree that didn't have a neighbor for about ten feet on either side. The base of the trunk was near the creek's edge. One of the lower limbs of the tree, just a few feet off the ground, jutted straight out from the trunk. The girth of the limb was enormous, especially for a pecan tree. Sitting atop the limb was a weathered, rickety tree house.

Behind the tree there was an abandoned garden shed. It was the sort of thing that could be bought from hardware stores in a flat cardboard box and only had to be pieced together with little to no thought or care. The door was pulled shut. Straggly blades of dallisgrass jutted up all around the base of the structure. Several tendrils of poison ivy crept up the sun faded, once dark green sides.

Levi stood there in the clearing and looked back at the tree house. As opposed to the garden shed, the architecture was made up of plywood walls and a silver tin roof. There was a rectangular doorway that had been cut into one of the pieces of plywood. There was no door that covered the entranceway and never had been. Of course by that point in time, the boards were badly weathered and had the gray pallor of aged, old timber. Some of the ones that made up the square frame of the structure were bowing outward and coming loose from one another. The tree house seemed to have seen better days, but Levi was surprised that it was even still standing at all. He had assumed that it would have long ago fallen from the tree and the boards would be a scattered mess across the ground. Back when the tree house had been constructed, Diesel's father had insisted that the kids build the house with treated lumber so that it would hold up to the elements. It must've worked, Levi thought.

On a summer day almost three decades earlier it had taken several hours for Levi, Diesel, and Claire to make a path from Diesel's house to the clearing that would be wide enough for a wheelbarrow. They had used a trio of machetes to chop their way through the brush. Over the course of that single afternoon they had transported stacks of lumber from the scrap pile behind the shop. Piece by piece the lumber was stacked atop the rusted wheel barrow. And load by load the boards wobbled and clambered together over the rutted path as the wheel barrow was pushed from the shop to the tree. The wheelbarrow's metal wheel screeched nightmarishly as each of the kids took turns pushing. The sound even woke Mr. Pratchett, an old man who lived two streets over, from his afternoon slumber. The man swore that it was a bobcat in heat that he was hearing and had called animal control. When the caged truck arrived to the scene, Levi and his friends laughed at the wild assumption.

After the pieces were relocated, the construction of the tree house took several more days, but it had been a huge accomplishment. It was theirs. Over the years the three of them spent many hours together in the tree house. It was where they wrote plays that they would perform together. It was where they had made a pact that the three of them would always be friends, that no matter what, no girl or boy would ever come between them.

The tree house looked so much smaller than Levi remembered. He approached the wooden step ladder that ran from the ground to the limb and ended at the open door of the house. Really the ladder was more of a series of steps instead of an actual ladder. The height of the limb where the tree house stood was only a little higher than Levi's waist. Just one look at the rungs and Levi knew that the weight of his body would bring the ladder crashing down. Back then, in an unknowledgeable decision, the rungs had simply been hammered on to the side boards of the ladder and a couple of them were now swiveling loosely by the rusted nails that barely held the hodge-podge together.

After deciding against trying the steps, Levi moved closer and leaned toward the door. He realized that as a grownup he would no longer have been able to stand up within the cramped construction anyway. And there was also the great possibility that like what he presumed would've happened with the ladder, the additional weight of both him and Craven would have brought the whole thing crashing down.

After his eyes adjusted to the chasm of darkness that was within the structure, Levi was surprised to see what had been left in the tree house and had remained there for all those years. In the far left corner there was a cheap piece of an old, moth ridden costume. The red cloak was the kind of thing that could be bought at almost any costume store. A wooden handled gardening hoe was lying on top of the wadded fabric just where it had been left. With a child's imagination, those two objects could become anything. Once, in a play that Levi had written about a magical kingdom, a young farmer (Levi) used the magic garden tool (the hoe) to destroy the evil king (Diesel) and rescue the princess (Claire) from his clutches.

On the opposite wall there was a drawing that was tacked to the plywood. The childish sketch had been done on lined notebook paper that was now yellowed with age. The sheet of paper was crinkled and curling around the edges, but the crayon image was still visible after all the years. Levi thought that the tin roof that they had put on the tree house must've been sufficiently effective against rain and weather.

In the picture, three kids stood underneath a large tree. A yellow sun was in the corner of the paper. The upper part of the tree was a green swirl of deep hunter green. Crudely drawn yellow squash were across the bottom of the page. One of the stick figure kids was supposed to be Diesel. He had a camouflage cap on his head. The middle one, Claire, had a curly mess of sunflower yellow hair. The third figure, Levi, had at some point in time been scratched through with a blood red marker. It appeared to be a hasty, angry scribbling that covered the figure's childish body.

Levi was surprised that seeing the picture didn't affect him more than it did. Granted, he didn't remember ever seeing it in its current state, with the angry scratches slashed over the figure that was supposed to be him, but he knew without a doubt who had marred the drawing.

And he knew better than anyone the events that had led to the juvenile act. He had been the harbinger of it all.

More importantly he knew firsthand all the nightmarish things that had happened later.

☐

The month of May, eighteen years earlier…

"WHAT ABOUT Diesel?" Levi asked.
 "What about him?" Claire shot back.
 "I don't know, I just -," he searched his mind for the right

words. "I just kind of feel bad about it, about everything that we're doing."

The two of them sat in the tree house. By that point in time it had become a spot where they never went anymore, but it hadn't taken long for the two of them to realize the potential of its seclusion. Some of the teenagers at school had their cars that they would drive out to the end of Hollyhock Road, past the deathly sharp and dangerous turn where the pavement curved around the pond, and they would park at the edge of the water and make out while being afraid that either their parents *or* the ghost of Anna Moore could appear at any time. In the fantasy world of teenagers, either scenario seemed like a possibility.

And while those kids had the pond, Levi and Claire had the tree house.

Their backs were leaning against opposite walls as they faced one another. An unlit flashlight lay between them. The sky on the other side of the plywood walls was black with night. A scattering of stars was sprinkled across the dark. It was Monday night. There was only two more days of school left.

"It'll be OK." Claire inched closer to Levi. "We'll figure something out," she said softly and placed her hand on Levi's bent knee. She looked at him and smiled. Levi's body responded quickly. Just that single touch, even through the denim, sent jolts of sparking electricity down Levi's leg and throughout the entirety of his being. It was the same spark that he had felt the night before. The spark though seemed to increase in intensity each time that they touched.

It was true that what they were doing had been bothering him for days, but when his eyes met with Claire's, Levi knew that the guilt that he felt was worth it. He just had to figure something out with Diesel. With Claire's hand on his knee, Levi thought about the pact that had been made in that very spot, that no matter what, the three of them would always be friends. No girl or boy would ever come between them.

It was crazy how things changed.

Before Levi had time to realize fully what was happening, Claire slid her hand underneath the soft black t-shirt that he was wearing. The skin contact sent his pulse racing. He was nearly breathless. In response, he reached out his own hand and grasped a mass of Claire's yellow curls in his fist. His other shaking hand reached under her pink tank top. He caressed her skin and gently tugged on the strap of her bra.

When there lips met it was with a devouring need and just a moment later they were covering each other with caresses and kisses. Claire reached to Levi's belt buckle with a trembling hand. She fumbled with the clasp and when she finally had it loose she was gasping for air.

"Are you sure?" Levi whispered below her. There was no question in his mind that he was ready for what they were about to do. This moment is what he had been anticipating for what seemed like forever and now it was finally happening.

And it was happening with her, Claire Carlson, of all people.

Claire nodded.

Afterwards they dressed in silence and then lay snuggled close together. It was getting late and they both knew that they needed to get back home, especially since they each had to take final exams the next day. They walked back into the throng of houses and then separated at the street corner, not kissing one another good night. Instead, they just simply looked at each other and smiled. Levi went in the direction of his house and Claire went hers, each of them taking the knowledge of the secret with them.

Inside the house, Levi's mother was still up. This simple fact alone surprised Levi. On weeknights Jill rarely stayed up past ten o'clock and by the time that Levi entered the house it was already ten thirty. She was sitting on the floor in the den. A section of white wrapping paper was rolled out in front of her. She was wrapping a wedding gift for a coworker. A closed cardboard box sat perfectly centered on top of the paper. Jill ran a sharp pair of scissors in a straight line across the paper, cutting it to the correct size. Atop the entertainment center that was pushed flat against the wall, a made for TV movie was playing on the television. Suspenseful music filled the room.

"Where've you been?" Jill didn't sound angry, just inquisitive. She folded one side of the paper over the box.

"With Claire." Levi shut the door behind himself. "We were at her house, studying." He sat on the couch behind where Jill was sitting on the floor.

Something didn't seem right. Levi could feel the uneasiness in the room.

Was it possible that the big, bad secret was somehow out and that his mother knew?

That he and Claire would soon be caught?

Jill didn't turn to Levi when she spoke. "Diesel's missing." She taped the paper to the box and then folded the opposite side over.

The word rammed into Levi.

Missing? The mere mention of the word sent chills all over Levi's body. It made him feel sick. He thought that the guilt that he felt was surely visible. It was a good thing that he was sitting behind his mother, out of sight.

"Missing? What do you mean?"

Jill turned to look at her son. "He's not been home all weekend." She stated matter-of-factly and shrugged her shoulders. "Janice and Tucker have no idea where he is." As she spoke about Diesel's parents, Jill had tears in her eyes. It was as if it was *her* son that was missing instead of one of his best friends.

"What – are they – is anybody looking for him?" Levi's voice trembled. He hoped that she couldn't see the guilt that was without a doubt covering his face.

"Tucker contacted the police, but it's a tough thing because Diesel's nineteen and technically an adult. He's free to do whatever he wants."

Levi stood from the couch. By that point he was trembling with nerves. He began walking toward his room. He had to call Claire. They had to talk.

"Levi," Jill started.

The speaking of his name stopped him cold.

"When was the last time you've seen him? Or Claire?"

With his back turned he spoke. "I just saw Claire tonight," he stated too quick, reminding her of what he had already said, that he had been at Claire's house and the two of them had been studying together.

"No. I mean, when is the last time that Claire saw *him*?"

Levi shrugged his shoulders, not turning around. He thought about something he had been told in school one time, that liars never look the other person in the eye. He swiveled his head and looked at her over his shoulder, in the eyes. "The other day I guess." As soon as he had done it he thought it had to have been obvious that the eye contact had been forced, that surely his own mother could see the lie in his eyes.

"She hasn't said anything to you about it?"

"No, I mean - she seemed fine."

It was all spinning out of control. He knew for certain that what they were doing would soon be found out. Maybe it was best to just come clean. The three of them had been best friends for their entire lives, so of course everyone would expect that he and Claire would be the first to know that Diesel was not around.

They *had* been best friends.

That was until Levi screwed it all up and decided that he wanted to be more than friends with her.

Calling Claire was the only thing that Levi could think of. He had to talk to her. He began to walk away, toward his bedroom. He would call her from the privacy within those four walls, where no one could hear.

Behind him, as he was walking down the hallway, his mother spoke again. "Tucker called Claire's house looking for him." There was a long pause in what she was saying that seemed to stretch on forever. "Her mother said that she hadn't seen him *or* Claire."

And so that was it. He had been caught in a lie.

After all, it was the truth. He had *not* been at Claire's house studying.

☐

"WHAT HAPPENED here on this piece of land changed everything," a deep male voice came from behind Levi.

Levi jumped and spun around from the tree house. He immediately recognized who was standing in front of him. The man was wearing a black suit. A white dress shirt was underneath the jacket, a pitch black neck tie was around his neck, and a frayed and faded black fedora sat atop his head. The old man's skin was not impossibly wrinkled and sagging the way that was expected for someone his age. Instead, his face and complexion was as smooth as Levi's own. If it wasn't for the white hair, the man could've passed for half his age. Levi was shocked that Mallard could even still be alive. He had seemed to have been ancient even when Levi had been a kid living next door to him.

"What? What did you say?" Levi asked, squinting through the bright sunlight. He could hear his own voice tremble at the strangeness of the situation.

It was then that Levi noticed the very large dog emerge from behind Mallard. It was a Rottweiler. As apposed to Craven's leather leash, the Rottweiler had a thick, clanking chain around its neck that Mallard held onto. The massive dog spotted Craven and growled as it lurched forward, yanking on the chain. Levi jerked Craven's leash, pulling his own dog back toward safety. Craven hid behind Levi.

"What happened here that night changed everything," the man said again.

Levi shook his head. "I – I don't know what you're talking about sir. I - "

"I think you know exactly what I'm talking about."

Levi began to walk away.

Was this man senile? Levi wondered.

Alzheimer's maybe?

Levi shook his head as he was backing away.

"No, I'm sorry, I don't. But I need to get back." Levi turned his back on the man and began to walk faster. From behind him he could hear that Mallard was still mumbling.

"I have a secret -," he was saying.

Levi's heart was pounding in his chest as he pushed through the overgrowth.

He wondered again, what was this man talking about?

Levi was far enough away by then that he could just barely hear what Mallard was saying from behind him.

"Come by my house and I'll tell you," Mallard said. It was the last statement that Levi could make out before the barely audible words softened into distant mutterings.

☐

LATER IN the afternoon, after it became obvious to Mallard that Levi was not going to take him up on the offer of dropping by his house, Mallard tried once again to reach out to him. Determined to tell what he needed to say, Mallard walked across his own yard to Levi's house. He was still wearing his suit and hat. After ascending the front steps, he tried knocking on the door, but got no answer. From inside the house there was only the loud barking and growling from the dog. He couldn't hear any sign of Levi being inside. There were no footsteps or shuffling of paper, nothing to indicate that he was at home. As Mallard stood there, he couldn't help but to peek through the window panes of the door. There was a sheer curtain on the other side of the glass, but by leaning this way and that, he could make out a few things that he saw. He wasn't *necessarily* looking for anything. He was just being inquisitive. Right away there was something that caught his attention. Next to the door, there was a stack of papers that were neatly clipped together and sitting on top of an antique chair. It looked like they were rubber banded to a laptop computer.

It was the top page that got Mallard's immediate attention: *The Story of My Family* by Levi Stanley.

As soon as he saw it, Mallard *knew* that he had to read it. He needed to know what it was about. Maybe what was inside would change things. Maybe, somehow, even though it was highly unlikely, Levi already knew the secret.

Standing up straight, Mallard looked to his right and realized how unobservant he had actually been in the whole ordeal. Levi's car wasn't even in the driveway. Mallard reasoned that the young man had probably run to the grocery store or somewhere to grab a bite to eat.

Mallard turned to look down the road, just to make sure that Levi's car, or anyone else's for that matter, wasn't approaching. He was in the clear, safe, but he knew that he would have to be quick. He reached his hand out to the doorknob and was surprised to find that Levi had left the door unlocked. In Devlin there was very little crime, but it still came as a shock, especially coming from someone that must've already become accustomed to big city life. Surely Levi wouldn't dare leave his door unlocked in the city, the old man thought.

Mallard looked over his shoulder once more, just to make sure that no one was looking and he only had to slip half of his tall, slim body into the house. Immediately, the dog was jumping up on him. Mallard grabbed the stack of papers, slipped them out from underneath the rubber band that made a *snap!* as it hit the laptop, and pulled himself back outside, shutting the door behind him. He looked at what he held and quickly fanned through the pages before holding the entire stack safely against his chest and scrambling back to the sublime familiarity of his own home.

III

THE NEAREST grocery store was out on Highway 22, just outside the town limits.

Earlier in the evening Levi had pondered different possibilities for dinner, but had ultimately decided on just going to the store. The store was situated in between two empty fields. Both of the fields were marked with construction site signs, indicating that new business would be coming soon, but the ground had yet to be broken on either side. The grocery store's parking lot only had a few vehicles parked in it, mostly pick up trucks. Levi parked on an aisle that didn't have any other spots taken. Grocery carts had been left at random spots throughout the parking area. Levi walked past a heavy set lady that was pushing a cart that rattled horribly on its wheels. A bobcat in heat, Levi thought and chuckled quietly to himself.

Once inside, Levi was greeted with curious looks from almost every employee and shopper. At first he thought that they must've all recognized him, but then upon thinking on it, maybe it was that they were simply staring because they *didn't* recognize him. In a town as small as Devlin, and so far away from the interstate, it mustn't have been very often that a stranger stepped into the store. It was a relief for Levi to see that most of the people that he wandered past were not ones that he recognized. Not wanting to make small talk or answer any questions about why he was in town, he thought it best to simply avoid getting into a conversation with anyone.

After grabbing a canister of coffee, a six pack of beer, and a frozen pizza, Levi walked to the front of the store where the cashiers were located. There were only three lanes open, each of them with comparable, short lines. One of the workers he had gone to high school with, another was his mother's age, and the third was a young teenager with bright blue hair. He chose the third. She was so young that there would be no way for her to know him. After scanning the items, the cashier looked up at him. Levi noticed that she had a silver hoop looped around her a bottom lip.

"Got your ID?" The girl asked as she was smacking on a wad of bright pink bubble gum.

The question caught Levi by surprise. He was shocked that at his age he was actually being carded for beer. He fumbled at his back jeans pocket for his wallet. "Yeah, yeah, here you go."

The girl studied the Georgia driver's license. Levi pointed out the birth date that she was searching for and failing to locate. The girl obviously didn't see a lot of out of state licenses.

She glanced back up at Levi. "You're Levi Stanley," she nodded. "I've heard about you."

Levi was perplexed by the statement. He didn't ask what the girl had meant, what exactly it was that she had *heard* about him. Instead he just smiled, grabbed his bag and left. What she had said clambered about in his head as loudly as the fat lady's shopping cart wheels all the way back to the house.

Back at the house Levi carried his groceries to the kitchen. He placed the pizza on the counter, took a beer out of the carrying case, twisted the top, took a long drink and sat the bottle on the table. The beer was OK, but he preferred the hoppy taste of craft beers, something that the stores in Devlin were sadly lacking. As he went to open the refrigerator to put the rest of the six- pack away, he noticed that the phone number for Calvin Harris was written on a small piece of paper and stuck to the front of the refrigerator with a magnet that was in the shape of the flower from a magnolia tree. Levi remembered that he had seen the number posted there before, on one of his infrequent visits home, and had asked his mother about it. She had informed him that Calvin had been helping her keep up with yard work. He remembered how Calvin had been the one to discover Jill's body. Levi removed the paper from the refrigerator, folded it in half, and slipped it into his back pocket.

After eating dinner and drinking a few of the beers Levi began preparing for bed. It was early. In fact it was so early that it was just beginning to turn dark outside. There was a steady hum of cicadas and crickets. Inside, the house was quiet. Levi wasn't usually one to take a bath in a tub, he was more of the shower type of guy, but the idea of soaking in the old claw foot tub was so inviting that he couldn't turn it down. While he was submerged in the warm, soapy water, Craven rested on the ceramic tile floor of the bathroom with his head on Levi's pair of jeans. Occasionally Levi would hear a creek deep within the structure of the house. Each time, there was an ever so brief thought that would shoot through his mind that his parents were in another room.

Could the thump of an old pipe actually be the setting of a pan on the stovetop as his mother began to prepare supper?

Or could the tree branches scratching against the old windows be instead the crinkle of his father's newspaper?

Of course these thoughts were instinct. It was his brain's uncontrolled way of associating one thing with another. Just then, just as Levi was thinking about the way that his memories were so intricately linked with sounds and smells, the slightest aroma of basil drifted past his nose.

It must've come in through the open bathroom window, he thought.

While the herb was believed by some to induce calmness, the smell was discomforting to Levi. It instantly brought to mind childhood and his teenage years. Over the years Levi had begun to detest the smell and taste of the herb, but every so often he had been surprised to find himself longing for the scent. He closed his eyes and inhaled deeply, savoring the aroma, letting it take him back in time.

Remembering that there was not a single basil plant currently growing in the yard, Levi wondered where the smell had come from or if he had only imagined it. He rested his head back against the curve of the tub and closed his eyes. He made a mental note of things that he needed to accomplish the next day, including contacting Calvin Harris. He planned on hiring the man to do the yard work in his absence, keeping the place looking tidy, just until the house got sold.

Moments later Levi nodded off into a brief, dreamless sleep and woke to the ear splitting sound of Craven barking. Since he had dozed off, the sun had completely set and the sky had turned black. The only light in the bathroom was coming in through the narrow, high window that was at the tip top of the wall. The moon and a nearby streetlight gave a soft glow to the mostly white bathroom. Being woken up by the dog's abrupt, earsplitting barking was always a bit alarming for Levi regardless of the cause or time and it usually sent his nerves jangling. It was obvious that the barking was coming from the front of the house. Levi wondered if someone was outside in the yard or on the porch. He wondered briefly if he had locked the door. He glanced at the clock and saw that it was only nine thirty in the night. In Levi's mind it was too early in the night for an intruder or anything bad to happen. It had *just* gotten dark. He knew that in reality those things could happen at anytime, but there were hours in the night that ever since Levi had been little he had reserved for bad deeds.

Levi stepped out of the tub and toweled off. Craven's barks were persistent as Levi put on pajama pants and a t-shirt. He walked into the living room and saw that Craven was at the door, looking through the glass, still barking. Levi stepped closer and flipped on the porch light, sending a soothing yellow glow over the front of the house. There was no one or nothing out there. Levi scanned the yard and the porch, searching for what could have excited the dog. He was expecting to see a stray cat or neighbor passing by on the sidewalk, but the only thing that he could find that was even *slightly* out of the ordinary was that the porch swing was swaying back and forth.

It was as if there had been a sudden gust of strong wind.

Or if somebody had just stood from the seat.

Levi opened the door and stepped onto the porch. As soon as he did it, the thought occurred to him that it was exactly that kind of thing that got people killed in the horror movies that he liked to watch when he had been younger.

But he didn't turn around. He did however leave the door standing open, just in case he needed to quickly make it back inside. Levi wasn't afraid of what he was seeing. It was more of a curiosity. He stood on the porch in the amber glow of light. Craven stood at his side, also observing. In front of them the swing was still gently moving, but it was slowing down as if it were about to become still once again.

And then something else caught Levi's attention. On the window sill that was nearest the right arm of the swing there was a wet ring of condensation where a drink had recently been sitting. It was near, if not exact, where Jill liked to place her drinking glass while she was sitting on the porch.

Levi approached the swing. He just stood there looking at it for a brief moment before he finally turned around and sat down, doing what he had been afraid of for so long. Finally he was facing his emotions head on. Levi was surprised to discover that he felt closer to her than he had in a long time. He could feel her presence.

It was like she was there with him. He propped his elbows on his knees and buried his face in his hands. Craven jumped onto the swing and joined Levi. The dog pawed at Levi's arm, obviously trying to get his attention. When Levi looked, Craven was looking back at him. The dog's eyes were full of sorrow. It was clear that the dog understood that Levi was hurting inside and wanted to comfort him. Levi wrapped his arm around the canine and pulled him close. Craven didn't tolerate the cuddling but only for a brief second before wiggling away, circling around on the seat, and finally laying back down and resting his head on Levi's leg.

The two of them sat just like that for a long while before finally turning in for the night.

☐

THE NEXT morning, Levi pushed the curtains aside and beams of the new day's light shone in through the windows. From where he stood inside the den, he looked at the swing and then at the windowsill where less than twelve hours earlier there had been a ring of condensation.

A fresh, steaming, hot cup of coffee was sitting on the table that stretched across the front of the couch. While the coffee had been brewing, Levi had stood in front of the open kitchen cabinet and studied the menagerie of coffee mugs. The shelf was full of pastels, flowers, and such. His mother had always had a thing for the most feminine mugs that she could find. The one that he had pulled out was white with a row of fluffy, sitting kittens lined around the perimeter. The felines were all colors; brown, black, white, calico. Each had its head tilted adoringly. And to top it all off, each of them had a pink bow tied around its neck. Levi lifted the cup from the table and sipped at the coffee, savoring it; he loved the first taste of coffee in the morning. Feminine mug with kittens or not, the coffee was good. Levi picked up his cell phone and dialed Paige. While he was waiting on her to answer he pressed the phone to his ear with his right shoulder and sat the coffee mug back onto the table. He picked up a disheveled blanket from the couch and began to fold it.

The previous night he had originally tried to sleep in his old room, but it had been too hot. He had even tried with the ceiling fan running at full speed and no blanket, but the heat had ultimately been just too unbearable. He found that it was just *that* room, his, the one where he had kissed Claire Carlson, that was intolerable. Walking throughout the house it was obvious that the AC had seemed to have cooled the rest of the rooms to a comfortable temperature. And so he had wound up on the couch. Outside the windows there had been the occasional hum of passing cars. As he lay there, his mind had been so wrapped up in thoughts; Jill, Claire and Diesel, the nonsense that the old man had been talking, the heat that he felt in his bedroom, the porch swing, all of it was swarming around in his head so fast that it had been difficult to get to sleep right away, but eventually, as always, sleep finally came.

That night he had dreamed of approaching the garden shed that stood in the clearing. In the dream the day was glaringly bright. When his hand reached out and pulled the door open, the inside was dripping with blood.

"Hello." Paige finally answered. Her voice was hoarse and sounded hung over. Levi imagined her just waking up. He knew that she liked to sleep in on Saturdays and that sometimes on Friday nights she liked to drink as if she were still a freshman in college.

"Hey Paige."

"Hey, how's it going?"

"Good." Levi paused, trying to think of small talk that would fill time before he asked what was really on his mind. "I met with the realtor yesterday and that seemed to go OK." Levi didn't mention all the changes to the house that the realtor had suggested. "But Paige, really I was calling for another reason."

"What's up?" Paige suddenly sounded more interested, perky even.

"I know this sounds crazy, but -", Levi paused. He knew that what he was about to suggest was so absurd that he couldn't even believe that he was considering it. "- do you believe in ghosts?"

Until the day before, Levi had been pretty sure that *he* hadn't. Throughout his life he had heard of the legend of Anna Moore and how her ghost supposedly lingers about the area surrounding Mercer Creek Baptist Church. According to the story, Anna is perpetually searching for the heart that had been cut from her chest and tossed into Hollyhock Lake. Over the years, Levi had heard rumors of numerous Anna sightings, but he had never seen or experienced anything firsthand. Even when he had been younger he had always passed the legend off as nothing more than small town lore. You have to see it to believe it, he had always thought, and now with all that had happened the night before, what he had seen and experienced, he was wondering if ghosts *were* real. It wasn't the existence of Anna Moore he was questioning though. He was wondering if he had come into contact with the spirit of his own mother.

An audible sigh could be heard from the other end of the phone. "Levi, you've only been there for a day, not even that, and you're already losing your mind."

"Really, Paige. It's a serious question."

"Why are you asking?"

"Well, you know I've told you before that Mom died in the porch swing right?"

"Yeah."

He told her about how Craven had been barking at something unseen and the way that the swing had been moving back and forth. He told her about the ring of condensation on the window sill. He told her about how he had sat in the swing the night before and felt that his mother was there with him, how it had comforted him and made him happy. He told her about the warmth that he feels every time that he steps into his old bedroom.

"Levi, please don't tell me that you're getting drawn back in."

"What? Paige, no, I'm not getting drawn back in, I'm just-"

"You hate it there, remember. And while you're there it's going to be easier for things from your past to start popping back up. Next thing you know you'll be telling me that you've seen that old girlfriend of yours. What was her name? Clara? Clarissa?"

"Claire," he corrected her.

"Whatever. My point is that you've got to let it go." Levi could hear the clink of ceramic and knew that Paige was about to fix herself her own cup of coffee. Then there was the sound from Paige's apartment of the cabinet door closing with a soft thud. "Just hurry up and sell the house so you'll never have to go back."

The doorbell rang and within an instant, from the other side of the room, Craven started barking and jumped up from where he had been resting peacefully on the floor. Levi stopped pacing and when he looked to the door, he expected to see the realtor standing on the other side, but who he saw through the curtains and panes of glass had a familiar head full of blonde hair. She was a reminder that things from the past *could* come back. Craven was running toward the door, wound up into a barking frenzy. His claws clicked with each hurried step. Rushing past Levi, the dog bumped into the corner of the coffee table on the way to greet the visitor. The coffee mug that Levi had sat there just moments earlier toppled to the floor and shattered on impact. Ceramic scattered across the hardwood and black coffee splattered outward like blood at a crime scene.

"Paige, I've got to go," he said. "I'll call you back later."

part two
a novella of romance

I

IT WAS the month of October when the garden shed first stood amid the green grass of Diesel's parent's backyard. This was seven and a half months before Levi and Claire kissed for the first time, seven and a half months before Diesel took missing. On that day, the two plastic doors on the front were standing open and the interior was dark and empty. It was big enough for a couple of chairs. The outside was already faded from years of standing in the weather. The walls were gray and the sloping roof was a deep red.

  Claire and Levi circled the modular object, studying it as if it were a pod from an alien spaceship that had somehow found its way to earth and landed in the middle of Devlin. It was obvious that the catawampus structure had just been dropped in its current spot with little to no thought on its placement. Its arrival was so recent that without being able to see underneath, Claire knew that the Bermuda grass below the bottom slat of plastic would be just as green as what covered the rest of yard. While Diesel seemed excited about the shed, both Claire and Levi studied the foreign structure with trepidation.

  Diesel walked the perimeter of the pieced together building in a proud strut, full of cockiness. He tapped his knuckles against the plastic side. The tapping resounded with a hollow thump. "I got it for free. Jackson's old man wanted to get rid of it and I thought, shit, why not." Jackson was Diesel's age and helped out at the shop.

  Diesel removed his camouflage cap and scratched at his short, matted down hair. Sweat beaded on his forehead. Even though it was the middle of October, the sun was still summer time hot and was beating down on the three of them with a fiery intensity. They stood at the very edge of the yard. The tall, red siding of Mr. Atwater's shop loomed beside them. Orange oak leaves scattered the ground. Diesel leaned against the side of the shed, placed his cap back on his head and crossed his arms.

Claire studied him. He wore a white t-shirt that he had at some point in time used a pair of scissors to cut the sleeves off. His arms were lean and muscled from working on cars and doing yard work. Recently, Claire had found herself drawn to Diesel.

In fact, over the past few months she had come to realize that she was drawn to both of them, Diesel *and* Levi. She had known both of them their whole lives and had always been friends with them, but recently things had begun to get more complicated with what she felt for them. She had no idea where this newfound attraction for each of them had come from. It just seemed like one day, out of the blue, it had happened. What she felt toward each of them seemed so true that it seemed like it always had been so.

"And what are you going to do with it?" Claire asked.

Diesel smirked. He placed his cap back on his head and stood up straight. "This'll be our new place to hang out, our beer drinking spot." He blushed when he said it.

Levi and Claire both laughed.

"Right here in your backyard?" Levi asked. They were at the age when they still hid drinking from their parents.

Diesel smirked and spit onto the ground. "Na, I'm moving it to the clearing."

Neither Levi nor Claire protested. At the time they didn't see anything disheartening about the idea of tainting that area of land with the ugly, store bought atrocity. As teenagers they didn't see the symbolism that could be discussed in book groups if the scenario that they were living was placed within the plot of a novel. The acre of land had long been a place of childhood innocence and imagination, but with the addition of the garden shed, it was on its way to becoming something else entirely.

By that point in time the three of them never went to the tree house anymore anyway. They saw it as childish, something they had outgrown. So the idea of placing the shed in the same spot as the tree house didn't seem like a bad idea at all. And Claire liked the boyish rebelliousness that the idea represented in Diesel.

She doubted that Levi would ever suggest something of the sorts.

And so, similar to the day almost a decade before when they had transported the timber that would become the tree house, with the help of a hand truck the three of them deconstructed and drug the garden shed piece by piece to the spot where it would sit for many more years. Over that same fall and winter the three of them hung out together in the shed a few times, but soon enough it became the spot where Diesel would go to be alone. It was where he went many nights to drink himself into oblivion. He liked the dark, cramped interior. Over a very short amount of time, the shed seemed to become solely his.

It was in that same garden shed where the police found him during the late spring of the following year.

☐

The next May…

BLOOD. THE cop said that it was the first thing that he noticed when he opened the door.

"There was blood all over the inside walls of that shed," he told the newspaper. "Somebody really had it out for that guy."

Later, both Levi and Claire would dramatically imagine the crimson dripping down the plastic walls and pooling on the floor.

Levi and Claire were sitting at the Stanley's kitchen table, side by side. The cop was standing across from them. His rectangular, silver name badge stated that his name was Cooper. The man didn't appear to be too many years out of high school himself. He had transferred to Devlin from a larger city a couple of years earlier and had been an instant heart throb among the young women of the town. His arm was leaning against the laminate countertop. Every so often there would be the crackle of static from the CB radio that was clipped to his black leather belt. It was just the three of them in the kitchen. Mr. Cooper had asked Jill to wait outside while he spoke to Levi and Claire.

It was the middle of the morning, the day of graduation. It was a day that should have been full of excitement and promise. Outside, the cornflower blue sky looked to be bright and happy. Stringy cirrus clouds floated across the horizon, indicating a clear day. Everywhere, all over town, the trees, flowers, vegetable gardens and farm crops were all vibrantly green, flowering, setting fruit, and already being harvested. There were people that were already loading their cars for a day at the lake while others were preparing to barbecue in their own backyards. To an outsider, all of Devlin looked to be perfection, but it was a façade, because inside the Stanley house the ambiance was anything but what the cheerfulness of the day suggested.

It was the day that Diesel was found in the garden shed. His head had been bashed with a metal pipe.

"I'm having a hard time understanding why you were not worried about where Diesel was for all of that time," Cooper spoke in a tone of authority and accusation. He walked to the table and stood directly across from Claire and looked her in the face as he spoke. "I mean, you're his girlfriend." He paused, letting both the words and the reality of the situation sink in. "If what I've been told by others is correct, the two of you have been dating for the past seven months or so. And if what I remember is still accurate, at your age, that's a long time to be in a relationship with someone." The cop stood up straight and heaved his chest out. "Now, if there is anything that you are hiding, you need to come clean about it now."

Claire knew that they would find out eventually and she had seen enough TV shows and movies to know that once they found out that she and Levi were hiding something then the outcome would only be worse, and so she told him. Sitting beside Levi, she told Cooper how the two of them had been fooling around for the past week, behind Diesel's back. As soon as she said it, she knew what it sounded like. She knew the assumption that the cop would have.

Cooper looked toward Levi and nodded as if it was all becoming clear. He looked back to Claire. "So would the fact of the two of you being together, behind your boyfriend's back never the less, give Levi enough motivation to commit a crime?"

"I didn't -" Levi started, but Cooper cut him off.

The cop pointed his finger at Levi. "I'm not talking to you. I'm asking her."

Claire was crying. She shook her head. "No."

"Maybe he wanted Diesel out of the picture all together?"

"He wouldn't do that." She looked over at Levi. His complexion was ashen. He appeared afraid of what was happening, what *could* happen.

"Well, if he wouldn't do it, then who would Claire?" The tone of his voice was aggravated and gravel-like.

"I don't know. I've already told you that I don't know."

The cop began to pace the kitchen floor. "Well, it's lucky for everyone that's involved in this ordeal that the doctors say that Diesel is probably going to be OK. As soon as he is well enough to speak and comprehend, maybe we'll be able get some answers from him." He looked back at Levi as he spoke. "What we're looking at is probably considered assault and battery. His parents want to press charges on whoever did this to their son."

Claire and Levi nodded in understanding.

"His alcohol level was sky high. I'm assuming, being his girlfriend and all, that you've been aware that he's such a heavy drinker?"

"He's been drinking a lot lately. It seems to be more though just in the past couple of weeks."

"Is he an alcoholic?" Cooper shot back. Not *do you think*, but *is* he.

"No – I mean I don't think so." The truth was that Claire wasn't sure. She had even begun to wonder the same thing herself.

That night, long after Cooper had left, Claire visited Diesel in the hospital. He still wasn't able to speak. The sight of him lying there motionless in the bed, wrapped in bandages, filled Claire with guilt over what she had done to him; that she had cheated on him with Levi, realizing that it was very likely that her actions had led to his current state. She should have been with him instead of Levi. If she could go back in time, just a few days earlier, she would have never even kissed Levi. It had been a stupid mistake, one that she would have to live with for the rest of her life. Looking at Diesel, thinking about it, she realized that she had probably even been with Levi at the time of the assault. The realization made her literally feel sick to her stomach. That same night she broke off things with Levi.

She told him that they couldn't see each other any more; that she had made up her mind and she wanted to stay with Diesel.

☐

The month of August, that same year...

THE NIGHT before Levi was to leave for college, Claire asked Levi to go to a movie with her.

"Just you and me, like we used to do," she said. The idea seemed innocent enough at first, but even when she said it, Levi knew that what she *really* meant was that Diesel would not be there.

At first Levi had been hesitant about going, but ultimately

decided that he would give it a chance. He hoped that even after everything that had happened between them that they could find a way to still be friends. Going away to college had been a last minute decision. Up until Claire had broken things off with him back in June, he hadn't been sure what he was going to do that fall. *Before* he had thought that maybe he would stay in Devlin and commute to the local Tech school. But then came the day that Diesel was found beaten and left for dead in the garden shed. At the time Levi had been in love with Claire, he knew that for certain. Afterwards he had been so heart broken that he couldn't wait to leave town and so the decision had been made; he would go away to school. He had spent the remainder of the summer alone.

    That night, Levi's last night in town, Claire picked him and drove to Augusta. The movie that they saw was a slasher with a whodunit twist at the end. They both enjoyed it immensely and talked about it all the way home. When they arrived back at Levi's house, Claire parked behind Jill's car in the narrow driveway. She got out of the car and walked with Levi through the gate and across the stone path that led through the yard. Jill had left the porch light on and the bulb cast a soothing yellow glow over the entire yard. A light breeze carried the faint but detectable scent of basil through the night air. That year, along with several bushes of summer squash, a wild abundance of the herb grew a good distance from around the base of the huge oak tree in the corner.

    Levi walked up the steps of the porch first. Claire followed him and they stood in front of the closed front door. Levi didn't sit on the swing at the end of the porch. He didn't want Claire to sit beside him. He knew that it would have been an invitation to begin talking. Instead he stood rigid. Through the pair of windows that flanked the door, the interior of the house was dim. Inside, only a single lamp had been left on. Levi knew that the lack of lighting was an indication that his mother had already gone to bed for the night.

    The American flag that was hanging on one of the posts of the porch was moving gently in the breeze. The mid-August night was pleasantly warm. Even though summer would last for another month, the change of seasons was on the horizon and could be felt in the air and seen in the color of the sky. Just in the past few days the impending season had become noticeable when people walked down the sidewalk of the town square during the daylight hours; their shadows had already began to appear longer than they had in the early summer. It was another sign that the angle of the sun was shifting, that things were about to change.

"I'm going to miss you," Claire told him. She was fidgeting her hands together, looking down at her feet as she talked. "Will you keep in touch? Email me sometime?" After the incident with Diesel and up until that night, the two of them had not spoken.

Levi nodded. He didn't have a computer of his own, but knew that there would be a computer lab on the bottom floor of the dorm where he would be staying. The special amenity had been so proudly advertised in the brochures that it seemed like it was the main draw of the entire campus.

"It's the same that it's always been, but I wrote it down just in case you ever forget it." Claire took a small, folded square of paper from the back pocket of her jeans and handed it to Levi.

Levi took the paper from her and without unfolding it, placed it into his wallet. They stood facing one another, arms crossed.

Claire uncrossed her arms and wiped a tear away from her cheek. "I'm sorry," she looked away from Levi. "I feel like there's the possibility that I'll never see you again, I mean with everything that's happened between us."

Levi stared off into the darkness of the yard, not answering Claire, not telling her that *yes* he would definitely try to keep in touch. At that moment Levi thought that it really was very likely that he would choose to never talk to her again.

How could he move forward if he didn't let go of his past?

"I need to go to bed. I've got a big day tomorrow," he said.

Claire nodded in understanding.

Then Levi smelled the rebellious aroma of cigarette smoke. The smell of burning tobacco was so strong that it overpowered the already fragrant smell of the basil that grew in the far corner of the yard. Levi immediately knew who the owner of the cigarette must have been. There was the sound of the gate latch and then the gate swung inward. Diesel stepped into the yard. His steps were uneasy from both the numerous beers that he had drunk and the slow process of recovery. Underneath the camouflage cap that he wore, his hair was finally beginning to fill in from where it had been shaved and the wound had been stitched back together with black sutures. The scar snaked out from under the cap, ran past his eye, and ended at his cheekbone. In the dark, Levi thought that he looked like a monster, one that he had helped to create.

Claire spoke first. "Diesel," she said. The tone of her voice was one that was supposed to sound as if she was happy to see him, but the innate dread could not be covered up by her pretending. She turned her back to Levi and stepped to the edge of the porch. Diesel was already across the yard and his heavy, mud caked boots were on the steps. Even though Claire was standing on the flat of the porch, Diesel was so tall and looming that he only had to stand on the bottom step before his eyes were level with hers. Claire wrapped her arms around Diesel's neck and kissed his cheek. She laid her head on his shoulder and Diesel followed suit and placed his chin on hers. From where Levi stood he could only see the back of Claire's head of tight blonde curls, but Diesel leered at him across the width of the porch. Underneath his cap, Diesel's glassy blue eyes glared at Levi. Claire and Diesel swayed and Levi knew for a fact that Diesel had been drinking before coming over. The unsteady, drunken, and unbalanced weight of him was causing Claire to sway uneasily. Diesel's left hand was placed low on Claire's back and his right arm was held out to the side. The burning cigarette was between his fingertips. Just a year earlier, the fact of Diesel showing up unannounced would not have been out of the ordinary. In fact it would have even been expected, but that night, the out of the blue visit held an air of menace and venom.

"I've been looking all over for you," Diesel told Claire, loud enough for Levi to hear. His voice was slurred. "And imagine finding you here of all places." He continued to look at Levi as he spoke. "I thought you were done with this twerp."

Diesel slipped out of Claire's grasp and walked away from her and across the porch, closer to Levi. He tossed the cigarette butt over the porch railing. "Tomorrow's the day?" he asked Levi, but Levi didn't respond. "Well, it's a damned good thing because I don't know if I could take much more of this. You running around with my girl's kind of wrong."

"We weren't - ," Levi began to defend himself but Diesel cut him off.

Diesel stepped closer to Levi. He gripped the collar of Levi's black t-shirt in his fist and pulled Levi toward him. There faces were inches apart. As Diesel spoke, Levi could smell the cigarettes and beer on his breath.

"When are you going to get it through your thick skull? She doesn't want you no more." When Diesel talked, spittle flung from his mouth onto Levi's face. "And if you ever lay your hands on her, I swear to God that it'll be the last time you will."

Anger boiled within Levi. Even though Diesel was nearly an entire foot taller than Levi and built with muscle, Levi pushed him. Diesel's grip was still on Levi's shirt and Levi felt the neckline stretch even further. He could hear the rip of thread and fabric. Diesel nearly lost his footing, but flung Levi back against the door, releasing his hold of him. The shirt was stretched so loose that it hung over Levi's prominent collar bone and drooped down to his thin chest, exposing the top bones of his ribcage. Diesel glared at Levi and Levi was sure that Diesel's tightly clenched fist was soon to pound into his face.

Diesel's chest was held out in authority as he shook his head. "I wouldn't do that again if I were you." He held his eyes locked with Levi's for a moment longer before turning back toward Claire and chuckled. "The next time you come into town, if you come anywhere near me or her -," Diesel nodded toward Claire and didn't finish the statement. Instead he left it for Levi's imagination to what would happen. Diesel stepped closer to Claire. He placed his hand on her back and led her down the steps. "You'll wish that you hadn't."

Levi was in the house before they even made it to the gate. He locked the door behind him and walked to his room, not caring if he stepped on the squeaking boards in front of the door. He shut his door and pulled the stretched and ruined t-shirt over his head. It had been a favorite shirt of his.

The walls of the room were bare. The top of the wooden dresser that stood directly across from the foot of the bed was empty. With the exception of his grandfather's old almanac that was lying flat on the surface, the nightstand was the same. Levi fell onto the bed, unable to sleep, reminding himself that as of the next day, everything that had happened with himself, Claire, and Diesel would no longer matter. All of it he would leave behind.

The next morning he was slouched in the passenger seat of his mother's car. He barely even glanced over his shoulder at the house that he had grown up in as the car began to back out of the driveway. Even though at the time Levi didn't care if he would remember anything of the house or its surrounding property, the truth was that he already knew all of it so intimately that every square inch of it would leave a lasting impression on his psyche nonetheless. Years later he would be able to recall every detail of the structure.

Even though the car was only just beginning to back out of the driveway, Levi already had his headphones over his ears and a CD in the player. He didn't care to hear the familiar pop of gravel underneath the car's tires. The music coming from the portable music player was turned so loud that Jill could hear the screaming vocals and screeching guitars of heavy metal music from all the way across the front seat of the minivan. Levi's head was propped against the passenger side window. Forever after, the triumphant day of finally leaving home would always be associated with screaming music and the smell of hot, vinyl car seats.

All of Levi's clothes and most important belongings were packed away in the back of the vehicle. It was a day that Levi had been impatiently awaiting for the entire summer, ever since he had made the final decision. That summer had been hell. He was ready to hightail it out of there.

"I need to cut that tree back," Jill said, referring to the massive oak as she craned her neck to each side, searching for any oncoming traffic. After she was sure that no cars were coming from either direction, Jill backed the car into the narrow street. It seemed to Levi that the car paused longer than it normally did. The house was on the right side of the street, the side where Levi's head was resting against the window. Levi caught a glimpse of his mother as she looked across the width of the car's interior and toward the house. It was almost like Jill was pleading for her son to look at it one more time.

"Levi, take your headphones off."

Levi could hear his mother talking from across the seat. He couldn't understand what she was saying over the music that was blaring in his ears, but he heard her muffled voice and knew that she was either trying to tell him something or ask him a question. Levi removed the headphones from over his head and looked uninterestingly toward her.

"What?" He shrugged his shoulders.

"Levi, just please talk to me on the way there, OK? It takes only a little over an hour to get to the campus. The least you could do is talk."

"What do you want me to talk about?" Levi turned to look at his mother, disapprovingly.

"I don't know. Tell me how last night went. Did you have fun?"

"I wouldn't call it fun."

"How was Claire?"

"She was fine."

"Were you smoking last night? I found a cigarette butt in the shrubbery," his mother asked as she veered the car onto the oncoming traffic of the main highway.

Levi sighed with frustration. He remembered how Diesel had tossed the spent cigarette over the porch rail just before he had grabbed onto Levi's shirt. "It was Diesel's."

"Oh." The mention of Diesel's name seemed to perk his mother's interest. She had made it clear all summer that she thought that the three of them should try and reconcile their differences. "Diesel came over? I didn't think you really hung out with him much anymore." *After what happened*, she implied.

The details had gone unspoken between the two of them but Levi knew that the gossip had spread all around Devlin and that his mother surely had heard about what he and Claire had been doing behind Diesel's back.

"I don't."

"Levi, the three of you really need to get over your differences. I don't really know what all happened, but they are *good* friends. I hope it's just a teenage thing that y'all are going through. You need to hold on to them. The three of y'all used to be so close."

"I don't want to be friends with them." Levi placed the headphones back over his head and again pressed the play button. He put his head back against the window and closed his eyes. He didn't watch through the back window of the car as the small town disappeared behind him. As far as he was concerned, he was already gone and had been for months.

☐

THE UNIVERSITY campus itself seemed to be several times larger than the entire town of Devlin. The dormitories alone were taller than any building in the small town where he had grown up. There was only one structure in Devlin that even remotely compared to the height of the buildings at The University, the old water tower that stood on the outskirts of town.

The day had turned brightly sunny and seasonably warm. From the passenger seat, Levi studied the entranceway to the campus. In front of him, the paved driveway led through two enormously tall wrought iron gates. The open gates were flanked on each side by two unusually tall weeping willow trees. An old, concrete sign stood to the right, nestled in the drooping branches of the tree. The sign was edged in red brick and stated *UNIVERSITY* across the cracked, gray front. It was where he would start anew. Nobody there knew him, and even though he was nervous about being on his own, he also liked the possibilities that awaited him.

Inside the gates there were studious looking academic buildings that had long ago been constructed from red brick. Vibrantly green grass covered the ground. Aged brick sidewalks lead to and from each building and stretched serpentine through the lush greenery. A multitude of oak trees gave plenty of shade. There were already students sitting under the shade provided by the canopy of limbs. Aside from the oak trees, the campus grounds were scattered with weeping willows just like the pair outside the gate. Everywhere there were cars waiting to park so the parents could drop off their sons and daughters. It was move in day and there were students and parents milling all around with campus maps in hand, searching for the correct dorm.

Jill drove through the campus until she reached the dormitory that Levi would be staying in. After parking near the dorm, Levi walked with his mother and studied the faces that wandered around him. Some of the students wore excited expressions while others appeared to be nervous.

For the next two semesters Levi would be staying in one of the freshman dorms that were located on the east side of campus. After lugging his belongings into the building and up the elevator, he finally said goodbye to his mother and began unpacking.

The room that he was staying in wasn't much bigger than his bedroom at home. One difference was that this one was going to be shared with another person. The four walls were made of cement blocks. The only pieces of furniture that stood within the confines of the room were two plain, wooden beds and a set of matching desks. Built-in wardrobes stood across from the foot of each bed.

He was in the midst of placing his clothes in the closet when he heard a female voice in the hallway. "I am totally going to kick his ass," the girl stated loudly. Levi walked to the open door and peered into the hall. A red haired girl, with her back turned to him, was standing in between two other girls, two blondes, and pounded on the door to the room across from his. The red head must've sensed his presence behind her because she spun around just seconds after Levi walked up. She was wearing a pair of black, intellectual type glasses. She looked Levi up and down.

"What?" she said.

Levi was speechless. The girl was so confrontational that it caught him completely off guard. Most of the girls that he had gone to school with and known back in Devlin were not like that.

"Is there a problem?" she asked.

"No." Levi shrugged. "No problem." He turned to go back into his room and heard the girl's fist beating the door again. A moment later, the girl growled with frustration and stormed off.

Levi's roommate arrived later in the day. His name was Jonny Statham. He, like Levi, was from a small town. The town that Jonny was from was in North Carolina. From across the room, Levi sat on his bed, pretending to read a paperback horror novel, and watched as Jonny unpacked his things. One of the first things that Jonny pulled out of his oversized duffel bag was a framed photograph of a smiling girl. He gently traced his fingertips over the glass before sitting the frame on his nightstand.

Levi wondered who the girl was, but didn't ask. He didn't want to come across as being nosy on the first day.

Not long after dusk had fallen on that first night, Levi and Jonny ventured out of their dorm. Outside, students were sitting on the benches that stood around the small common area in front of the dorm. Many of them were smoking cigarettes. The distinct smell of clove drifted along the air.

Together he and Jonny walked across the campus to the cafeteria. This building didn't match the rest of the campus. Instead, it had a 1950's feel to it. Inside, people were bustling about, carrying trays of food, searching for a place to sit. It was while they were standing in the serving line that Levi spotted the girl with the red hair. She was walking toward the cash registers with her tray of food in hand. She looked over and studied Levi as she passed. Levi turned his attention away and tried not to look again in her direction, not wanting another confrontation.

Minutes later, Levi and Jonny were sitting in the dining hall at one of the tables that rested against a set of looming windows, eating, when the girl came over.

"Hey, my name's Sophia." She introduced herself as soon as she walked up. Sophia looked at Levi as she spoke. "Don't call me Sophie." She fluttered her eyelashes and rolled her eyes, "so juvenile."

Levi laughed at the girl's aggressiveness. "I'm Levi and this is my roommate, Jonny." He nodded across the table.

"There's a party tonight at the Delta house if you want to go."

Levi shrugged his shoulders and looked at his roommate. "Yeah, I guess so."

"Be there at eleven?"

"OK."

Sophia, not Sophie, Levi reminded himself, walked away.

College was weird. For one thing, Levi wasn't used to random girls that he didn't know walk up to him and invite him to parties. He was also surprised at his own willingness to agree to such things. It was only the first day of being there and he was already surprising himself and making new friends.

Putting the past to rest was going to be easier than he had originally thought.

Back at the dorm, Levi finally asked Jonny about the girl in the photo.

"My girlfriend," Jonny said and left it at that.

At quarter till eleven they were standing in the hallway and Levi was locking the door to the room when the door behind him, the one across the hall, the door that Sophia had been banging on earlier in the day swung open. Levi looked over his shoulder and saw that the guy that walked out of the room was wearing only his underwear. He obviously played sports and worked out every chance that he got. He was the type of guy that had the body and confidence to walk around in front of strangers wearing nothing but his briefs and caused normal guys, like Levi, to feel agonizingly inadequate. Levi watched as he walked down the hall toward the bathroom.

For a moment Levi wondered what he was getting himself into. If Sophia knew *that* guy and had any reason to be mad at him, as she obviously did, should *he* really be going to meet her at a party? What if that guy was her boyfriend or an angry ex? What if

Mr. Underwear found out? Judging by the looks of him, Mr. Underwear could kick Levi's ass in a minute flat. It would be just like what he had gotten himself into with Claire and Diesel all over again. And he had learned from his mistake. He wasn't about to willingly put himself into *that* situation again.

Outside, students were wandering about in storms of excitement, presumably on the way to parties. Many of them had obviously been drinking already. Levi and Jonny walked across campus and with little trouble found the location that Sophia had invited them to. This area of the campus had old fashioned lamp posts spaced apart along the sidewalk. Yellow bulbs shined from the glass canisters at the top of each post, illuminating the night. The lamp posts had been there when the university had first opened. In fact, this area of the campus was where the school had started; it was the heart of The University. All the rest was from the years of expansion that followed.

The house was an old two story structure with several white columns on the front. A massive statue of an open book stood in front of the house. A guy and girl were standing near the statue talking to one another. The statue was as tall as either of them. The page on the right side was curled at the top corner as if it was being turned by an unseen hand.

Levi could hear the music pumping from inside of the house as he and his roommate walked closer. Several partiers were hanging out on the porch. Some were sitting on the porch rail while others were standing, leaning against the side of the house, and sitting on the steps. It seemed that every one of them had a drink of some sort in their hands. Like those outside the dorm, most of them also held a burning cigarette.

Once they entered through the front door, it didn't take long for them to find Sophia. She was standing in the kitchen with the same two girls that she had been with earlier in the day. She introduced her two friends to the roommates as they walked up. There names were Stacy and Rebecca.

Without being asked to do so, Sophia turned around and reached her hand into a cooler full of sloshing ice. She pulled out two beers. She handed a can to Levi and one to Jonny. The can was ice cold in Levi's hand. A semi melted ice cube floated in the water that was pooled on the top. It was the first beer that Levi had since Halloween night the year before.

The four of them stood that way for a while, talking and drinking. Sophia and her friends smoked cigarettes and offered them to Levi and Jonny who each declined. As opposed to most everybody else at that particular party, Sophia smoked cloves. Before coming to The University, Levi had never known anybody that smoked them. At home, everybody'd smoked your normal, run of the mill cigarette. He immediately assumed that cloves were popular among the artier, more intellectual type. He had noticed it with the students outside of the dorm and now with Sophia. The scent was overpowering as it drifted toward him and seemed to stick to his lips. He licked his lips and could actually taste the sticky flavor of the cloves. It made him wonder what it would be like to kiss her. As the night spiraled further into an alcohol induced haze, Levi's attraction to Sophia grew, but the image of Mr. Underwear, the muscled guy that lived directly across from him on his floor, kept threatening him. He too vividly remembered what it was like to be in this same situation.

"Is that guy your boyfriend?" He finally yelled over the music to Sophia, wanting to make sure that it was safe to proceed.

Sophia leaned closer to him. "What?"

"That guy that lives on my floor. Is he your boyfriend?"

Sophia straightened up and laughed. She looked over at each of her two friends. One of them was talking to Jonny and the other was talking it up with a new guy that had wandered over. Sophia grabbed Levi's arm. "Let's go outside!"

Together they burst through the front door of the house and into the night. They ran. Sophia still had Levi's arm grasped within her hand as she led him. They didn't go far, only past the statue of the book and across the sidewalk until they came to a grassy square. Sophia hit the ground first, she didn't sit as much as she fell, and Levi sat across from her. It was quieter there on the grassy square. No other students were around. The buildings that surrounded the block were made up of classrooms and administrative offices. Through the windows, the interiors were dark. There was only the occasional glow of nightlights and that of the red exit signs that were hanging above stairwell doors. The square itself had a few lampposts. The Delta house was off in the distance. Levi and Sophia were close enough to where the music could still be heard.

"Are you a freshman?" Levi asked and sipped from his beer.

"Sophomore, but you were asking me about Justin. That's

his name by the way and no he's not my boyfriend. He's my kid brother." She said it like the year that separated them was twenty instead of one.

It was a relief to know that the guy was her brother. "And why are you going to kick your brother's ass?" Levi asked her, referencing what he overheard her saying earlier that day.

Sophia's cheeks turned red with embarrassment. It was surprising to Levi that she would become embarrassed so easily. Up until then she had been so opinionated and outspoken. "You heard me say that?" She giggled. "OK. This is the deal." She said up straighter and wiggled closer to Levi. "Justin is the biggest whore you'll ever meet."

Levi laughed.

"I'm serious. I mean, already, he's been here just one day and has already managed to sleep with one of my best friends."

"What? When did he even have time to do that?" Levi thought about how over the past twelve hours he had been so busy moving his things, finding his way around campus, and unpacking that he couldn't even fathom how he could have found time to hook up with somebody.

"From what I've been told, it doesn't take long, if you catch my drift." She raised her eyebrows over the frames of her glasses. "Anyway, so tell me about you." She touched his knee.

With all the alcohol in his system, Levi opened up. He told his new friend all about Devlin. He told her details about Claire and Diesel. He told her all that had happened over the summer, what they had done and how Diesel had been attacked.

"And they never found out who did it?" she asked, referring to the assault on Diesel.

"No. Not yet anyway. Diesel insists that it was a woman that attacked him."

They sat there for a while longer. Overhead, through the drooping branches of the weeping willow trees, white stars sparkled in the black sky. It felt good to talk to somebody new. Levi could already tell that he liked this girl named Sophia. She made him laugh. And while they were together, he was able to forget about Claire and Diesel. Even when he had been talking about it with her, the past seemed less pressing.

"What are you here for?" Levi asked her.

"Here? As in, here with you?"

Levi laughed again. "What are you majoring in?"

"Actually I'm not going here this year. I leave tomorrow to go to England to study abroad. I'm an art major. I was just here today helping Justin get situated, as if he needed any help at that." She rolled her eyes. "Tonight I'm staying with my friends."

The revelation that she was leaving the very next day was disheartening for Levi. He had seen something special in her. Even though they had met only several hours earlier, he liked her already. She seemed like somebody that he could be with. He liked her dramatic statements and expressions. She made him laugh.

"Come on, I want to show you something." Sophia stood up and grabbed Levi's hand again. She pulled, helping him to his feet. Together they ran again, across the grass and the sidewalk, and in between buildings. They emerged from an alleyway that was sandwiched between the brick walls of two buildings. A large reflection pool stretched out in front of them. The water was still in the calm, dark night. The illuminated steps to the campus library stood on one side. Sophia led him around to the opposite side where a concrete platform jutted out into the water similar to the way a wooden dock stretched over the water of a country pond.

They walked onto the platform, all the way to the end where an unoccupied bench sat, forlornly overlooking the water. Together they sat on the bench. As opposed to the side where the library stood, the view from this side was full of trees, mostly more weeping willows.

"See that?" Sophia asked as she pointed straight ahead.

Levi looked in the direction that she was pointing. In the distance, through the willow branches he could see the statue of the open book. The giant tome was illuminated with the yellow glow from the pair of lamp posts at each side.

"The two pages that the book is opened on are blank," Sophia said. "I like the way that the one on the right is curled and the one on the left isn't. It's like you can't go back and change *anything*. All of those pages have already been written, done, caput. It's like it is just waiting for you to fill in those two so the page can turn. You can only go forward, not knowing what each page or chapter will contain." She straightened up and looked at Levi. "All those previous pages greatly influence what we're writing now, but they're done. It's like we're writing the story as we go. Like there's no stopping the future, but what we do now, on this page, will determine what is on the next page and so forth," she looked like she was getting confused at her own drawn out analogy. "You get what I'm saying?"

What Sophia was saying was so far removed from any conversation that Levi had ever had before, that fact combined with the numerous beers that he had drunk throughout the night was making it difficult to comprehend what it all meant. "So that book is life," he stated, trying to grasp his head around the analogy. "And what kind of book is it?"

"It doesn't have to be contained to any one genre, Levi. It can be made up of all sorts of things." Sophia stood. "Romance, mystery, humor, horror, literature, it can contain all of those."

"So you're saying that what we are doing right now, in the present, we are writing as we go. We can make the story go anywhere and that it could end any way we want."

Sophia sat again. "Yes and no. I mean I think that every little thing that we choose to do leads us to the next word, sentence, paragraph, and chapter."

"But that book right there," Levi nodded. He felt drunk now. "You can't even go back and review those pages," meaning that the statue was one solid piece, that in reality the pages couldn't be flipped backward, *or* forward for that matter.

"Exactly. It's the way we remember the past, what we take away from it that writes the rest. I mean, think about the way that you remember *anything*. Some things you remember in great detail, while others are hazy. Memories of certain things pop up at unexpected times. Years from now, one day you might remember *this*, what we are doing right now, while everything else that happens between here and there might be," she searched for the right words, "one sentence paragraphs if you will. At some point in time, tonight might be what you *need* to remember. The past shapes us and guides us. Sure," she nodded, "there will be letters, and diaries, and email to help record everything, but-"

"But those are all written words. How do we know if what is written is even accurate? How do we then know if it's truth or fiction?"

"Folktales, myths, and legends, all of it is passed down through generations and over time it becomes jumbled, changed, and distorted, but I think that there is always a seed of truth that remains."

"So what are you saying?"

"Why are you so hung up on the past, Levi? If it's meant to be, it'll be."

Despite knowing that she was leaving the next day, Levi leaned over and kissed her.

The next day she was gone.

By the time that fall arrived, everything involving Claire and Diesel was slowly drifting away, piece by piece. Each orange and yellow leaf that fell from the trees around the campus took one more piece of the past along with it until winter arrived, and by then it had all crumbled to nothing, just as the leaves on the ground crunched and broke apart underneath Levi's feet as he walked from class to class. As Sophia had taught him, it was all history. It was what he took away from it that mattered.

Over those first few months, Levi only went home a few times, once over fall break and then again at Thanksgiving. Christmas break was the longest that he spent in Devlin. Not on any of those three visits did he see Claire or Diesel. He didn't want to. None of it mattered anymore.

When he went back to the campus in January, a few things had changed. Justin was no longer there. He had managed to flunk out after just one semester. Jonny didn't bring back the framed photo of the girl. He said that they had decided that the long distance thing wasn't working out. He told Levi that she had left the decision up to him and he had decided to end it.

"It just seemed right," he told Levi as they were heading out to class one morning. "I feel like this is what I need to be doing right now. And you never know," he shrugged his shoulders. "We might even get back together one day. Who knows, you know?"

☐

Mr. and Mrs. Bradford Watkins request your presence at the marriage of their daughter, Claire Carlson to Mr. Diesel Atwater
June 15th – 7:00 pm
Mercer Creek Baptist Church

BY THEN Levi and Jonny were sharing an apartment off campus. They were each working various part time retail jobs in order to pay rent and utilities. That day, after coming home from the mall, Levi checked the mailbox and was surprised to see the square, white envelope that was unmistakably the envelope holding a wedding invitation. He flipped the envelope over and on the back, where the flap was sealed down, there was a sticker. The sticker was a silver rectangle and held the emblem of what looked like a sprig of basil with several leaves sprouting out from the stem. After ripping the envelope open and reading the invitation, Levi stared at it a moment longer in disbelief.

Did they really expect him to go to the wedding?

Or was it some kind of sick joke that either Bradford or Diesel was playing on him?

He didn't go.

Nor did it affect him in the least.

It had already been three years and he had long since moved on.

Levi and Jonny remained friends and roommates all the way up until graduating. After graduation Levi accepted a job in Atlanta. And Jonny moved back home to North Carolina. They kept in touch over the years. Jonny didn't get back together with his high school sweetheart. Instead, years later, he ended up marrying Rebecca, Sophia's friend that he had met for the first time on that first night at The University. They had gotten married at a private ceremony at the courthouse in the small town where they now lived.

For the next thirteen years, Levi lived in Atlanta. He was happily living on his own. At first he rented a small apartment in the heart of downtown, and then a few years later, after he had moved up within the financial company that he worked for, he bought a townhouse on the edge of the city. The small house was just outside of the downtown area, but still held the close allure of city life. It had a small yard in the back where Levi tried his hand at growing summer squash. Admittedly, he was the first to find it peculiar that as much as he had wanted to get away from Devlin, he was now trying to grow the very vegetable that the town was so well known for. His crop was *very* slight, and was nothing compared to what the residents of Devlin would have been able to produce on the same number of plants. When he would have friends over for cookouts, they were all surprised upon spotting the plants in his backyard, and to learn that the small town where he had grown up was known for producing squash. They laughed when he told them about the annual festival that the town held in the square.

"That's cute," a girl named Adrianne that he had never met before that night said when he told her about the town where he came from. "Quaint," she added.

He had girlfriends off and on, but was never in a relationship that was very serious.

Over those intervening years he went to Devlin occasionally, for holidays and birthdays, but mostly he stayed in the city.

Not once, until the day of his mother's funeral, did he see Diesel or Claire.

☐

ON THE day of Jill Stanley's funeral there had been an overwhelming sense throughout all of Devlin that anything could happen. It was a day where many of the town's residents awoke and instantly looked toward the future. Reginald Jackson, who had just turned seventy the day before, woke up to the brightly sunny morning and wrote the first words of a novel that had been clanging around in his head for years. Loretta McGee, a lady who had always dreamed of owning her own restaurant, exited through the courthouse doors on her lunch break and never returned to the county job that she had loathed for years. It was a day that many felt the sudden urge to play the lottery because the jackpot had just reached one of the highest amounts in history. Even those that had never once experienced the mere seconds of hope that came with scratching a ticket piled into the nearest gas station for their chance at becoming filthy rich.

And for Levi, now that both of his parents had passed away, a time that had once seemed unforeseeable, any other surprises that life could throw his way now seemed like a possibility. His father had died when Levi had only been eleven. It had been an auto accident. Levi could only remember bits and pieces of the funeral. And now his mother would be buried right at his side.

By noon the clear blue skies of the morning had disappeared. The sky was overcast, but the day was warm. The most recent weather forecasts from the television stations in Columbia and Augusta didn't call for any significant rainfall and each of the weathermen had said that most of the clouds would be out of the area by dusk. That was of course if everything went according to the way that was expected, but so far everything about that day was out of the blue.

Just a few days earlier, all had been normal in Levi's life. He had been happy and comfortable with his job in the city, he had a beautiful girlfriend, and the most pressing thing on his mind was the question of where the two of them would have dinner later that night. Even though he had been in the midst of an intensely important business meeting at the time of the phone call, he had made the drive to Devlin as soon as he received the news. He rushed from the office to his townhouse where he packed a bag and abruptly hit the road. After dropping Craven off at Paige's condo, he and Adrianne, who had become his girlfriend by then, had ridden in near silence while the police officer's voice echoed in his head.

Over the phone the deputy had introduced himself before breaking the bad news. It was Cooper, the same cop that had questioned him and Claire all those years before. All Levi could hear repeated over and over as he drove were the words that Cooper had spoken.

"Your mother, Jill Stanley, has passed away."

Levi knew as soon as he had started the drive that he couldn't tolerate the idea of staying in the house, and so for the next few days he and Adrianne would be staying at an inexpensive motel in a larger, neighboring town, but the house in Devlin was where they went first.

Outside, the yard and flower beds were tidy. Even though it was early in the season, the squash plants were already bursting open with orangey, yellow blossoms. Levi observed that there was newly planted basil in the ground. Aside from the lush greenery of the plants, another color stood out prominently. Yellow pollen coated every surface of the outdoors. Even the red hummingbird feeder that hung from a hook on the fence was covered in the stuff.

On the inside of the house everything was just how Jill had left it. It was the little things that Levi noticed the most. Even though no candles were currently lit, the house smelled of lemon verbena. Clocks still hung on walls, ticking away the seconds of life. The most recent paperback romance novel that Jill had been reading was dog eared and sitting on the small table at the end of the couch. In the kitchen, an upside down plastic tea pitcher sat atop a yellow dish rag where it had been left to dry on the countertop. In the starkly white farmhouse sink there were two drinking glasses, a fork, and a butter knife. The entirety of the house seemed as if Jill had only just stepped out to the grocery store and could return at any minute.

The house did not yet seem to know that it was now vacant and its own mourning had yet to set in.

As Levi took in the house's surroundings, Adrianne walked in silence throughout the rooms, looking at the artwork and photos that hung on the walls. Minutes later, together the two of them stood in the hallway.

"Who are they?" Adrianne asked from behind Levi, without breaking her focus of one photo in particular.

Levi turned around and looked toward the photo that she was studying so closely.
It was right next to the one of his grandfather, next to a row of various framed insects.

"They were my two best friends growing up," he said, acknowledging the picture of Claire and Diesel. In the photo, the three of them were standing just outside of the Stanley house. He and Claire must've been around sixteen at the time. Levi stood in the middle and had his arms wrapped around each of the others' necks. The sunlight from that day gave the photo a warm brilliance.

After speaking their names out loud it was the first time that Levi even thought that he might see either of them while he was in town. Truthfully, he had been so caught up in everything else that was going on that he hadn't even thought about the possibility. If so, it would be the first time seeing either of them since the night before he left for college and Diesel had delivered those threatening words.

Mercer Creek Cemetery was located just off Hollyhock Road, one of the main roads that ran through the center of town and looped around the large pond that was situated on the outskirts of the town limits. Old and weathered granite tombstones and monuments stood across the green, grass covered ground. Various sizes of magnolia trees grew on the property. The mid-April breeze caused the thick, rubbery leaves of the magnolia trees to quietly clatter in the branches. The cemetery stood next to the wooden church and was believed to outdate the church by several years. This was the newer of the two churches. The ruins of the original, the one that was supposedly haunted by Anna Moore, was further in the trees, nearer the edge of the pond. It had been abandoned decades earlier when the congregation had become too numerous for the one room structure.

Jill's grave was not within the black wrought iron fencing that surrounded the interior plots. Over the years, the number of graves in Mercer Creek had far exceeded the original planned space of the cemetery and there were now graves neatly lined all across the grounds.

During the service, the preacher stood at the head of the grave and spoke about mortality and transcendence. Behind him, far off in the distance, a dark storm cloud was approaching. Levi kept his head down, listening to what the preacher was saying, trying to let the words sink in.

"As we leave this world, we go on to the next," the preacher said, "moving on to something far greater."

Without looking, Levi could feel the many eyes of sorrow that would occasionally glance over at him. Surrounded by the many faces that he recognized from his past, it was the sound of a familiar sniffle that caused him to look up from where he had been staring blankly at the parched dirt of the earth. The unexpected sight of the woman that stood across the width of the grave sent Levi's heart to thumping and the hairs on the back of his neck to stand on end. Even though the seed of possibility had entered his mind when Adrianne had inquired about the photo, it was still startling to see the figure from yesteryear. It was as if a ghost was standing amid the cemetery looking back at him. She was wearing a simple black dress. Her spray of blonde curls fell well past her shoulders. He had not seen her in sixteen years.

Throughout the rest of the service Levi had kept his head down and his eyes away from scanning the crowd that had gathered to say their goodbyes. Most importantly he didn't want to make eye contact with *her*.

When the service concluded, some of the mourners passed by where Levi was still standing. For the most part they were all faces that he recognized from years past. He was surprised that he could still recall a lot of them by first and last name. A few of the women hugged Levi and some of the men had shaken his hand. It was when one of these men that Levi had gone to school with was shaking his hand that he spotted Diesel off in the distance. He was walking along the edge of the tree line, away from the cemetery and toward the gravel parking lot.

Diesel didn't look in Levi's direction. Instead, he kept his head down and hands shoved deep into his pockets. Even though it had been years, Levi could feel his body tense just at the sight of him.

He wondered if it would be possible for Diesel to still hold a grudge against him after all that time.

Diesel got into a rusted green pickup truck. Levi watched as the truck started in a roar and eased over the gravel as it drove away. As the truck turned, he could see that Claire sat in the passenger seat. The tension in Levi's body finally began to ease as soon as it was visible that the truck was pulling away from the cemetery.

After all the mourners had gone, Levi remained a while longer and stood at the edge of the grave. Adrianne was by his side with her hand awkwardly placed on his lower back. Now that the crowd had dispersed, details of the scene were more clearly visible. Sprays of colorful flowers were arranged intricately around the gravesite. Loose, recently placed dirt was piled atop his mother's final resting place. Pretty soon a drenching rain and high winds would pound onto the dirt, flattening it, washing the loosest bits away. The delicate petals of the flowers would soon be scattered across the ground. The grass and dirt would soon be exquisitely messy with pieces of gladiolas and geraniums.

From the steadily approaching black cloud in the west there was a rumble of thunder that was quickly followed by a sharp bolt of lightning that caused Levi to finally turn away from the gravesite. Huge rain drops began to pelt down upon them and when Levi grasped onto Adrianne's hand, a flock of black birds fluttered from the highest branches of an oak tree that was just beginning to put on its new, green leaves.

By the time that they got back to his car, that by that point stood alone amid the gravel covered and deeply rutted parking area, the rain was a downpour. The weatherman's forecast of clear skies had been incorrect. Just as Jill's passing had been a shock, how could one predict something as enormous and unexpected as a southern thunderstorm? In South Carolina during the spring and summer months, storms of the type could pop up with little to no warning, putting a hiatus on the most elaborate garden parties or family trips to the lake.

The windshield wipers of Levi's car could barely keep up with the amount of rain that was pouring down even when they were set on the fastest speed. Levi had to drive slowly as he exited the cemetery and along the rough driveway that led the way back to the main road.

    The rain had slowed to a drizzle by the time that he got to the house. He reminded both himself and Adrianne that he was just there to check on a few things, to make sure that all the doors were locked, that all the lights were off. On that unimaginable day, it was normal, everyday things that he needed to take care of.

    As he pulled into the driveway he noticed that there was another car already parked there and so he parked alongside the street, leaving the driveway clear so that the other car could easily back out.

    Levi wondered who the visitor could be.

    Could it be that the preacher had come to give his final condolences?

    Immediately upon standing out of the car, Levi pushed up the gunmetal gray umbrella that he kept underneath the driver's seat of his car for such occasions. Adrianne ran around the car and together they huddled underneath the safety of the umbrella. They entered the back yard side by side. Levi glanced up and saw that the visitor was standing on the porch. It was Claire. In the yard, the rain was not as heavy underneath the thick canopy of the oak tree that grew in the corner. Together he and Adrianne walked along the stone pavers and to the porch where Claire was standing, waiting. Levi lowered the umbrella and shook off the excess rainwater onto the bushes beside the steps.

    "I'm sorry," Claire said as Levi stepped onto the first step. Claire was as beautiful that day in melancholy as Levi had ever seen her. The shock of first glimpsing her in the cemetery had worn off and now he was actually kind of happy about her being there. It seemed comforting. It felt right. It felt good to see someone that he had been so close with for such a long period of his life, but all the mixed emotions that were raging within him was too much. First his mother had died unexpectedly and now he was seeing Claire for the first time in over a decade and a half.

    "What can I say? It was so unexpected and everything. I mean, I was shocked." He told Claire as he climbed the steps. He wondered where Diesel was.

    Claire nodded in understanding. Levi, Claire, and Adrianne stood under the shelter of the porch as the rain continued to slowly patter on the tin roof. By then the bright sun was just beginning to peak out of the dark clouds. The sun, along with the recent rainfall, would soon cause the day to become unbearably humid. The pollen that had coated everything just moments earlier of that same day had been mostly washed away. On some surfaces the rain had only caused the pollen to run. The windows of the house were streaked with yellow, making it appear as if the house itself was finally allowing itself to cry for its recent loss.

It is common knowledge that news travels fast in small towns, and it travels especially fast in those towns that happen to be nestled within the southern part of the United States. North Carolina, South Carolina, Alabama, and let's not even get started on Georgia, are all susceptible to this type of gossip. So of course by then all of Devlin had heard what had happened. It was likely that Claire had even heard the details of how Jill had died in the porch swing well before Levi.

"Hey, I'm Claire." Claire held out her hand to Adrianne and smiled.

The two women were in stark contrast to one another. While Claire's hair was blonde, curly and unruly, Adrianne's on the other hand was dark and straight. Claire's complexion was fair and Adrianne was tanned a golden bronze.

Adrianne hesitantly placed her hand in Claire's. "Adrianne." She smiled as she introduced herself. "Have you known Levi very long?"

"We've known each other our entire lives." Claire looked from Adrianne to Levi and smiled. "Ever since we were toddlers."

"Oh, how cute," Adrianne smiled at Levi. He knew the expression on her face. He had seen it many times before. Just as sure as a black cat crossing your path was a precursor to bad luck, the look on Adrianne's face could only mean one thing. He knew that it was a portent to a discussion that they would surely be having later.

The three of them stood in miserable silence until Claire finally broke the stillness.

"Look, if you need anything, or anybody to talk to, I just want you to know that I'm here," she told Levi.

"Thanks, I'll be OK." Levi quickly turned his back to Claire and was reaching up to remove the hanging baskets of flowers from the eave of the porch. Each of the baskets was filled with vibrantly purple petunias that had just began to blossom for the season.

"Those are so beautiful," Claire said regarding the flowers.

The petunias were of the hearty, old fashioned variety that came back year after year. All around the Stanley house they had grown in hanging baskets, terra cotta flower pots, and randomly throughout the yard, wherever the seeds ended up, for as long as Levi could remember. Many years they even survived the winter.

"Yeah, I just don't want them to die hanging here. It would make the house look so unkempt."

Levi busied himself with placing and shoving and rearranging the baskets on the corner of the porch until he heard the sound of Claire's shoes on the porch steps.

When Levi straightened up, Claire was already standing amid the wet grass of the yard. By then the rain had completely stopped. The only water that was falling were those sporadic drops from the tree branches, every so often making a soft ting against the roof.

"Well, I just wanted to stop by and say how sorry I was to hear about it. Take care, Levi." Claire looked at Adrianne. "It was nice meeting you," she said.

"You too," Adrianne responded and smiled half heartedly.

"Take care," Levi echoed Claire's words back toward her. He wanted to tell her more. That it was good seeing her again and to thank her for dropping by, that they should keep in touch, but by the time that he had finally built up enough courage to do so she was already gone.

Levi shuffled around the inside of the house for a few minutes and then, since he had already planned on staying around the area for another couple of days to take care of things and begin packing up the place instead of making the drive back to Atlanta that evening, he and Adrianne went back to the motel that he had already paid for in advance for the duration of time.

Later that night Adrianne had fallen asleep with relative ease, but Levi lay there atop the blanket, wide eyed and full of thoughts. The sound of Adrianne's steady, rhythmic breathing beside him didn't do much to coax him into slumber, instead it kept him alert. Every time that he begin to doze off his mind would wander back to Devlin. It was as if even over the miles that distanced him from the town just then, the knowledge that the house was standing vacant for the first time in decades gnawed at him. Since seeing her, images of Claire swirled and crashed tornado like through his mind. It was as if everything from his past was beckoning him, plotting for his return.

When he finally did fall asleep, he dreamed that he was standing alone in an endless field of squash. The green vines were covered with orange blossoms. Bees and butterflies hovered about. Overhead, the sun was bright in the clear, blue sky. Nothing was said; nothing was heard. It was perfectly serene.

☐

"YOU'RE STILL in love with her."

"What? Adrianne, that's ridiculous. I haven't even so much as seen her in sixteen years." Levi gulped from a waxy cup of soda. The plastic lid lay where Levi had haphazardly tossed it onto the diner's table just moments earlier. He had never been one to drink out of a straw.

Thankfully, Adrianne had waited until the two of them had arrived back to Atlanta before she had brought up the awkward situation dealing with Claire and everything that was on her mind in those regards. It was a Saturday. They were sitting across from one another in a corner booth at a popular local diner. The restaurant had retro blue tables and vinyl covered booths. A griddle stretched along one wall behind a counter top where several customers sat waiting on their order to be served. The cook was busy frying eggs, flipping burgers, and crisping bacon. Several waitresses were bustling about with notepads and coffee pots in hand.

Adrianne was speaking so matter-of-factly that it seemed as if she was a fortune teller sitting across from him and Levi was there to have his innermost feelings unveiled. "I could see it in your face when you first spotted her, Levi. And I could definitely tell that she still loves you."

Levi chuckled. Everything that he was hearing was so absurd to the point that he couldn't believe that it was actually happening. "We grew up together. We had a short fling when we were teenagers and she broke my heart. That's it, end of story." Levi maneuvered uncomfortably in the booth. "Like I said, that was the first time that I have even *seen* her since the year that we graduated high school and even by then we had already been done with."

Adrianne traced the tip of her finger around the top of her own cup. It would have been easy to replace the plastic lid of the cup with a martini glass, transforming her into a glamorous movie star. "Levi, have you ever heard about stories of eternal love? Soul mates, if you will?"

Before Levi had to time to answer, the waitress, a heavy set, middle aged woman, walked up and placed a plate in front of each of them. Levi had ordered a chili dog with a heaping side of fries and Adrianne had opted instead for a garden salad.

"Anything else for y'all?" The woman said, unenthusiastically.

"No, I think we're good." Levi answered and the waitress sauntered away.

Levi looked at Adrianne disapprovingly, returning to the topic of eternal love. "Are you about to lecture me using some modern vampire crap as an example?"

It was no hidden fact that like Levi's mother, Adrianne was very fond of reading all sorts of sappy romances. She would read young adult titles, retro, paranormal, futuristic, it didn't matter. She was even in the process of working on a book of her own. Spin that around with the fact that her career was that of a couple's therapist, throw in a dash of interest in mythology and what came out each and every time that she began to speak about someone's love life never failed to astound Levi.

"Listen. I have a PHD, OK? It's a real thing," she replied, stabbing at a cherry tomato with her fork. "Anyway, Plato had a theory where he talked about two halves. It means that we are constantly looking for our other half. Everybody has one. He said that in the beginning, all beings started out attached to another. Originally, we had four legs and four arms, and that at some time or another we were all divided into twos. Ever since then, we, humans as we know them, have wandered the earth seeking our lost half. It is when we find the other part of us that we will become whole again."

Levi chuckled. "So you think that Claire and I were born as Siamese twins." He bit into the chili dog.

"Levi." She rolled her eyes and sounded increasingly frustrated. "It's figurative."

"I know Adrianne. I know it's not to be taken literally, but c'mon, soul mates? And Claire?"

Adrianne leaned back in her seat. "I'm just saying." She crossed her arms. "Let's not forget that I do this for a living. I know people and I know what I saw between you two. I mean I'm not necessarily suggesting that it needs to be anything sexual. I just think that it's obvious that the two of you have a very strong bond with one another. It could just be a friendly relationship that would end up being enough. And even though it has been –"

"Sixteen years."

"-sixteen years since you have seen her, I think that the bond, that connection is still there. I really truly think that all of us have certain people that are meant to be in our lives. She is supposed to be part of your life in some capacity or another. And I think that it would be very beneficial and healthy for you to have her around, if you would allow yourself to, and invite her back into your life."

Levi rolled his eyes.

"She obviously means a lot to you," Adrianne added. "And there is a whole subgenre of romance novels that deals with two characters reconnecting after spending years apart, rekindling the romance that they once shared."

Levi thought about it and realized that he had often seen novels with exactly those kinds of storylines sitting around the house when he was growing up.

From that moment on, the way that Adrianne acted around him seemed different. Soon they were not sleeping together anymore. After a couple of weeks, on the last night of April, Levi tried his best at making it up to Adrianne, proving once and for all that it was she that he was truly interested in, that Claire held no amount of interest for him whatsoever. And it was true. All of that was in the past. That night, he showed up at Adrianne's apartment with a bottle of the nicest red wine that the store offered and six long stem roses. She answered the door and instead of looking excited about Levi's attempt at being romantic, she appeared to be more frustrated.

"Levi." She turned and led him into the apartment. Levi closed the door behind himself. "I've been trying to find the right time to tell you this." She turned to face him. "I just don't think that the two of us being together is going to work out." She sat on the arm of the couch. "I'm sorry for not mentioning it earlier, I just -"

Levi nodded in understanding and finished her thought for her. "You wanted to wait until everything else had smoothed over, when I wasn't as upset over everything else that had happened." Levi sat the wine and roses on the coffee table. "You can have these," he said. He shrugged his shoulders. "I bought them for you anyway." He turned and let himself out of the apartment.

That night Levi slept fitfully. When he finally fell into a deep sleep his dreams took him away to Devlin.

In the dream it was dark. He was walking alone. The house stood vacant amid the night sky. From within the structure of the house an orange glow was emanating. Levi stepped onto the porch and the front door flung inward. He stepped into the living room. The door slammed shut behind him and the deadbolt clicked.

The next day was sunny. It was a day where long ago people used to dance around a May Pole in celebration of the birth of a new spring. It was a day of renewal. Levi walked with Craven to the city park. The basset hound was still young and tugged excitedly on the leash as he walked in front of Levi down the city sidewalk. Despite numerous people that were on the grass enjoying the warm temperatures, the park felt like a welcome sanctuary from the busy, hectic life of the city. Craven knelt down and rubbed his head against the grass. Levi gently tugged on the leash and urged him on until they got to the particular spot of the park that they had come for.

Before leaving Devlin, Levi had gone back to the house and got one of the hanging baskets from the porch. The next day he had carried the basket full of purple petunias down to the park and planted them in the ground. It had only been a couple of weeks but the plant was now flourishing. The stems and leaves were a deep, healthy green and numerous vibrantly purple flowers were open all over. Levi sat on the ground near the flowers. The sun shone down on him. Even after several weeks, he was still surprised that he hadn't been caught by a security officer and told that he couldn't plant anything within the public park, but somehow he had managed to do it and the plants had even survived.

It felt strangely good to have a piece of his old life there with him.

☐

SOON AFTER she had seen Levi at Jill's funeral, Claire knew that she was going to end her marriage with Diesel.

Even before then, she had known for a long time that she wasn't happy in the relationship that she had with her husband. She wasn't planning on ending it so that she could go after Levi or anything as dramatic as that, it was just the simple fact of seeing Levi again after all those years that had brought the whole thing into focus. She had known all along that she had made the wrong choice, that way back then she should have broken things off with Diesel instead of Levi, but the guilt that she had felt over what all had happened, over what she and Levi had done, how it had led to Diesel's assault, had ultimately outweighed rationality, and so she ended up in a decade long marriage where she was never truly happy.

She had realized long before then that she was no longer in love with her husband. She loved him, but what she felt for him was a different type of love, not the kind that she should feel for the person that she was married to. Deep down she had known it for years, but for whatever reason, she just hadn't been able to allow herself to accept that reality. She *had* been in love with him at one time, she knew that, she would have never married him if she hadn't been, but she knew now that at that time in her life she had confused love with being *in* love. She also knew that in the summer after graduating high school, before *the incident* as she had come to think of it, it was Levi that she had really been in love with. And then after the incident, she just couldn't see any way out of the cloud of shame and guilt that she had gotten herself into except to stay with Diesel. *She* had been the bad guy through this whole ordeal. *She* had been the one that cheated on her boyfriend. And every night when Diesel took off his cap before getting into bed, because of the scar, Claire was reminded of what she had done.

And then there was Bradford. He was also a big hindrance in her leaving Diesel.

Her step-father, Bradford Watkins, a local farmer, married her mother when Claire had been five years old. Her real father had died in a hunting accident when she had been three. Mr. Watkins had been friends with Diesel's father for as long as Claire could remember. The two men had opened up an auto shop together when the kids had been younger. Years later, Diesel's father died in an auto accident when Diesel was fifteen and Mr. Watkins took over running the shop. As Diesel had gotten older, he began to spend more and more time with Bradford. His mother had remarried, a man named Tucker, but he and Diesel had never hit it off. At first glance it seemed that the older man was acting as a father figure to the teenage Diesel, but it was far more than that. Even though twenty years separated them in age, the two of them behaved more like friends, drinking, smoking, and ogling girls who were much too young for Bradford. Eventually, the auto shop became Diesel's, and Bradford remained on as co owner.

For as long as Claire could remember, the man had never liked Levi. Bradford seemed to tolerate him well enough when he and Claire had been kids, but as soon as puberty struck and Claire began to express even the slightest bit of interest in boys, her step father had made it very clear that he didn't approve of Levi; that he wasn't going to be the right kind of man for her. Bradford let it be known that it was Diesel that he wanted his step-daughter to be with. Over the years, Bradford had pushed hard for Diesel and Claire to be together and eventually even got his wish to come true, no matter how short lived it wound up being.

Less than a week after the funeral, when she told Diesel that she wanted a divorce, he simply nodded in understanding. They had been sitting out on the back porch of their small brick house. Dark woods stood at the edge of the yard. It was at night and the sky was impossibly black and scattered with shining white stars. Sitting across from her, Diesel took off his cap. The pink scar from that night long before was prominently visible as it snaked out of his thinning hair. He cried at what she told him and then reached over and hugged her tightly. "Thank you," he said, "for being honest with me." He told her that he had already sensed long before then that she didn't love him, but was hoping that what he thought he knew was true would in the end turn out to be wrong. He said that he had hoped that she did love him still.

That same day, Claire called her mother and said that she had something very important that she needed to tell her. Together they agreed on a time to meet at her mother's and Bradford's house. Claire knew that her mother probably assumed that she was pregnant or that there was something wrong, that she was sick and that she needed to tell her face to face. They sat on the brick patio in the backyard. Blue jays and cardinals flittered about, occasionally taking seed from the multitude of bird feeders that her mother had hanging in the branches of the old oak trees that scattered the yard. Overhead, the ceiling fans that were attached to the beams of the patio cover were whirring round and round.

"That's a brave thing to do," her mother said after Claire told her of her decision to file for a divorce. "I'm glad you have the courage that it takes to walk away when you know that you're not happy."

Bradford, on the other hand, was not as sympathetic and understanding. "Are you out of you ever loving mind?" he yelled across the kitchen that same afternoon. He picked up a glass full of lemonade from the counter that he had just minutes earlier poured for himself and threw it across the room. The glass shattered on impact with the kitchen cabinet. Lemonade poured down the white cabinet door and pooled on the floor. Glass, ice, and several lemon slices scattered across the tile.

Claire's mother came running into the kitchen upon hearing the shouting and the breaking glass. Bradford spun around to face his wife. He pointed at Claire. "Has she told you? Has your daughter told you what the hell she is planning on doing?"

"I'm not *planning* on doing anything. I've already done it." She shrugged her shoulders. "I don't love him and I never have. Not like a husband anyway."

"Claire," Bradford was pacing the floor. "How can you say that? If I were you, I would rethink everything that you are doing. Diesel is a good man." He pointed his finger at her. "He has been there for you, even when ya'll were kids and you screwed up everything you had with him and fooled around with that little Stanley shit, that man stood by you."

Even though Claire's mother had tried to clean up the mess of lemonade and glass later that night, the next morning there was a steady line of ants that had marched into the house seeking out the sugary sweetness.

Claire packed her things and left the house that she and Diesel had shared during their married years. She wasn't sure how she was going to be able to make it completely on her own so she reluctantly moved back in with her parents until she would be able to stand on her own two feet. The two story brick house was so much bigger than the house that she and Diesel had lived in. It was weird being back there, in the house where she had grown up. The first night that she slept in her old bed, she was taken back in time. Instead of eighteen years, it seemed like it had only been eighteen *days* since she had been lying in that same bed, listening to music, avoiding homework, trying to decide which boy she liked best.

It didn't take long for Bradford to simmer down. One day he was with Claire in the kitchen. They were sitting at the table, sharing breakfast. He told her that no matter what he would always think of her as his daughter.

As opposed to Bradford's slow acceptance of what had happened, Diesel's outlook on life in general spiraled steadily downhill. His drinking only got worse. Many people of Devlin thought that the alcohol consumption was due to the stress and heartache caused by the divorce, but there were others that knew that those things were just excuses, that Diesel would have eventually found a way to the bottle no matter what. Just like his father, and *his* father before him, Diesel seemed destined for alcoholism. The drinking spun so far out of control to the point where he was arrested with a DUI. Even afterwards, he would often be spotted stumbling around town, drunk in the middle of the day. Due to being hung over most days, he began to make mistakes at work. One day he had been doing a simple oil change, but had forgotten to cap the oil afterwards. The woman's car had ignited in the middle of the street. News quickly spread, and the people in town soon became hesitant about taking their cars to his shop. Many longtime customers even quit going all together.

Along with the drinking, a deep depression also settled over him. It was evident by his demeanor. Soon, Claire became so concerned for him that she began to check on him regularly, showing up at his house unannounced, just to spend time with him and make sure that he wasn't doing anything foolish. Even though she didn't want to be married to him, she did want him as a close friend. If he wound up doing something as stupid as killing himself, Claire didn't think that she would ever be able to come to terms with the role that she had played with leading him there. She knew that if that were to happen then the guilt that she had already felt before would only be tenfold. The unthinkable act had began to seem like such a possibility that she had even rattled her brain wondering if she would then be able to even live with herself. One night when she got to Diesel's house, the TV had been left on, empty beer bottles were standing along the coffee table, and Diesel was nowhere to be seen. She tried calling his cell phone, but on each ring she got no answer. Her heart was hammering in her chest as she walked through the house, searching each room.

"Diesel?" she called out through the house, redialing his phone at the same time.

She called Bradford just to confirm that the two of them were not together. They weren't.

After searching through the house and discovering that he was definitely not there, there was only one other place that Claire could think of that he may have been.

She parked her car on the side of the road and with a flashlight held out in front of her she walked through the briars and overgrowth until she came to the garden shed. The door was closed. As she approached the structure and the beam of light from her flashlight danced over the faded sides, she was hoping that she *wouldn't* find him inside there. Memories of that summer night when they had been teenagers jabbed through her. Unwanted, jolting visions of the interior walls splattered with Diesel's blood flashed through her mind. If he was in there, Claire was afraid of what she might discover that he had possibly done to himself.

"Diesel?" She said again and reached her hand out to the door. She paused for a moment, took a deep breath and then pulled the door open.

Empty.

☐

DIESEL HAD not come to the tree house to kill himself. He had gone there simply to think about things. First, upon arriving in the clearing just after dusk, he had gone to the garden shed. Inside, it smelt dank. It was a sour, vile smell that must've been intensified from standing under the sun, unopened for all those years. The girly posters were still taped to the wall. Empty beer cans littered the floor. He had sat in the cramped interior for a while before stepping back outside, closing the door behind him, and walking across the several feet of ground that separated the shed and the tree house. It was like going back in time, going from one structure to the next. As opposed to the tainted interior of the garden shed, the inside the tree house held an air of innocence. The tree house was *before*, before drinking, or kisses, or the metal pipe that had smashed against his head. The abandoned props in the corner, the ones from that stupid play from when they had been kids; the robe, crown, and the magic scepter (the garden hoe) was a reminder of what they used to think, that good would *always* triumph over evil.

He had brought a six pack of beer with him. In addition to the beer and liquor that he had already downed before leaving the house, he thought that six should be plenty. He knew that his drinking had gotten out of control all over again. Before he had gotten married, when he had been younger, it had been bad, but somehow after becoming a husband he had managed to successfully lock the monster of impending alcoholism away. Over the years that he had been married, he had successfully been able to control his drinking. He had done it for Claire and he knew that he had done a damn fine job of it. Hell, now that he was thinking about it, most of everything that he had *ever* done was for her.

And now she was gone. It hadn't even been a full thirteen days yet since she had left him, but just in that short amount of time, he had fallen back into the drinking, just like he had never truly left it behind. Of course he had never *completely* stopped. Even while they had been together, he had allowed himself the occasional beer or whiskey, but during those years he had not gone any further than that. In the marriage, he had known that he couldn't have both, Claire *and* alcohol, and so he had chosen what was more important to him. He had chosen his wife. Now that she was no longer around, the alcohol had taken control over his life once again just as it had when he had been younger. When it came down to it, the alcohol was all that he really wanted anyway. It was what he lived for all day long.

He chugged the rest of the beer and tossed the empty bottle into the corner where it clanged against another. He lifted the third bottle from the cardboard pack at his side and immediately twisted the cap off. The beer was getting warm, but it still tasted OK. It only meant that he would have to drink faster, before they got too warm to enjoy. Diesel thought that what Claire had done had to have been because of Levi. The out of the blue decision for her to want a divorce *had to* have been fueled by seeing Levi at the funeral earlier in the month.

Was it possible that seeing him just once had awakened that long buried desire that she had for him?

The truth was that Diesel had always been jealous of the bond that Levi and Claire seemed to share. He had seen firsthand how Levi and Claire had been able to get along so well with one another. Even after Diesel and Claire had started dating, he had seen the way that they seemed to fit together seamlessly. And then when he had discovered what the two of them had been doing behind his back, something sinister had begun to stir within Diesel. The darkness of rage had spread throughout his entire being.

Diesel looked up and saw the curled drawings that were tacked to the slatted wall of the tree house. He yanked one of them down. The tack remained in the wall and ripped through the paper. The drawing was of himself, Levi, and Claire. They were standing underneath the oak tree in Levi's yard. Diesel thought back on the day long before when the three of them had sat in the same spot where he sat now and drew the pictures.

"Always friends," they had agreed to one another that summer day. "No girl or boy will ever come between us."

Diesel knew that all three of them had been so naïve when they had been kids. Little did they know back then that one day they would tear *themselves* apart. Diesel thought about ways that things could have turned out differently. If this hadn't happened, or that, or if he hadn't said this to her or that to him, would he be happy now? Would he and Claire still be together? Would he not be sitting alone in the tree house drunk with a broken heart? It was impossible to know. All of it *had* happened, but he also realized that it was all in the past and there was no way to change any of it, but oh how he wished that he could.

Diesel looked through the open door of tree house. In the dark, the acre of land was still and quiet. He remembered the day when they had been kids and had started construction on the tree house. It caused him to wonder, if they hadn't built the house, would things still be the same? If they hadn't tried to claim the acre of land as their own, would the three of them have ever made that stupid, unrealistic pact? If he had never opened a bottle, would he have ever thought that he needed a "beer drinking spot" in the first place, would the garden shed have ever made it to the clearing?

But they *had* built it, and they *had* made the pact. One day he *had* taken his first sip of alcohol and sealed his fate. It had all led to where he was now.

Diesel traced his fingers along the length of the scar. It was all because of Levi. Every damn thing that was wrong in his life was because of Levi.

With a red crayon that had been left on the floor of the tree house from a long ago childhood day, Diesel scratched through the sketched figure of Levi that was on the piece of paper, leaving himself and Claire without harm. Even as he was doing it, he knew that it was a childish, immature action that was more than likely fueled by the alcohol in his system. But it felt good to let out his aggression in some sort of way.

Again the thought, all of this, every bit of it, was because of Levi.

Diesel hated him. He knew that for a fact and had known it for years. And he also knew that if he ever saw him again, that if he was in his current frame of mind on the day that he did, he might even just kill him.

His thoughts were interrupted by the sound of his name being called from the other side of the wall. "Diesel?" He immediately recognized that it was Claire's voice calling out for him. The sound of her voice caused his heart to jump.

Through the slats of the tree house boards, Diesel could see the flashlight beam that was dancing around the ground. He could here her feet crunching through the thick weeds and grass.

"Diesel?" She said again.

He heard the unmistakable sound of the garden shed door opening and then there was an audible sigh from Claire. Was it a sigh of relief?

Diesel stood. The soles of his boots were loud on the wooden floor of the house.

From the other side of the walls, he could hear Claire speak again.

"Diesel, is that you?"

A second later, Diesel emerged from the dark interior of the tree house.

Claire walked the short distance that stood between them. "Diesel, I've been looking everywhere for you. What are you doing out here?" She glanced down at his hand and saw that he held a bottle of beer. It was obvious that it wasn't his first or even his tenth. "Diesel, it's late. Let's go home," she said as she walked toward him and wrapped her hand around his forearm. The skin contact made Diesel's body come alive. She still cared for him, he thought. Why else would she be all the way out there in the dark, looking for him?

As they began to walk, he stumbled on his feet. He stopped, reached his hand to Claire's cheek and leaned in to kiss her.

"Diesel," she said abruptly and turned her head away. She pushed him back. "You've been drinking and don't know what you're doing. You need to go to bed. C'mon." She gently tugged on his arm.

"I know what I'm doing." He leaned in to her again. "I want to go to bed with *you*." Because of the alcohol, his speech was horribly slurred. His breath was rancid with the beer and liquor. "Remember, like we used to do. All the fun we had…"

"Stop it, Diesel." She pushed him back, harder this time and he fell to the ground.

Claire gasped at what she had done. She brought her hand to her mouth, shocked at her actions. Both the sight of him on the ground and that of the moonlight illuminating the scar jabbed at her heart. "I'm sorry," she said and turned her head as if she was looking for a way out.

"Would you love me if Levi wasn't in the picture?" It was a pathetic, pleading question. He was beginning to stand back up.

"This has absolutely nothing *at all* to do with Levi." She was becoming more frustrated with Diesel's drunken stammer every second that passed. She threw her arms up in exasperation. "Diesel, what are you even talking about?"

"I just think that if he had never been around, then things might have turned out to be different for the two of us."

II

Friday...

"WHAT WAS that?" Paige asked. "Did something break?"

Levi looked toward the mess of spilled coffee and pieces of the ceramic mug that Craven had clumsily knocked from the coffee table in his hectic move to get to the front door. One piece of ceramic held the image of several of the kittens' tilted heads and the respectful, fluffy bodies were on one of the other jagged shards that had spun out of control and eventually stopped underneath the table. The pink bows that were around each of the kitten's necks had been split between the pieces. Craven was now sitting in front of the door, peering through the lowest pane of glass, still barking at the woman that stood on the other side.

"Yeah," Levi said. "I need to go."

"Call me when you're on the way back," Paige said in a hurry. It was obvious to her that Levi was trying to rush her off the phone. "Let's do dinner."

"I will, but Paige, I need to go," he said again. "I'll talk to you later." He ended the call and sat his cell phone on the coffee table.

Levi looked from the mess on the floor and toward the door again. Through the thin curtain he could see the silhouette of the blonde woman that stood on the other side. Momentarily ignoring the spilled coffee, he carefully stepped his bare feet around the shards of ceramic. When he reached the door he pulled it open.

"Sophia," he said, genuinely surprised at her arrival. "You're early."

She was supposed to get there around six that night, not eight in the morning.

"Surprise," she said and walked into the house, closing the door behind her. After acknowledging Craven, she stepped closer to

Levi and hugged him.

☐

THE RECONNECTION had started several weeks earlier. On that day, Levi had just left a job interview and was walking down the busy city sidewalk. Even though it was mid morning, people were already bustling about. A guy on a bicycle zipped past on Levi's right. Business men and women were hurrying along at break neck speed. Nearly every one of them had their cell phones out, checking email and texting. The sun was scorching already. Levi loosened his necktie and rolled up the sleeves on his shirt. He could feel the beads of sweat trickling down his back and making the fabric of the shirt stick to him. After he passed by a coffee shop and an Italian restaurant, he stood on the street corner, waiting on the light to turn so that he, along with the other crowd of people that had gathered around him, could cross safely. The building on the corner was plain and nondescript. It had a set of large glass windows on the front, but the other side of each of the panes of glass was blocked by velvet like black curtains making it impossible to see inside. There was a schedule taped to the glass door. Amid several artist names, it was one of them on there that stood out among the others...

Featured Artist – Sophia Forrest
Gallery Show June 1st 7:30 pm

Even though he had never known Sophia's last name, just the first name alone caught his attention. He stepped away from the crowd that was still increasing around him and walked closer to the door to the building. Below the announcement was a photo of a smiling woman. She wore a pair of black rimmed glasses. Instead of the red hair that he remembered, her hair was blonde and fell past her shoulders. He read her bio. University, England, South Carolina, it was her. His eyes fell to the time and date. The show was that night.

He had never been to an art show before that evening. He didn't even know what one wore to such an occasion. He only had what he had seen in movies and TV shows to go by. The men there always seemed to wear trendy, slim fitting shirts and pants. The only clothes that he had that even remotely fit that description and that he even thought would be appropriate for such an occasion were the ones that he was currently wearing.

When Paige came back to the apartment on her lunch break, Levi was sitting on the couch in his pajama pants and an old t-shirt. Craven was resting his head on Levi's leg.

"How did it go?" she asked, inquiring about his job interview.

"I think I bombed it to be honest with you." During the interview, Levi had been so caught off guard and unprepared for some of the questions that he didn't know how to answer them and was still not confident in the approach that he had taken.

Paige, hearing the thump of the clothes dryer, looked toward the hallway closet where the washing machine and dryer were located. She wore a confused look on her face. It was unusual for Levi to do laundry in the middle of the day. Just a moment later, the dryer chimed, indicating that the cycle was complete. Levi stood from the couch and went to the closet. He was placing the shirt on a hanger when Paige passed by the open door on her way further down the hall toward the restroom.

"Do you have another interview?" she asked, curious about why he was washing the dress shirt in the middle of the day.

Levi shook his head. "I'm going to an art show tonight."

"An art show?" The way she said it was obvious that she found it to be an out of the ordinary event for him to attend.

"One of my friends from college is in town and is showing her work tonight, I though it would be good to see her again."

"And you don't want company?"

"You can go -," Levi started.

"Nope," she cut him off, shaking her head. "I'm not stupid. I can see where you intend on this going."

"What do you mean?"

"C'mon Levi, I wasn't born yesterday. I know men your age have certain needs that need to be taken care of."

Levi laughed. "Needs?" He repeated.

"Yes, needs. And I don't want to be the one to blame when those needs go unfulfilled."

There weren't as many people at the show as he thought there would be. The other men were dressed very similar to what Levi wore, a dark pair of jeans, a gray button down shirt, and a black neck tie. Levi thought that the women were dressed a little fancier.

Most of the dresses that he saw were what he thought seemed appropriate for weddings, or based on the large number of black fabric, funerals.

The admission price was what Levi had found to be staggering. Not long before, he would have easily paid the admission without thinking twice about how much money it was that was coming out of his checking account, but with his current financial status, it was a large chunk of what he had, cutting his balance in half.

Levi walked around the gallery, every so often peering past the other people to glance the photos and paintings that hung on the wall. The title of the exhibit was *Small Town Lore.* There were black and white photos of old, ramshackle buildings and various landscapes, both woods and water. Most of the photos were paired with vibrantly colored paintings of ghosts and unusual creatures. It amazed him to think that all the artwork was Sophia's. The bar was in the back corner. There were a couple of people waiting in front of him. Each of the two people in front of him, a man and a woman, had walked away with elegantly stemmed glasses of red wine. Levi had never been much on wine; he would drink it if he had to, but preferred the hoppy taste of beer. When he stepped up to the bar, there were several bottles of beer neatly lined on top of the white tablecloth, examples of what was offered. He chose one he had never had before. It was one from a local brewery.

He was looking at one of the paintings when somebody to his right spoke his name. The painting was of a rust colored fox and had been hung next to a photo of a large tree stump. In another grouping there was a photo of a metal cage next to a creature that was combination of tiger and man.

"Levi?"

He turned around to be face to face with her, Sophia. She was wearing a figure hugging black dress that had been accentuated with crimson accessories: a bracelet, earrings, and a cameo necklace. A pair of thick, black framed glasses was perched perfectly on the bridge of her nose. She looked just like he remembered, except for the hair.

"I'm a natural blonde," she would tell him over coffee several days later, explaining the color change. "I don't know why I ever thought it would be cool to dye my hair that crazy color of red."

"Sophia, hey," Levi said. He could feel his smile widen

across his face.

She hugged him. It was a quick, nice to see you after all these years kind of embrace.

"You do still go by Sophia right? Not Sophie?"

She laughed and rolled her eyes, obviously a little embarrassed by the statement that she had made at one time concerning her name. "Nowadays, sometimes it *is* Sophie, it just depends on how much time I've got on my hands I guess, but yeah, usually I still prefer Sophia." She smiled at him. "How have you been? It's been what, nearly eighteen years?"

Levi sighed. He didn't tell her about his current predicament of unemployment, or that several months before he had had to sell his townhouse, and was now about to sell the home that he grew up in, or that despite how many times he sent out his resume and went on interviews, he couldn't seem to land a job. "Pretty good," he said. "But you, it seems that you're doing *very well*." He looked around the gallery, acknowledging the beautiful artwork that hung on the walls and the people that were standing in front of each piece, seemingly impressed with what they were seeing.

"Right now, yeah, but who knows what the future holds you know? I'm just trying to enjoy *this* moment." She looked around at her own success. "It took me a long time to get to this and who knows what it will eventually lead to, if anything."

"It must take time," Levi responded. "And I'm sure you'll continue to do great things with your talent."

"Well, listen; I've got to circulate around the place a little bit. This is *my* art show after all." She laughed. "Why don't I give you my business card?" She held a small, cream colored card out to him and Levi took it. Not sure why, but he glanced at her ring finger and saw that she was not married. "Call me sometime. I would like to keep in touch."

Over the next few days they talked a few times over the phone.

"Devlin, the town where I grew up, has a ghost story of its own," Levi told her one night, referencing the folklore inspired artwork that her show had been centered around. He told her about the ghost of Anna Moore and how it had always been said that she haunts the area surrounding the old church and pond, searching for her missing heart.

"After spending so much time on town legends, I've been

thinking about doing something a little different this time. I think if I work on another project that involves a quant little town square I might just throw up."

Levi laughed. "Well, I hate to break it to you, but there *is* a square in Devlin."

"As long as it's not going to become part of my artwork I'm OK with that."

"So what is it that you're thinking of doing?" Levi asked with genuine interest.

"Lately I've been pondering ideas about a project on family folklore and narratives. I took a class on folklore when I was in college and aside from the small town lore, I found the topic of family lore to be equally compelling," she explained her interest in the material. "Does *your* family have any stories and lore that gets passed down through the generations?"

"That's easy," Levi said. "I have an almanac that's been in my family for nearly a hundred years," he told her right off the bat. "Then there's a small triangle of paper that's supposedly the corner from a page of a nearly *two* hundred year old almanac."

"That's neat," Sophia said, sounding genuine.

"And I also have a pack of squash seeds that were my grandmother's. I've always been told that the pack of seeds is magical, that it is able to reveal the truth. My great grandmother was a mermaid and I have a sea shell that belonged to her husband, my grandfather. The oak tree in my back yard was planted by my great, great, *great* grandmother when she moved from Vermont in a summer that it snowed."

The next time that they saw each other, it was raining. They met in a café on the edge of the city. It had been little over a week since the art showing. Face to face, Levi explained his current state of unemployment. They talked about him selling the house. He told her how he had been having dreams lately involving his grandfather, the house and Devlin.

"Well, it seemed out of character for you anyway." Sophia said.

"What do you mean?"

"I don't know, even back then it just seemed like you were majoring in finance because it seemed like it would be an easy way for you to find a job after you graduated. It didn't suit you."

The truth was that Levi didn't know what *suited* him. He

was already in his mid thirties with a failed career, no family, and to top it all off he had no idea what he wanted to do with the rest of his life. "How did you know that you wanted to be an artist?"

"It started out as a hobby," she said.

Levi thought about his hobbies, if there was anything that he could turn into a career, and it occurred to him, did he even have a hobby?

He liked to drink beer, did that count?

"You should write a book," Sophia said.

Levi chuckled at the idea. He had never even considered such a thing. "Write a book?"

"Yeah, I think you'd be good at it."

"Talk about out of character." Levi wondered what he had said over the few conversations that they had ever had together that would make her think that he would be able to write a book. The only thing that he could think of that had *ever* written that had not been for school was that one, silly play way back when he had been a kid.

"Well, don't look at it as out of character. Instead, think about it as a turning point, a plot twist if you will. I think you'd be good at it."

"Why do you think that?"

"I just do." She shrugged her shoulders. "Everything that you've told me so far about Devlin and your family has definitely stirred my curiosity. I've been thinking about it and I think I could do a series of paintings and photos surrounding one or the other, or both; the two are so intricately meshed together. It could very easily be my next big project, *and* it would be the first time that I've collaborated with someone on one of these folklore pieces. It would be *your* folklore and my artwork."

"So what do you want me to write about?"

"Write a family narrative."

Levi looked at her, not sure what she was talking about.

"Like I was talking about the other day, family stories that get passed down through generations; myths, facts, and lore about the family's past all intertwined with one another," she explained.

"I think you're the one that should be writing a book."

"Give it a whirl and see what happens."

Sophia rented him a cabin on a lake that stood midway between her house and Atlanta. It was going to be his for the weekend, under the promise that he would complete a novella while he was there.

"A what?"

"A novella," Sophia began to explain "is longer than a short story, but not quite long enough to be a novel."

"And what's shorter than that?" Levi laughed. Even after agreeing to give the writing a try he still couldn't imagine being able to put enough words together to be *anything*.

Sophia answered quickly. "It's a novelette."

It was decided that he would write about the history of his own family, starting at the beginning, the *very* beginning. It would be a somewhat fictionalized account of the family through the generations. Names, dates and places would stay the same, as close to accuracy as he could get based on what he knew and what he could find on the internet, but a lot of the rest would have to be constructed around the stories and lore that surrounded the family. That's what a family narrative was anyway, he reminded himself. It was just stories that have been told countless times, legends if you will. As far as he knew, what he was about to do would be the first time that any of the stories had ever been written out on paper.

By the time that they arrived, the lake was at one of its highest levels in history due to the historic amount of rainfall over the past month, and it was still raining. The weekend that Levi was to spend at the cabin, the edge of the lake's water was near the back porch. Motor boats and jet skis zipped past. People were fishing both off paddle boats and from the shore.

The inside of the cabin was simple, not overly decorated. A large print of bass and crappie hung over the wooden mantle of the fireplace. The living room had a couch, entertainment center, chair, and desk. All the furniture was made of pine. The kitchen joined the living area and a bar separated the two rooms. Upstairs there was a single room loft. This is where the bed was located.

Outside, the cabin had a back porch that held two rocking chairs. There was a private wooden dock that stretched out over the water. Tall pine trees loomed overhead and the ground was covered with pine needles. When he and Sophia attempted to walk to the dock, tiny baby frogs that couldn't have been any larger than an adult's thumb nail scattered about everywhere that they stepped. That day he and Sophia couldn't get onto the dock because the water had risen high enough to where it overflowed the first ten feet or so of slats.

"I'll be back early Sunday," Sophia told him a little later as they stood in front of the house. The rain had finally stopped and the sun was peeking through the gray clouds for the first time in days. A moment later, Sophia's car sloshed through the mud puddles that stood in the driveway and meandered past a dense line of pine trees until it was out of sight.

Levi spent most of Friday and Saturday writing. At the start of each day, before he started tapping away at the keyboard, he spent the mornings sitting outside on the back porch, overlooking the lake, drinking coffee. It was relaxing, just sitting there alone, thinking about things. All sorts of things jangled around in his head. He thought about his job situation, selling the house in Devlin, the newly rekindled friendship with Sophia; but most of what he thought about was what he was writing. The words and story clanged around his head most of the day and well into the night, making it difficult to fall asleep. But over those two days he had ignored both TV and reading. He hadn't even allowed himself the simple pleasure of drinking a single beer. He had made a promise to Sophia that he would have it complete by Sunday and it was a promise that he intended to keep.

By the time Sunday arrived, Levi had written more words than he ever thought he would have been capable of. He had read over the story several times, overall pleased with his work. Sophia arrived mid afternoon, carrying a six-pack of craft beer, a bottle of wine, and a canvas shopping bag that was stuffed full of groceries.

"It turns out that the cabin was available again for tonight, so we're staying." She said matter-of-factly and sternly. She was already placing the groceries in the refrigerator. She handed one of the beers from the six-pack to Levi and poured herself a glass of wine.

Over the weekend, the rain had completely stopped and the sun had been shining. The water level of the lake had receded somewhat over those couple of days. Everywhere though the ground was still mushy under their feet from the unusual amount of rainfall. Levi knew that the wet pine straw and standing puddles of water would become breeding grounds for mosquitoes. In fact, an abnormal amount of the insects were already buzzing about and landing on whatever bare flesh that they could find. The sun was setting as Levi and Sophia walked outside.

"It looks like we can go out there now," Levi said, nodding toward the dock.

Their feet splashed in the inch deep, cool water that stood over the first several feet of slats where it had yet to completely clear off. The entire length of the dock didn't have any sort of rails on either side. It was just a simple, wooden platform that stretched out over the still, glasslike water. They walked to the end where there were two empty Adirondack chairs awaiting their arrival. The chairs had at one time been painted white, but were now weathered and turning gray. Levi sat in one and Sophia took the other. She placed her glass of wine on the wide, flat arm. Together they looked out across the lake and at the horizon. The sun was falling behind the line of pine trees that stood on the other side of the water.

"I wonder if the statue of that book is still at The University," Sophia said, remembering the one night that they had spent together and how they had sat at the edge of the reflecting pool at the library and looked at the book through the branches of the weeping willow trees. In a way, it had been a close similarity to where they sat now on the end of the wooden dock.

"You know, I don't know. We should go check it out sometime."

Just in the amount of time that it had taken for them to say those few sentences; the sun had descended well past the pine trees. The sky was a smash of orange, blue, and pink. Now the sun's descent was so fast that it was actually visible. It was those last few moments before dark. Just a few seconds later, the entirety of the sun had disappeared behind the pine trees and the only evidence that it had ever been there at all was that some of the orange glow still bled into the darkening sky.

Sophia slapped at a mosquito that was on her arm. "I'm getting eaten alive," she said.

"Me too," Levi stood and reached his hand out to Sophia. He pulled on her arm, helping her out of the chair. "Let's go inside."

A little while later, Sophia started cooking dinner. Levi sat on one of the barstools at the laminate topped bar that connected the kitchen to the living room. The entire cabin was filled with the delightful aroma of the beginnings of a home cooked meal. It was something that he didn't have very often and hardly ever prepared by someone else. Sliced onions and mushrooms were waiting on a wooden cutting board next to the stove. A pan was on the stovetop with a couple of tablespoons of hot olive oil ready to go. As Sophia placed each of the chicken breasts into the pan, Levi watched and talked briefly about what he had written.

"So tell me," Levi peeled at the label on his beer bottle, "are you seeing anybody?" It was the first time that Levi had broached the subject since they had met at the art show. He had already noticed that she didn't wear a wedding ring, so she mustn't have been married.

As Sophia removed the browned chicken from the pan, she explained how she hadn't been in a relationship in over a year, and that her last boyfriend had been too self-centered. "I guess dating is just something that I haven't really had much time for," she said. By then Sophia was adding the onions and mushrooms to the pan juices and would soon place the chicken back in with the vegetables

After dinner, they sat across from one another, Sophia on the couch and Levi in the chair. They talked and drank more.

"Whatever happened with you and that girl that you were telling me about?" Sophia had her legs pulled up underneath her bottom on the couch.

It surprised Levi that she had remembered so much of what they had talked about that one night at The University.

"Claire? I never saw her again until two years ago actually when I had been in town for my mom's funeral. You know, its funny, the girl that I was dating at the time, her name was Adrianne, met Claire and then broke up with me afterward because she thought that I was still in love with her."

"Are you? Still in love with her?"

"No, I mean she's not even part of my life anymore." He thought about what Sophia had told him that night at The University after they had discussed Claire and Diesel. She had said that if it was meant to be then it'd be.

"So can I read it? What you wrote."

Levi stood and walked to the old, pine desk where he had been working all weekend. The laptop computer was shut down and closed on top of the smooth, flat, and impeccably polished surface. A neat stack of typed pages sat on top of the computer. A thick, black binder clip held them together. Levi picked up the manuscript, walked over to the couch and handed the pages to Sophia.

"While you jump into that I'm going to go ahead and turn in for the night," he told her.

As he was climbing the steps to the loft, he paused and glanced back over his shoulder at Sophia. She already had the pages unclipped. He watched as she lifted the title page and smiled when he could see that she really was interested in what he had written. He knew that he wanted to be more than friends with Sophia and wondered if she felt the same way about him. He knew that he could easily use the seclusion and privacy of the cabin to his advantage and make his move right then. Actually, he wondered if it was part of her intentions of wanting the two of them to stay the extra night. But he didn't want to rush into anything. There was something about the idea of the two of them being together that felt right and he didn't want to ruin it with jumping ahead. He wanted to take it slow, one step at a time, the way that he thought it should be.

"Sophia, we should go out on a date sometime," he said from the steps.

She lowered the pages and looked up at him and smiled. "I'd like that," she said.

Levi smiled back. "Good night," he told her.

"Night," she said.

Levi stepped all the way into the loft as Sophia began to read.

The Unclaimed Acre, the Story of My Family
by Levi Stanley

IN THE year 1816, the month of June brought snow storms throughout various parts of the world. It would later be declared by scientists that the unusual and alarming weather incident could have been triggered by the eruption of a volcano. Because of the eruption they would say, the environment had been altered.

The effects of the cold were felt in places as far away from one another as France and Germany, Switzerland and North America. All over the land crops were failing under the frigid temperatures. Animals were dying. That year, the harvest of vegetables, if there were to be any, would surely be slight. Much of the population was becoming hungry. Many people feared the end of the world.

In Vermont, snow began to fall on June the ninth. Seven year old Sarah Lincoln stood at the edge of her family's farm and watched as the first flurries began to drift down from the gray clouds. No one could have predicted the freakish weather. It was June! Even the published almanac for that year did not predict the snow fall.

Sarah was bundled to defend herself from the cold. In the field that stretched before her, the thick green leaves of the corn stalks were already beginning to catch the falling snow. Some of the leaves were already starting to sag and droop from the weight that was accumulating on them. Sarah liked snow, but knew that what she was seeing was a bad sign and she feared the worst. She had heard stories of vegetable blights and too much rain. She knew of the hardships that farm families faced whenever their crop did not produce the bounty that they needed. Sarah knew that it was the corn that her family depended on, and without it…well it would be hard to imagine.

However horrible of a future the snow covered corn stalks signified, it was the sight of the summer squash that truly broke Sarah's heart. In front of the rows of corn stalks, there was a slim hill of squash plants. The tender yellow flowers on the squash plants were not able to hold the weight of the snow. Each flower was flattened to the ground. Squash had been her mother's favorite vegetable, especially yellow crook necks like the ones that were planted in front of the corn.

Sarah's mother had died the previous autumn when the falling leaves of the dogwood and maple trees were red and orange. Even though months had already passed since her death, within Sarah's heart she could still feel the same empty harshness of impending death that she had experienced while sitting in the room with her. Sarah could remember sitting on the edge of the bed as her mother gasped for breath. On that day, Sarah's father had been out in the field, working on the final harvest of the summer. Through the open window, the land was a beautiful array of the season, just the way that it was supposed to be, but inside the bedroom, everything was wrong. There was a pressing that seemed nearly to shatter everything that Sarah knew. The white blanket was pulled up close around her mother's neckline. The sturdy wooden headboard was draped with a bunch of herbs that was supposed to bring calmness to her passing. When she died, a single orange leaf drifted in through the open window. The leaf landed on the bed clothes. When it was finally time to leave the room, Sarah lifted the leaf from the sun kissed white linen and carried it with her. Later that night, after her mother's body had been taken away, Sarah pressed the oak leaf between the pages of her Bible. She placed the book on the wooden table at her bedside and snuffed out the candle that she so often used to read by. She fell asleep and dreamed of an evening funeral procession in which her mother's body was carried in an oak casket through a dense area of trees. Squash of various shapes and sizes hung from the lowest branches of the trees. Each of the squash had been hollowed out and now held a lit wax candle within its cavity, lighting the way as the six nameless and faceless black dressed men carried the casket through the trees and toward the cemetery. Sarah and her father followed, each of them wiping a tear from their cheeks.

"Sarah! Come in! It's cold out here," her father yelled from the porch of the weathered, wooden house. Sarah turned her back from the field. Unlike every previous year of Sarah's life, the plants that Sarah was turning her back on had not been planted by her mother. Earlier that spring, she and her father had used some of the seeds that her mother had collected toward the end of the previous growing season, just as she had started getting sick. The seeds had been started with the drying process and placed in the pantry where she intended to retrieve them the next year, but she had died before the seeds were even completely dry. In the spring, well after the danger of frost had passed, Sarah and her father planted the seeds in the soil, just as her mother had done every year before. It was a way of remembrance. It was a way to keep the steady flow of their lives normal even though everything had been changed beyond repair. The seeds that they had planted were the last, except for a small packet that Sarah had secretly stashed away in her bedroom.

Inside the house, all the windows were shut. Even though it was the beginning of the summer, a fire was crackling in the fireplace. The entire town was filled with the smell of wood smoke. It hinted at memories of Christmastime and winter. This smell though was different. It wasn't the same aroma of burning wood that had been cut and left outside to dry all through the summer and beginnings of fall. The wood that was burning in the fireplaces of the community was more freshly chopped, some of it just a few days old.

"Abraham says that this is not right," her father told Sarah about what the town blacksmith had mentioned to him earlier that day.

Just hours earlier, the two men had stood in front of the blacksmith shop. It had not started snowing yet, but was unseasonably cold nonetheless. The men's frigid breath puffed out in the air between them as they talked. "We should all be worried. Elizabeth says that she saw Eleanor earlier today and that something about her eyes didn't look right."

Eleanor was an old woman that lived alone at the edge of the woods in a ramshackle house. Rumor insisted that the elderly woman was a witch. Many people of the area feared women that they would consider to be different. Eleanor had long gray hair that she never washed. The hair trailed down her back in a matted together mess of tangles that often had crumbling pieces of leaves and small twigs caught within. Some children had even said that they had seen spiders crawling out from the unkempt hair. The stories that people told about the woman had kept Sarah up late many nights. In one particular nightmare, Eleanor had been standing amid the dry cornstalks of the field behind Sarah's house. It had been night. The woman's eyes reflected the white glow of the moon. She held her arms straight out in front of her like she was reaching toward Sarah. The hair of Eleanor's head began swarming about in a twirl. Spiders the size of Sarah's childish hands skittered from the gray. Bats fluttered out. All the creatures swarmed toward Sarah in a hungry and desperate determination. That night Sarah had bolted up in bed, covered in sweat, full of fear.

Eleanor had been one of the only town members that had visited Sarah's mother before she died. On the day of the visit Eleanor had tied the bundle of dried herbs to the bed's headboard. "This will help in her passing, it will assure that she leaves this world calmly and arrives safely into the next. It will also soothe the loved ones," the old woman had told Sarah as they stood in the room together. Sarah no longer feared the old woman and learned that she had actually been friends with her mother, that they had spent a lot of time together.

"I'm afraid of what they might do to her," her father told Sarah as she was taking off her heavy coat. "The town will come after her, Sarah. They're going to think that this is all because of Eleanor." He walked to the window and glanced outside at the heavily falling snow. "She was your mother's friend. I just can't let her life be in danger." He looked toward the woods and took note of the slim trail of smoke rising from deep within the trees and knew that the smoke was coming from Eleanor's chimney.

That night Sarah went with her father into the cold and through the woods. They had waited to start the mission under the blackness of the night so that no one would see them. They didn't want the rest of the township to think that they were harboring a witch. They used a single lantern to light their way. The snow was not as thick under the canopy of green leaves in the woods, but out in the open it was as thick as winter. When they knocked on the door, there was no answer and when Eleanor finally swung the door open, there was a look of fear in her eyes. Sarah knew that the woman must have thought that the visitors that she would be faced with on they other side of her door were accusers that had arrived in the dark of night intending to do her harm.

The next day, the snow flurries continued and the fate of the crops throughout the town was one of certain doom. All around there was a sense of fear and worry. Everyone was looking for somewhere to place the blame for what was happening to them. Without their crops, how would they survive the rest of the year? Surely hunger would strike the community and would lead to what? Burglaries and death most assumed.

Everywhere, the whispers of dark magic circulated. It didn't take long for some of the more vengeful men to take action. With guns and knives in hand they busted down the door of Eleanor's house only to find the interior empty. Various dried herbs and candles were scattered among all the flat, wooden surfaces. In the fireplace, the fire that Eleanor had lit the previous day had all but diminished. All that was left were ashy, glowing embers. One of the men held up a burlap satchel. He ripped the bag open with his hunting knife and the contents scattered to the wooden floor. Small bones clattered at the men's feet. A collective gasp came from the four of them. The fifth man, one that had stepped outside to search the surrounding property, burst into the house. "I found something!" He exclaimed. "Foot prints!"

The five men followed the three sets of footprints through the woods. Since the trees were thick with green leaves, the trail of foot prints through the woods had not been covered over by the falling snow. They followed the steps all the way to where they emerged from the tree line and into the corn fields of Edgar Lincoln's property.

Sarah opened the door and knew without asking why the men were there. The one in front, one Sarah only vaguely recognized spoke. "Where is she?" His black, handlebar mustache had melting snow flakes caught within its wiry hairs.

"I – I don't know –," Sarah started.

The man kicked the door inward. Sarah stepped back as the heavy wood banged against the opposing wall. He stepped over the threshold. "Don't fuss with me! Where is she?" He reached out toward Sarah and grasped her thin, tender arm with his callused hand.

"Daddy!" Sarah screamed for her father who was already pounding into the room, obviously alarmed by the racket.

The man spun Sarah around and pulled her to him. In one fluid motion the man held the serrated hunting knife to Sarah's throat. He glared over Sarah's blonde hair at her father. "Tell me where the witch is or your bastard child dies." As he spoke, Sarah could feel his hot breath on the back of her neck. She closed her eyes. She was crying. When she reopened her eyelids, she could see the contemplation on her father's face.

"Daddy, don't," Sarah pleaded softly through her tears.

"Sarah, I – I'm sorry," her father's eyes left hers and landed on the man that was standing behind her. Sarah watched as her father pointed toward the bedroom. She felt the cold metal of the knife blade fall away from her neck. The man shoved her to the side. She crashed into a wooden table and fell to the floor. She sat on the floor and cried as the other four men followed through the house. Their feet were heavy and determined on the wooden slats of the floor. Sarah felt sick as she heard Eleanor's screams in the other room. She could hear scuffling and shouts of the men to "Get her! Stop her! Don't look in her eyes!" Sarah flinched at the loud crack of the gunshot as it echoed through the house. Eleanor's screams abruptly stopped and the smell of gunpowder drifted past Sarah and through the open door.

That night Sarah couldn't escape the image of the men dragging Eleanor's lifeless body through the house, leaving her and her father to clean up the blood. Neither she nor her father was able to sleep that night. Outside, the land was white and their livelihood was dead. Inside, they felt haunted by what they had witnessed.

"I don't know if I can stay here anymore," Sarah said as she faced her father in the quietness of the night. The fireplace was ablaze behind her. It was the only source of light in the room. "With what happened to Momma and now this."

Her father nodded in agreement. With the farm destroyed, his wife already gone, and his daughter wishing to start anew, he saw no reason to stay. In addition to the all the misfortune that had already happened, now the rest of the town would view him as one that had assisted in hiding Eleanor, who they already assumed was the catalyst with the summer snow. He felt guilt for pointing the men in the direction of the old woman, but it had been his daughter that had a knife held to her throat. What else was he supposed to do? The future for him and his daughter did not look promising. "We'll take the first available wagon away from here. I have a sister that lives down in South Carolina. Her husband grows cotton. We'll go there and begin a new life." He looked toward Sarah and spoke assuredly. "We'll be OK. I'll make sure of it."

Sarah and her father had to board a horse drawn wagon that would take them to their new home. The driver helped with the luggage. After several days, the buggy finally traveled through roads that were lined on either side with pecan trees. Fluffy white cotton was in abundance in the distant fields. Even at that moment workers were in the fields picking. Sarah watched all the scenery as she passed. The cotton was such a difference from the tall stalks of green corn that Sarah was used to.

When the horses finally trotted into the town, Sarah was filled with excitement. A wooden courthouse stood on one of the streets. A gazebo was in front of the building. Sarah was told that the town of Devlin had been established in the mid 17oo's. The horse pulled the buggy down another dirt road. Houses stood on each side.

Compared to the house that Sarah had grown up in, the plantation house that the carriage finally stopped at was massive. Tall, white columns that reached from the ground all the way to the roof's eve stood on the front. All the windows were flanked on both sides by slatted black shutters. Purple wisteria hung in the trees that stood in the front yard. Pink and white camellias were blooming everywhere that Sarah looked. When Sarah stepped out of the wagon she felt like she was in the process of entering another world. Of course she thought that living in the house would only be temporary, but it was an experience that Sarah looked forward to.

Her aunt was a tall, slender and elegant woman who rushed

down the steps of the house and scampered barefoot across the dusty yard where she hugged her brother that she had not seen in many years.

"Edgar, it has been so long. Too long," she stated dramatically. She turned toward Sarah and smiled. "And you must be Sarah."

That night, supper was served in the dining room of the house. Sarah and her father were there as well as his sister and her husband. Sarah's uncle wasn't what Sarah pictured when she had been told that he was a cotton farmer. He wasn't rugged the way most farmers were that she had grown up seeing. He was a dapper man, clean shaven and plump. Supper was roast pork with all the fixings.

It wasn't until after they had arrived in South Carolina that Sarah finally asked her father what the man with the mustache had meant when he had referred to her as a "bastard child". They were seated in the front parlor room of Aunt Margaret and Uncle Frank's house. Sarah was by the window. Her father placed his hand on Sarah's leg.

He told her how that when she had been a baby, she had been left on the porch of his and his wife's house. Nobody knew who Sara's real parents were. He and his wife had been married for a while and they had been trying to have a baby of their own for years, but were never able to conceive. The discovery had been made on a clear, sunny morning. Mrs. Lincoln had opened the front door of the house. The sun was just coming up over the horizon. Roosters were calling. She nearly tripped over the small basket that the baby was lying in, wrapped neatly in a hand woven blanket. When she looked down, the baby was sound asleep. Mrs. Lincoln's initial reaction was one of horror and confusion. She wondered who would abandon their baby in such a cruel way.

"Edgar!" She turned back toward the interior of the house and yelled again for her husband. "Edgar, come quick! There's a baby out here. Somebody left their baby!"

When Edgar had rounded the corner and saw the beautiful baby girl that lay in the basket, his heart nearly stopped. "My God," he told his wife. "She's beautiful."

Mrs. Lincoln's yelling for her husband had awakened the baby, but the girl was not crying. She looked up at the man and woman. Mrs. Lincoln kneeled down at the basket. Scribbled on a piece of paper, there was a name. *SARAH* the note said.

"Sarah. Her name's Sarah." Mrs. Lincoln turned to face her husband. The paper was still in her hand. "They even named her."

Sarah was confused about the confession. Of course she wondered who her real father and mother were, but as far as she was concerned, her true parents were those that had raised her and took care of her throughout her life.

"But everybody else knew? The man that day, the one with the knife, he knew?"

"Yes, the whole town knew. It wasn't like we were trying to keep a great big secret from you or anything."

It was ten years after she and her father had moved to Devlin that Sarah met a boy by the name of Thomas Hollister. The first time that Sarah had seen Thomas it had just been something about him that made her eyes linger. She had been in the midst of the hustle and bustle of town center where the farm trade was at its most intense. It was a rare thing for her to be there among the farmers, all of them men. Usually she was at home with her aunt, tending to domestic chores. That day, her father was making a deal with another man from Augusta, when out of the corner of her eye Sarah spotted him. She watched as he easily hoisted a cotton bail onto his shoulder and carried it to a wagon. When Thomas turned around, Sarah quickly spun away from him. She could feel her face blushing. She never expected the feelings that were coursing through her body. Of course she knew that she was expected to find someone to marry and have children with, but until that day, she never thought that she would crave a man's companionship the way that she did then.

She spotted him several times over the next few days. Sarah began slipping away from the house to specifically search for him. It was discovered that his family owned the farm on the opposite side of town and sometimes he would be found there. Once, she had stumbled upon him sitting on the ground, leaning against a massive oak tree. His hat was off his head and covering his face. His body was covered in shade from the tree and must have been a welcome relief from the heat of the sun. Each time that she saw him, he didn't notice that she was watching until one day where she must've stared too long.

Sarah had been standing behind the massive circumference of a large tree that day, peeking around to watch the boy at the edge of the field as he was swinging a wooden handled hoe into the dirt. His muscles were tight under the white shirt. Sweat was making the fabric adhere to him. After one swing, he paused and looked toward Sarah. His eyes locked with hers. Her face was on fire as she ducked behind the width of the tree. Her nerves were jangled as she pressed her back to the rough bark. She breathed heavily, telling herself that she couldn't stay hidden there forever, but not knowing when it would be safe to move. Finally she ever so slowly peaked around the tree to see if he was looking. What she saw was that the hoe was lying on its own in the newly loosened dirt and the boy was nowhere in sight.

From behind the tree, and barely peaking around the side, Sarah scanned the landscape that stretched out in front of her. Fluffy rows of cotton extended nearly to the end of her vision. A line of trees stood on the other side of the field. There were several houses within sight. Tools were scattered about all across the ground, but she still couldn't find what she was looking for. She turned her head to search the other direction.

"My name's Thomas in case you're wondering." He was standing right beside her.

Sarah felt her cheeks ignite at the sight and closeness of him. It was then for the first time that she noticed the dimples on his cheeks when he smiled. Sunlight reflected off his hair that was as black as raven feathers.

"I'm Sarah," she said coyly.

By Thomas's insistence they spent the rest of the day together. They walked through the woods behind Sarah's house to a narrow creek where they sat and stared off into the trickling water. The ground was covered with dandelions. Most of them had yellow flowers while a few had already turned fluffy white. They talked to each other, telling things about themselves. Thomas was two years older than Sarah. He was turning nineteen that year. He loved to go fishing. He had a dog that he called Weevil, as in boll weevil, because of the canine's affinity for destroying cotton plants with his teeth and mouth. His family owned the farm where she had been seeing him work. Like Sarah, he was an only child.

Sarah watched him as he told her all of this. Occasionally he would glance at her, but most of the time he looked at the water, almost as if he was concentrating on what he was saying, wanting to tell her all the right things.

Sarah told him that she was an orphan and that nobody knew who her real parents were.

Thomas was quiet for a moment and then looked at her as he spoke. "I am too." He told her that unlike her situation, his parents had died in a fire right after he was born. He had no next of kin that anyone knew of so he was given to his current parents. "But they are the only ones that I have ever known," he said.

"Who owns this strip of land?" Sarah asked as she looked at her surroundings. The trees, the water in the creek, the dandelions, all of it was beautiful.

"No one," he told her and shifted the way that he was sitting. He leaned forward and pulled a book from the back pocket of his brown trousers and placed it between himself and Sarah on the creek's grassy bank. Sarah glanced to the book and saw that it was a journal of some sorts.

"What's that?" she asked him.

"It's my almanac. It predicts weather patterns, planting times, and various other things pertaining to the farm."

They spent the afternoon laughing at one another. Thomas made Sarah a crown of dandelions from the ones that were growing by the creek. She felt like the queen of everything at the moment when he leaned toward her with his arms extended and placed the crown of flowers on top of her head. She knew at that moment that she had fallen in love with him.

"This way you won't walk away from here with nothing," he told her.

When Sarah finally got home it was nearly dark. She still wore the ring of flowers. The sky was orange around the setting sun. Her father wanted to know where she had been.

"I went out for a walk," she told him and went to her bed.

That night, Sarah couldn't sleep. Every time that she closed her eyes she could see Thomas as he leaned toward her, placing the flowers on her head. Even though they were now hanging in a ring around her bed post, it felt like they were just now leaving his fingertips.

The next day, Sarah couldn't find Thomas. She looked for him at the farm and at the creek. What she *did* discover at the edge of the creek though was that he had accidentally left the almanac there. The next time that Sarah saw Thomas was a couple of days later. He was sitting on the bank at the same spot where they had spent that first afternoon of getting to know each other. He was leaning against the tree. Once again, an open book was held in his hands. At first, Sarah thought that it must have been another almanac, but the closer that she got she saw that it looked like a novel. Those were not common in Devlin at the time.

"What are you reading?" Sarah asked as she approached.

Thomas was so engrossed in the story that he hadn't even heard Sarah approach. Her voice startled him and he looked up at her. He smiled. "It's called *Frankenstein*. It was written by an author by the name of Mary Shelley. It's about a doctor who creates a monster with discarded body parts. I think probably in the end though the monster is just misunderstood."

"Well, it sounds horrendous."

Thomas closed the book and laid it in his lap.

"We'll I've been searching for you all over. I wanted to return this." Sarah held the almanac out to him.

"I've been looking for that," he told her with a chuckle of relief. "I thought that maybe it was lost." He took the almanac from her and flipped through the pages.

In the distance, thunder began to rumble. Both Sarah and Thomas looked up and across the creek. Through the trees of the woods they could see the approaching storm clouds. Thomas put his boots back on and began lacing them up.

"The rain's coming quick. It'll be good for the crops," he told her.

"Was that predicted in your book?"

"I don't know. You've had it," he said with a laugh.

A loud crack of lightning striking a tree was heard in the distance and preceded the first rain drops only by seconds. Thomas quickly gathered both his novel and the almanac from the ground and held them tight to his chest. He and Sarah began running through the woods. By the time that they emerged through the tree line that separated an empty field and the woods, the rain was a downpour. Together, they ran toward Sarah's house that was already visible across the field. Sarah wasn't thinking about how she would explain Thomas's presence to her father. She was only caught up in the moment with Thomas as they ran through the rain. She screamed with laughter as the rain water soaked through her clothes, every so often glancing at Thomas who was also smiling and wet. Sarah tripped and fell into the freshly plowed, wet dirt of the ground. It wasn't quite yet muddy, but was wet enough to cling to her white dress. Thomas stood over her and reached his hand out to her, offering assistance in helping her back to her feet. Sarah stopped laughing as her eyes met his. She reached to his hand and before he had time to pull her up, she resumed her shrill of laughter and yanked his arm downward, causing his feet to slide across the ground. He fell down on top of her. Both of them were silent as his face hovered inches above hers. Water dripped from his hair onto her face. He lingered there, looking contemplative. Sarah grasped his face in her hands and pulled her lips to his. She didn't care if she was lying in the dirt with rain pounding down on them or of the fact that they were easily within view of her father if he was looking out one of the westward facing windows of the house.

Thomas was all that mattered.

Later, when they walked into the house it was still raining. Sarah's father looked at her and Thomas questionably. She thought that she must've been gleaming with happiness. Later that night, after Thomas had gone, Sarah lay in bed by candlelight thinking about him. She wanted to remember forever how it felt to kiss him for the first time, and just to think that it was her initiative! She wanted to always be able to go to that spot in the field where it had happened and be able to look at the ground and remember how happy she had been.

Sarah leaned over to her bedside table and pulled her Bible from the shelf. She opened the pages to where the she had placed the oak leaf on that long ago day when her mother had died. The Bible's spine was so creased from her frequency of opening it to that same spot that it naturally fell open that way. After ten years, the leaf was fragile and brittle. It had lost most of its color and was now a color of brown that could be crumbled so easily. In between the same pages was the folded brown paper that had the squash seeds held within.

The next day was sunny. It was a welcome relief from the rain, even though for the rest of her life, rainy spring days would always be a comfort to Sarah just as snow would bring about a sense of dread and sadness. Sarah was standing in the empty field across from her house. She dropped the wooden handled trowel onto the ground. She looked around at the distant house and the trees of the woods, judging the proximity and checking her vivid memory of the day before to assure herself that she was in the right spot. Satisfied with the location, Sarah ripped the brown paper open and dropped the seeds into the earth. A tear dropped town her cheek as she crumbled the leaf into the soil. Next, she took the crown of dandelions and placed it in the ground. She covered the hole with dirt and patted it down. That night it rained again, soaking the earth, germinating the seeds of squash.

By the beginning of the summer, the vines had spread like crazy. There were so many bright yellow blossoms on the vines that they were difficult to count. Sarah knew a good bit about the plant from her mother. She knew that some of the blossoms were female and some were male. It was the female ones that would produce the vegetables. Looking closely she could see the small, barely formed squash at the base of the female flowers. Sarah understood the pollen covered pistons that stood erect within the flowers. She watched as bees hovered around the plants, transporting the pollen from one to the other. Some days she and Thomas walked through the field together. Neither of them ever said "this is the spot, this is where we first kissed," but both of them knew. It was a silent sentimentality between them. Years later, they would tell others the significance, letting the fable be passed down through generations.

Even though the squash marked the spot of the first kiss, Sarah new that the unclaimed land at the creek was where she had fallen in love with Thomas as they had spent time there together. As they walked across the field, toward the creek, Weevil was at their side, occasionally wondering off, sniffing at the ground until he found where he wanted to rest in the cool dirt at the edge of the squash vines. Next to where the dog lay, there was a sprout of another kind of plant that was just pushing up through the dirt. It was a very young oak tree.

At the end of the summer, Sarah and Thomas were married. Autumn was on the horizon. The squash plants, along with many of the other crops of the town were nearing their final harvest. Even though neither Sarah nor Thomas's family had enough money to buy her a special dress for the occasion, she still deliberated heavily on what she would wear. What she decided on was the dress that she had worn on the day that she had ventured to the creek to return the almanac to Thomas, the dress that had been soaked by rainwater, the same that had been filthy with dirt, the dress that she had been wearing when they had first kissed. She spent what little money she had to purchase a yellow ribbon that she tied around her waist. On her head she wore a fresh crown of dandelions.

Thomas was wearing his nicest waist coat and a top hat that had belonged to his grandfather.

The celebration ended in the field. Sarah's father had laid down wooden planks so that people wouldn't have to stand in the dirt. A local banjo player was seated at the end of the platform. Surrounding the temporary floor, poles had been erected and twine ran across them. Hollow squash hung from each length of twine. Each of the vegetables held a flickering candle within, giving a yellow, soothing glow to the late summer night. Sarah and Thomas danced under the moon while Weevil, who was intent with lying by the young sprig of a tree, would occasionally howl into the night.

After getting married, Sarah and Thomas Hollister had remained in the large plantation house with her aunt and uncle until the older couple's passing two years later. Both members of the elderly couple had died within a month of one another. Thomas took over the farm. Sarah and Thomas were heirs to the house and it was where they raised their own daughter, Emma. Sarah and Thomas had watched as Emma had grown up and gotten married to a man that had been passing through town on business.

George Fuller had been steering a wagon through the town when Emma had first seen him. When Emma introduced Mr. Fuller to her parents, her mother had been a little bit put off by her daughter's potential suitor. The man had been so different from the young Thomas that *she* had fallen in love with soon after moving from Vermont to South Carolina. While Thomas had been laid back, polite, and always smiling in his youthfulness, this Mr. Fuller was full of tension and had an air of recklessness about him. One thing that was most troubling to Sarah about her daughter's love interest was the mustache.

George Fuller wore a handlebar mustache much like the one of the man that had held Sarah so tightly in his grasp and pressed the cold blade of a knife to her throat when she had been younger. Even after all those years, she still had nightmares about all the things from that night, the knife, the gunshot, the blood. Every winter when it looked like there was the slightest chance of snow, the gray clouds filled Sarah with worry. Like snow, George Fuller's mustache was another thing that triggered her horrible memories.

Something else that Sarah though was a little discouraging was the fact that George never removed his hat when he was in the

Hollister's home and in the presence of the ladies of the house, Sarah and Emma. In those days it was a sign that he was ungentlemanly. It meant that he could be a heavy drinker and more than likely liked to frequent barrooms. Sarah wanted the best for her daughter, but Emma insisted that George was a perfect gentleman when he was alone with her and that she was in love with him.

They got married in the spring. Emma was not yet twenty three years old and George had been twenty years her senior.

Soon after their marriage, Emma and George built the house in the vacant lot that stood by the plantation house. It was near the oak tree that marked the spot where Sarah and Thomas first kissed. By then the tree was huge. The house's construction was finished late in the summer. The original house was built with only three rooms in its entirety. There was a parlor and two bedrooms. Within the first two years of living in the house, Emma had given birth to a baby boy that she named John.

By the time of his tenth birthday, John already had his grandfather Thomas's dimples and the pitch black hair that was the same as both his father and grandfather. John liked to climb up into the oak tree in front of the house and pretend that he was a pirate on his ship's mast. John was mesmerized by the stories that his mother would tell him about how *her* mother, John's grandmother, Sarah, had planted the tree herself. She also told him that his grandparents had buried their dog underneath the tree and that the dog's name had been Weevil.

John always laughed at the name.

John had been a very quiet baby, but as he began to mature, he became more and more restless. In his mind's imagination, John lived a very different life than he did in reality. He was fascinated with the ideas of travel and the fact somebody could go all the way from Vermont to South Carolina like his grandmother had done many years earlier was simply astounding. He had seen hand drawn maps of the United States and had been shown by his grandmother the state at the top right. It was the one where she was from. Sometimes John would sit on the floor in his room and study the map by candlelight. He would imagine himself in different states throughout the country, what life would be like there. What interested John the most about the map was the massive expanse of water that stretched all around the perimeter.

He had heard about the ocean in school.

Back in those days school had been a one room affair, filled with kids of various age groups.

According to his studies, the ocean was a large body of water that held many different types of creatures. The books held drawings of large fish, whales, and sharks.

The only bodies of water that John had seen so far in his young life was that of the small trickling creek that ran through the woods behind his house and into the large pond that stood behind the church.

John was afraid to go to the pond because that was where legend had it that Anna Moore, the infamous ghost of Devlin, was said to linger about. His father told him that she haunted both the area of land that surrounded the body of water and the old, abandoned church that stood near there. There had been numerous reports of townspeople stating that late at night they had seen the ghost of Anna looming around the water's edge.

In particular it was the ocean that was off the edge of South Carolina that held John's interest the most. He thought that since it was the closest, it would be the most likely for him to ever travel to. On the map it was only a few inches away, but John had no idea how he would get there. He had heard about railways and steamboats, but there was not a waterway or railroad nearby. It would be years later until a train track would be laid down in Devlin. He had never learned to ride a horse like his father who needed the mode of transportation to support his family.

George was a salesman and stayed gone sometimes for weeks at a time. He traveled to and from various places selling pots and pans out of the wagon.

Sometimes John liked to walk to the creek and pretend that he was at the sea. In his mind, the water seemed endless. He liked to dig around in the dirt, pretending that it was sand, and find small shards of rock that in his childhood imagination he was sure were shark's teeth. It wasn't only the fish and real life sea creatures that captured John's imagination. It was the idea of ghostly pirates and mermaids that sent his mind running wild.

After being gone for several weeks, John's father returned late in the day. After hugging both John and his wife, George opened his satchel and from within the bag's interior he pulled a large sea shell and handed it to his son. John's face lit up at the treasure. Up until that point in his life, John had only seen illustrations of sea shells. He had never had the opportunity to see one in person, much less hold one within his hands.

"Thank you! Thank you!" John screamed with excitement and wrapped his arms around his father's neck.

George took the conch shell from his son's hands and held it against his own ear. "If you hold it to your ear, you can hear the ocean," he told John and handed the shell back to his son.

John's face was filled with wonder. Just the sight of the shell was proof that the ocean *did* exist and wasn't just something that was drawn on a map and talked about at school. John held the shell to his ear and listened closely, mesmerized by what he heard.

For a long time that night John sat on the floor in his room with the sea shell lying next to him. Candlelight flickered against the four walls. While he liked spending time playing at the creek, being inside the family house when his father was at home was his favorite thing. It was those times that made him think that he *never* wanted to be anywhere else. It made John feel safe and secure knowing that his father that had worked so hard building a home for his wife and unborn child had returned and was there with them.

Through the wall John could hear the unmistakable sound of lapping water coming from his parent's bedroom. He imagined that it was the waves of the ocean coming ashore, but knew that it was really his father lying back in the wash tub that his mother had just filled with warm water. Bathing was only done once a week and George usually bathed upon his arrival home. It was that night that John first felt the foundation of his home unsettling. From the other room, in between the sound of water, he could hear his mother speaking.

"You've been at the leg show, haven't you? While you're gone, that's what you do. I can smell the alcohol on your breath."

"Emma, I haven't." There were more abrupt, louder, angrier sounding splashes of water.

John knew that his father must've been standing from the wash tub.

"I just want everything to be OK. I'm afraid of losing you, George."

"Emma –," that was the last word that John could understand. What was said next was nothing more than whispers.

John dreamed of tipping the conch shell to the side and letting sand pour out from within its depths. It wasn't only a small amount of white sand in the dream. The sand just kept coming. It was so much that it covered the floor of John's room. On the other side of wall he could hear the lapping of water, but instead of the soft, familiar laps of the water in the wash tub, it was becoming more of a rhythmic pounding against the other side of the wooden wall until the wall began to split into. A wave of foamy, salty water tore through the boards, crashing onto John, pulling him under, and sending him plunging far into the depths.

John woke and saw the flicker of candlelight coming through the crack at the bottom of his door. He opened the door and went into the parlor room where his father was sitting in a chair with a half empty bottle next to him. His father looked up at him. It was the first time that John noticed how his father's eyes had become so different. The pupils were still hazel, but the whites had turned red. John knew that the liquid in the bottle changed people; that it made them do things that normally they wouldn't. He had heard from other people around town that the stuff in the bottle caused an addiction that sometimes was hard to let go.

"I'm going to be leaving again tomorrow, John," George said. "This time I don't know when or *if* I'll be back."

John felt his heart thud. Tears were nearly falling from his eyes. He knew that it must be something serious, that it wasn't business that was the reason that his father was leaving this time. It was then that John knew that it wasn't only the liquid in the bottle that had caused his father's eyes to turn the alarming and scary color of red. He was sure that his father had been crying.

"Your mother told me that she doesn't want me coming back."

"Why?"

"It's my fault, John. I messed up. Someday maybe you'll understand."

John fell asleep in his father's arms and the next morning woke alone in his own bed. When he emerged from his room, his father had already left. John ran back into his room. At that moment in time he hated his father. He picked up the sea shell that George had given him and flung it against the wall in hopes of destroying it. The shell didn't even crack. It just fell onto the bed. In tears, John flung himself on top of the mattress, not realizing that the shell was right there where he was falling. The sharp edge of the shell sliced into his cheek, causing a deep gash that would leave a scar.

As John got older he began to understand the accusations from his mother that he had heard years earlier, but didn't know what the truth had been until a day when it had been raining and caused John to think about water and the ocean and the shell and his father. John was already turning twenty and had taken up a lot of the work around the house. He had assumed a lot of responsibility with his grandfather's farm. His grandfather was getting older and needed the help with the cotton and squash. By then the squash had become a large part of the farm. And it wasn't just Thomas Hollister; others in Devlin had also started growing the vegetable in abundance.

"What was it that made him decide to leave?" he asked his mother as they sat underneath the covered front porch and watched as the rain pelted down onto the field in front of them. It was summer and the leaves of the squash vines were lying flat against the wet ground.

"He said that he had decided that it was best both for me *and* you. And him too, I guess." She told John how his father had finally admitted to seeing other women while he had been out on his business trips. He had blamed it on the alcohol, but it was she that insisted that it was his own fault. Through many tears and deliberation it had been decided that it would be best if he leave.

John nodded in understanding. He didn't know why the details had been kept from him for so long or why he had never asked, but respected his mother for being forthright with him.

Five years later John was completely in control of his family's farm. On a night in the winter when it had been snowing, which was a rarity for South Carolina, both of his grandparents had perished in a horrible house fire. The smoke and flame had woken both John and his mother, but it was already too late. By the time that they rushed into the yard, the plantation house of his grandparents was already engulfed in hot, orange flame. As they stood hopelessly in front of the inferno, John held onto his mother as her body was wracked with heavy sobs.

Amid the ashy remains, John found his grandfather's almanac. The book was lying in a still smoldering heap of debris, and when he went to pick it up, all that he was able to pull free was one piece of it, a corner from a single page. The rest of the book crumbled into ash. Remembering a story his mother had told him about the book being from the summer that Thomas and Sarah first met and that each of them had held it very close to their hearts, John stood there, holding the small piece of paper and cried. His tears landed on what was left of Thomas Hollister's almanac, staining the paper forever.

The plot of land where the plantation house had once stood was cleared and remained in the family for a healthy number of years until it was sold and another house built in its place. On the night of the fire, as they sat in the parlor room in front of the fireplace, John's mother told him that she couldn't wait until the spring when it would be time to plant squash. She told him that she would then feel closer to her parents.

The next year, one of John's long forgotten fantasies finally came to fruition.

There was a traveling carnival that came to town in the summer of that year. On the edge of the town limits, huge tents had been constructed in an open field. Within the tents there were games and sideshows. It was a poster on one of the tents that caught John's attention as he was walking through. *LIVE MERMAID!*, the sign proclaimed in red and yellow letters. John eagerly paid for his admittance, and when the carnival attendee pulled the curtain back, he was mesmerized by what he saw. Lying on the table at the front of the tent was a woman who appeared to be about John's age. Her hair was a blondish green, a color that John had never seen on a woman before. Her top half was bare with the exception of a brassiere made out of two large sea shells. The rest of her costume was an obviously fake, shimmering tail of aqua that started at her slender waist and covered her legs. Every so often she would move her legs, making the tale appear to flap. Even though the tent was full of men who seemed enamored by the beauty of the woman, the mermaid smiled when her eyes met John's.

John tried to work himself closer, to get a better look at her. He pushed his way through the other men and removed his derby hat from atop his head, showing how gentlemanly he was. A carnival attendant held him back as he pressed his body against the rope that separated the mermaid from her audience.

"My name's John," he said over the shouts and hoopla that surrounded him.

The mermaid smiled, but didn't break character. She never uttered a word.

"Move it along mister," the heavyset attendant told John.

John waited outside of the tent until he saw the woman again. As soon as he caught a glimpse of her out of the corner of his eye he knew that it was her because of the hair. He looked around to make sure that there were no attendants that would accuse him of harassment and proceeded to walk up to her, again removing his hat.

"My name's John," he said again. "I just wanted to introduce myself."

The woman laughed. "I'm Bonnie." Her cheeks were blushing.

John learned that the carnival would be in town for the rest of the week. Every night John and Bonnie spent time together. She told him that she too had always dreamed of going to the ocean. When she had joined the carnival it had been with the dream that it would take her there, but so far there hadn't been a stop any where near the sea.

John took her to the creek and told her how his grandparents had liked to go there together. He showed her the house that his father had built. Bonnie loved the story of the oak tree. John showed her the piece of paper from the almanac that had belonged to his grandfather. Bonnie said that she would have liked to have met his grandparents. By the end of the week when the carnival was packing up, it was on the night before Bonnie was supposed to leave that they made love for the first time. Afterwards, Bonnie traced her fingertips down the scar on John's face.

"Where did this come from?" she asked him, knowing that it didn't matter, that whatever had caused it would not make her think any less of him. Even if it was something bad.

"I cut it on a sea shell when I was little."

Together they walked through the woods and to his house. His mother was inside asleep. John and Bonnie sat on the porch with their arms wrapped around one another. Moonlight and stars were the only source of light. The yard was full of dandelions. The smell of squash plants along with that of the fields of cotton drifted along the nighttime air. The wind was blowing and when they closed their eyes they could imagine that the rustle of leaves in the tall oak tree was the sound of crashing waves.

For the next several years the two of them kept in touch and saw each other occasionally whenever the carnival would come through town or make any stops any where near there. Eventually, John and Bonnie married and they didn't have children until seventeen years later, just after the turn of the century. Their first child they named Constantine. Three years later, Bonnie was surprised to learn that she had become pregnant again. This time it was a baby boy that they named Maxwell.

"I hate, hate, hate this place," Constantine shouted over the music coming from the gramophone type record player that was standing upright in the corner. "I can't wait to hightail it out of here."

The house had belonged to and had been built by her grandparents, George and Emma, who were both deceased by that point in time. Constantine lived in the house with her parents and her brother. By then squash had become the main crop that was grown in Devlin. Everybody said that the soil around town held the perfect balance of nutrients for growing anything in the cucurbit family. And it wasn't only the yellow summer squash that were produced in such abundance, it was winter squash as well; pumpkins, butternut and the like that were grown almost everywhere that space permitted.

The Fullers operated one of the largest squash farms in the town. There used to be miles of farmland around the Fuller house, but now there were other homes that had been constructed in close proximity. The farm that the family owned was located a ways from where they lived. It was a piece of land that John's grandfather had purchased when he had been younger. Over the course of John's life, much had changed around Devlin. Land had been purchased and sold. There had been a lot of construction, both on the town square and on the streets surrounding the town. During John's life, the road that the house stood on had been appropriately named Cucurbit Street. Recently there had even been a house constructed next door on the plot of land where the enormous plantation house of his grandparents had once stood. Not long after the fire that destroyed the house, Emma had sold the property.

Several years after getting married, John had built the kitchen onto the back of the house. Years later, when Maxwell was born, John didn't see any opportunity to add onto the house any further. There just didn't seem to be enough room in any direction to add another room, so it was decided that one of the two already small bedrooms in the house would be divided into two. It was a relatively simple construction, a wall and door were added and suddenly the house had a third bedroom.

Just recently, it had become possible to have electricity added to the house and so without much contemplation the wiring had been snaked throughout all the walls. Soon every room had glowing light fixtures, the kitchen had electric appliances, and there was even a house phone. Outlets were located in each room and reading lamps were plugged in on each end table.

"If you hate it so much, why don't you leave?" Maxwell asked as he stood in the doorway to Constantine's bedroom that shared the thin wall with his. Every light in the bedroom was on; the elaborate overhead fixture, the reading lamp by her bed, and the nightlight that was plugged into the wall socket were all shining bright. The record player in the corner was spinning. Jazzy swing music filled the room. Constantine was lying on her bed, reaching her hand up toward the ceiling. The flowing yellow housedress that she wore cascaded down her arms and pooled around her on the white bed. She flipped over onto her stomach and propped her chin on the back of her hand. She looked at her brother and smiled.

"Maybe I will. That's what I'll do; I'll go to college and never look back."

For years Constantine had been talking about how she was going to leave the town behind on the very first chance that she got. She was always saying what she was going to do once she left. She planned on getting a college education and afterwards finding a nice office job. In a condescending tone, she told everyone how she was going to make something out of her life. She made it very clear to everyone that she knew that she didn't think highly of Devlin and that she thought of herself as being a cut above the rest of those that lived there.

Unlike Constantine, Maxwell didn't mind living in Devlin; and truthfully, he actually liked it. He was already seventeen years old and had his future set out for him. He would take over the farm. It was what he had always known that he would do anyway, ever since he had been a little boy. The work didn't bother him. He quite enjoyed it. Like his grandfather Thomas had years earlier, Maxwell often referenced a farming almanac to help with the farm. On the margins of the pages, each day he wrote details for future reference. Planting time, weather patterns, first blossoms, and the first harvest were all documented. He liked the way that he could watch the squash go all the way from seed to table in just one growing season. Something else that he liked about the farm was that the work gave him muscle and it was those muscles that he thought had helped him to land two of the most beautiful girls in Devlin.

Actually, he knew that it was the muscles *and* the car.

It was a glossy black convertible with silver and white trim work. Maxwell loved the car. He was among the first people in Devlin to even own an automobile. He had paid for it himself with the money that he earned from helping out around the farm. Cruising around town and down the country roads with the top back, letting the air blow over him filled him with a sense of pride, especially when one of his two girls was in the car with him. He loved to be driving the car and look over at her, whichever one of them it would be at that particular moment, and see her blonde or auburn hair blowing behind her in the wind.

The two girls were named Lucine and Violet. Whichever one of the two was first Maxwell couldn't remember. He thought it was Violet, the blonde, but he had been with each of them for the first time in such close proximity that he couldn't be for sure. The girls knew about one another, everybody did, but how much each of them knew of what was going on with the other no one knew for sure.

"We're just friends," he would tell Constantine, referring to one girl or the other, whenever his sister brought the subject up.

"You're using those girls Maxwell. You can't keep doing that," Constantine would respond back to him. "You have to choose one."

He had been with Violet on the night that the love triangle finally came to a head.

Well after sunset, with Violet in the passenger seat, Maxwell had driven his car down Hollyhock Road and around the large pond that stood on the outskirts of town. The body of water that had recently been given the moniker of Hollyhock Lake wasn't big enough to officially be a lake, but was bigger than most ponds around the area. It had gotten its name because of it being located near the end of Hollyhock Road, a stretch of highway that in the spring and summer months was covered on each side with its namesake flowers in full bloom of pink and purple. It wasn't an official name for the pond, but one that had recently been coined by the town's more social and outgoing residents. Even though the name was a stretch, Maxwell thought that it was better than what many other people called it. To a lot of people it was still referred to as Anna's Pond, in reference to the infamous ghost that was supposed to linger around there. Hollyhock Lake was where many people of Devlin went to lounge on the bank by the water. They took beach chairs and snacks with them. The men and women wore swimsuits like they were at the ocean instead of sitting by the murky water of a pond. At night, it was where the teenagers of Devlin went to make out. Like others his age, Maxwell had done it many times before. On that particular night there were too many other cars parked around the pond for the two of them to enjoy any kind of privacy, so Maxwell sped around the sharp turn back toward town. The bend in the road was notorious for causing car accidents and a guard rail had recently been constructed on the edge of the road near the water. After safely making his way around the curve and arriving at his destination, Maxwell parked the car in a wooded area near Mercer Creek. Maxwell took Violet's hand in his own and guided her through the trees and to the edge of the water. His other hand held a silver flask that was full of dark brown liquor. As far as they knew, the area of land at the creek didn't belong to anyone, so they didn't have to worry about being accused of trespassing or being interrupted. Maxwell took swigs from the flask and intermittently handed it to Violet who also drank from it. Violet wrapped her arms around Maxwell's neck and kissed him on the mouth. Above them, the moon was full and reflected brilliantly against the dark water.

Through the trees there was a sound that interrupted their kisses. From where Maxwell and Violet stood, it sounded like footsteps. There was the snap of a twig and what sounded like the rustle of feet moving through the tall grass. Both Maxwell and Violet looked up at the same time and saw the figure that was approaching them through the outstretching tree limbs. They each recognized her immediately. It was Lucine. Like her name implied, Lucine seemed to change with the phases of the moon. That night, under the full moon, her hair was blonde like Violet's.

"Maxwell?" Violet said, seeing the anger in the other girl's eyes as Lucine was stepping closer to where they stood.

Violet wrapped her arms tighter around Maxwell, afraid of Lucine's intent. By then Lucine was already face to face with them.

"I'm not going to keep putting up with this, Maxwell Fuller. It's either me or her," Lucine said and looked at Violet. "You decide right now which of us it's going to be."

Maxwell drank from the flask. He was glaring at Lucine, letting her words and the ultimatum that she had given him fully sink in. The decision was hastily made. He grabbed Violet's hand. "Come on Violet, let's go," he said and led her back through the trees from where they came. They walked away from Lucine, leaving her standing alone on the edge of the creek in the moonlight.

Later that night, after her parents had gone to bed, Constantine was the first to hear what had happened. She rushed through the house, her sheer housecoat flying behind her. "Wake up!" she yelled to her parents. "Get up! There's been an accident."

After rushing away from the scene at the creek, Maxwell's car had crashed into the guard rail around Hollyhock Lake. Both Maxwell and Violet had died on impact. Rumors began circulating almost immediately that Maxwell must've seen the ghost of Anna Moore on the road and that was what had caused him to crash. The more realistic residents of Devlin understood that the crash had been fueled by both the liquor that Maxwell had been drinking and the stress of the love triangle that he had created for himself.

Just like she had always dreamed of doing, Constantine went away to college in the fall. At The University, she was able to transform herself into what it was that she had always wanted to become. The more she studied, the more liberated she became. The promise of being more than what her life had seemed it would be for all those years that she had spent in Devlin began to become closer to a reality with each passing day. She became friends with a couple of vicarious girls from up north that lived on her floor in the women's dormitory. There names were Dorothy and Alice. The three of them were deep into the women's movements. They liked to participate in the protests and marches that were held across campus.

The hall that Constantine lived on in the dormitory had one phone that was located in the central area that all the girls shared. It was early in the evening one night when the phone rang with a caller for Constantine on the other end. The girl that had answered the phone gently tapped on the door to Constantine's room. Constantine was sitting at her desk studying.

"Yes?" she called out toward the closed door.

The door eased open. The girl on the other side of the threshold peeked into the room. "The phone's for you."

Constantine stood from the desk and walked down the

hallway to the phone.

"Hello?"

"Constantine, there's some news." It was her mother.

"Well, don't keep me waiting. What is it?"

"You're going to be an aunt soon."

It turned out that Lucine had become pregnant just a few days before Maxwell's car had crashed into the guard rail. The baby would be due in the next few months.

"Isn't that great?" Her mother asked.

Constantine saw a double standard. If it was she that had become pregnant out of marriage then it would have been a different story, but this involved Maxwell so it was OK. "Yeah, that's peachy."

The months passed.

It was a girl. Lucine named her Jill.

"Sell it! I'm going to sell it all!" A few years later, after both John and Bonnie had passed on, the house and all the farmland had been left to Constantine, their only child now that Maxwell had died. "I have no need for it," she told Dorothy and Alice as the three of them were sharing cocktails. She knew that if she kept the house it would only be a burden; that it would hold her back from the things that she really wanted to do with her life. "There is nothing for me in Devlin. Owning the house and land would just be a hassle." She shrugged her shoulders. "I don't want it and the amount of money that would come with selling it would be staggering."

On a bright and sunny day, just before selling both the house and the farm, Constantine visited Lucine and Jill. She parked on the street. She had a medium sized cardboard box in her hands as she walked up the paved driveway to Lucine's small, brick house. A large pair of sunglasses covered her eyes. The yard was tidy with a perfectly green and freshly mowed lawn. Constantine had to walk around a spray of water that was coming from the rotating sprinkler that had been placed in the grass. A green water hose ran from the sprinkler to where it was attached to the spigot on the side of the house. Lucine's cousin, a tall man named Kenneth, answered the door. It was early in the afternoon, but he was wearing a set of blue and white striped pajamas and holding a martini. His hair was neatly parted.

"Yes?" he said, studying Constantine. It was the first time

that he had even seen her.

"I'm here to see Jill," she said. "I'm her aunt." Constantine didn't remove her sunglasses.

"Well, she's not in. She's gone out with her mother. Is there something that I can help you with?"

"Just give this to her," Constantine said and handed the box to Kenneth through the open doorway. "It's some things that I thought she would like to have. I have no need for any of it."

As Constantine drove away, she imagined Jill opening the box and studying its contents. It was a box of things that she thought Jill would want to have: a sea shell, Maxwell's almanac, a poster of Bonnie dressed as a mermaid, and a photo of Maxwell. It was the most recent photo of Jill's father that Constantine knew of. In the picture he was wearing a white shirt and a pair of suspenders; he was smiling brightly at the camera. Constantine wondered what the young girl's facial expression would be when she discovered the torn corner of Thomas Hollister's almanac tucked securely into the pages of her own father's book.

All of these things Jill had seen countless times before when she would go to the house on Cucurbit Street and visit her grandparents. Each and every time, each of the items had held an enormous amount of wonderment for the young girl. She knew that the shell had belonged to her grandfather and had been the cause of the scar on his cheek, there was a picture of her grandmother (!) of all people dressed as a mermaid. Of course in the advertisement Bonnie had been much younger than Jill ever knew her to be, but it was her grandmother nonetheless, and Jill thought it was hilarious to think that the older woman ever did something as outrageous as putting on a mermaid costume. Since she had never even seen her father, the photo of him was all she had to know what he looked like, and the simple fact that the triangle of paper was a piece of her great, great grandfather's *anything* was just astonishing.

Constantine returned to the house on Cucurbit Street one more time. She looked around at everything. Every nook and cranny was empty and pretty soon, with her signature, all of it would be out of her hands. Every board and speck of dirt of the entire property would belong to someone else; from then on it would be *their* burden to carry.

Jill grew up in Devlin and while riding her bike would occasionally wander past the house where her father had grown up.

Sometimes she would stop in front of it and recount all the stories that she had been told about the place. The house was where her grandmother had told her the stories. The new owners had moved there from out of town. They were very private and kept to themselves. Not long after being there they had planted a yard full of purple petunias. They had a young toddler that had not yet started school. Other than that no one knew a lot about them. Jill often wondered if they had any idea how important the house was.

One day when Jill was across the street with her left foot planted firmly on the ground and the right still on the bike's pedal, she noticed that Mallard, the creepy man that lived in the neighboring wooden house, was standing across the street, staring at her. He was wearing his usual black suit and tie. A fedora was on his head. Mallard had seemed old even then, but Jill was only thirteen so most adults seemed that way to her. The man gave her the creeps, more so than the old ghost story of Anna Moore ever would. She had heard about his fascination with dead, stuffed animals. She would often see him at various places all around town. He would always look at her, sometimes smiling. That day when she was on her bike and spotted him, he opened his mouth to speak, but no sound came out. Jill was terrified of what he could possibly be about to say and so she began pedaling faster than she ever had before. By the time that she reached home, she was out of breath.

"Jill, are you OK?" her mother asked. Lucine was in the middle of taking an apple pie out of the hot oven and quickly placed it on the stovetop. She reached her oven mitt covered hand out to her daughter.

"Mallard," Jill tried to catch her breath. "He was about to say something and I -"

Lucine laughed. "Jill, that man is OK," she assured her daughter for what seemed like the millionth time. "He's not going to hurt you."

After graduating high school, Jill went to the local college. She commuted back and forth. It was there that she met Thomas Stanley who was from Georgia. They fell in love and got married soon after earning their degrees. The timing couldn't have been better, because right before the wedding day, 3 Cucurbit Street went on the market. Jill was ecstatic. Thomas was hesitant at first. He had thought that the house was too small for starting a family, but Jill insisted that it would be the perfect place for a baby.

"Others have done it," she said. "My own family."

And so they moved in by the end of the year. It felt great being back in the house after so many years. She could barely remember what it had been like when she had visited her grandparents there when she had been a little girl, but not much of it seemed to have changed.

Mallard still lived next door, but now that Jill was an adult, she no longer saw him as being creepy. She now thought of him as being *eccentric* and to her it was a good trait for someone to have.

Over time, Jill and Thomas made the place their own. Jill told her husband the stories of every item in the box that Constantine had given her when she had been little. Along with the rest of the family photos, she hung the one of Maxwell on the wall in the hallway. Not too long after, Jill became pregnant. She and Thomas took down the dividing wall in the bedroom and transformed the larger, original space into a nursery. After the baby was born, when she would go into the room at night Jill would carefully step over the creaking board that stretched across the threshold of the nursery's doorway, not wanting to wake Levi while he slept. Standing over his crib, she often imagined that he was dreaming of the fantastical bedtime stories that she often told him as he was going to sleep. While many kids were read fairytales from thin paperback books, the mythical stories that Jill told Levi were from memory. They were the same ones that her grandmother had told her when she had been a young girl, the stories about their family.

□

WHEN LEVI woke the next morning, there was a brief moment of confusion about where he was.

Was he at home? No. The bed and the room that he was in were unfamiliar.

Then he remembered that he was at the lake and that Sophia was there with him.

From the bed he could see outside. On the other side of the windows of the cabin's loft, the lake was still, a sheet of glass. The early morning sun reflected against it like a mirror. There was only the occasional movement on the water. Every so often a fish or bug would hit the surface, causing a circular ripple to spread outward from the epicenter.

From where he lay in bed, he could hear that Sophia was already up and stirring about downstairs. He could smell brewing coffee. He stood from the bed. After throwing on his jeans, he stood in front of the freestanding mirror that was in the corner of the room and put on his cap. He walked down the steps to join her.

Sophia was standing at the couch folding the blanket that she had used to sleep under the night before. She was still in her pajamas, cotton pants and a tank top. She looked at him and smiled.

"I liked it," she said. "It was good. I wanted to tell you last night, but you were out like a light."

Levi knew that she was talking about what he had written. It made him happy to know that she had come up to where he slept.

Sophia tossed the blanket onto the back of the couch.

"From what you've told me so far, I can see a lot of *you* reflected in those pages," she told him. "It mirrors your life."

III

MALLARD PLACED the manuscript pages down on top of the wooden desk where he was sitting. It was the second time that he had read all the way through it. The first time had been just the night before. He was hunched over in a straight back chair that had been pulled up close to the edge of the work surface. The frayed black fedora that usually sat atop his head was now resting on the edge of the polished wood of the desktop, next to a taxidermy squirrel. The blue bird feather that was stuck in the wide band of the hat stood out prominently in the rays of sunlight that were shining in through the window behind the desk. It was a bright dash of color in an otherwise drab setting. Without the hat, several strands of startlingly silver hair stuck out in wild shoots on the man's nearly bare head.

    He looked out through the sheer, lacy curtains. The Stanley house stood directly across from him. His own house had been built where the original plantation house that burnt down once stood. The plantation house had been the one that Sarah had lived in when she had first moved from Vermont. The current house was where Mallard had lived his entire life. From there he had watched from afar as both Maxwell and Constantine grew up next door to him. The three of them had been about the same age, but were not friends. In fact, he and Maxwell had been enemies throughout most of their lives. But all of that had been a long time ago. Since Maxwell's death, Mallard had watched the house next door to his be sold by Constantine to another family and then eventually sold again, this time to Jill and her new husband. With a sigh, Mallard removed the lopsided, wire framed glasses from his face and sat them on top of the papers. He rubbed at his eyes and pinched the bridge of his nose with his fingers.

    The writing of the manuscript seemed shaky, amateurish at best. It was often repetitive and some things relating to the lore of the family seemed a bit far fetched. Like taking a horse drawn wagon from Vermont all the way to South Carolina seemed like something out of the range of possibility. He didn't know if the use of phones and electricity would have been accurate for the time period where Levi had included them in the story and he didn't have time to recount or do the math on his fingers. Would someone in Devlin have had a copy of *Frankenstein* at the time? And squash seeds that had been kept for ten years before being planted and yet they still germinated and grew into squash? It was ten year old seeds that started the still thriving squash business of Devlin? That didn't seem likely. Not to mention an oak tree growing from a single, dry leaf.

But what did he know? He was just an old man.

But putting all of the technicalities aside, Mallard realized that if that was the way that Levi wanted to tell the story then that was the way that it should have been told. Those things weren't really what the story was about anyway. All of that just served as filler and set decoration. As ridiculous as some of it was, so much of what Levi had written in the story was very close to the truth, the major points were hit just as Mallard himself had always heard them, yet it was glaringly obvious that other things Levi had obviously created out of the lore that surrounded the family.

Mallard understood that in order to connect this fact with that, there had to be some sort of artistic liberty with constructing the storyline, but what he knew, the secret that he had carried for so long, would surely change things. Once Levi found out, things would take on an entirely new perspective. And he *wanted* Levi to know. He thought that he *deserved* to know. For years he had wanted to tell either Jill or Levi, but there was a promise that had been made that the secret would never get out. That was what he had been about to do on that day many years earlier when Jill had been across the street from him on her bicycle. When he had opened his mouth and no sound came out, it was because the secret had gotten caught in his throat.

And Jill had thought *that* was creepy?

Just the day before, when he had seen Levi arrive at the house after so many years of being gone, he had known that it was time. He had tried reaching out to Levi at the tree house that stood on the land where long before then Maxwell's fateful decision had been made, to tell him, but the young man had seemed uninterested and had scurried away as if he had been frightened. Several hours later, Mallard had stepped over to the Stanley's house, but Levi hadn't been there.

Mallard hadn't set out the night before with the aim of stealing the manuscript and he *hadn't* stolen it; he had only *borrowed* it with the intention of giving it back. In fact, he hadn't even known that the pages existed until that night. While standing on the porch and knocking on the door was when he had seen through the window the stack of papers sitting on the chair on top of the closed laptop computer. It was part of the title that had immediately grabbed his attention, *The Story of My Family*. Mallard knew at that moment that he had to read those pages. He had to see what Levi *thought* was the truth.

There was movement and the sound of distant mumblings from outside that jolted Mallard into attention. He stood from the desk. The chair legs screeched across the hardwood floor. He walked around the sharp corner of the desk, closer to the window, and with just one of his long, bony fingers he pushed the thin curtain aside. He looked across his yard. Lacy, his Rottweiler, was lying in the shade of the wooden picnic table, happily panting in the summer heat. Since the rain, healthy, wild onions had shot up all over the yard, reminding him that he would need to cut the yard soon. Looking past Lacy and across the chain link fence he could barely see the bright yellow car that was parked in the driveway. Just moments earlier, a pretty blonde woman with thick framed glasses had gotten out of the car and stepped into the yard. He had watched as the woman went onto the porch and disappeared from his sight. Now she was walking with Levi along the sidewalk, away from the house, and toward the center of the town.

□

THAT MORNING was the first time that Levi had seen Sophia since the night at the lake house. The day after leaving the lake, Sophia had gone out of town to an art convention. It was part of her work. In her absence, Levi had been surprised to discover how much he missed her while she was gone. Of course they talked to each other on the phone, but he wanted to see her, to be able to talk to her in person. And he still owed her that date.

It had been Sophia's idea to visit Levi while he was in Devlin. After she read what he had written, she said she would like to see the town and all the locations for herself. She wanted to take some photos and do some quick, preliminary sketches of what she saw. She said that it would help with the creative spark that she needed to get started on her next series of art, the pieces that would be centered on Levi's family.

When he had opened the door earlier that morning, just the sight of her standing on the other side had made him giddy with happiness. It really was a surprise to see her. She wasn't supposed to arrive until late in the afternoon. It was a good surprise. And then there was the fact that she had an overnight bag thrown over her shoulder that had caused his pulse to race with wild abandon. It was the possibility of *more* that excited him.

Together they walked next to each other along the cracked sidewalk. Sophia had her camera held securely in her hand and the crimson colored strap was around her neck. She had her hair pulled back and wore a charcoal gray tank top that left her shoulders and neck bare. Levi's hands were shoved into his jean pockets. The tree branches that reached out across the sky above their heads were full of thick, lush greenery. The density of the foliage gave a welcome relief from the already rising temperature. They walked until they emerged from the canopy of overhanging branches and into the town square. The annual Squash Festival was scheduled for the next day, Saturday. All around the healthy green grass of the square, there were already numerous tables that had been set up. Each of the tables were currently empty, but would be filled with handmade arts and crafts within the next twenty four hours. Several food vendors had already parked their trucks on the black asphalt of the road next to where the tables stood. The roads that ran through the main part of town had already been blocked off by police barricades indicating that thru traffic needed to detour around the area. The white gazebo in the center of the scene was draped on all sides with yellow sashes. American flags hung from each power pole that stood along the street. Numerous terra cotta planters that held large, leafy citronella plants had been placed around the area in an attempt to ward off mosquitoes, at least during the day of the event.

As they walked, Sophia occasionally paused to take pictures. Each time, Levi stepped to the side and let her do her thing. He watched her as she became more and more enamored with her work. It was the first time that he had seen her work, and it was obvious to him that what she was doing was something that she loved.

"I thought you were done with town squares," Levi said jokingly, referencing the comment that she had made several weeks earlier about how if she ever worked on an art project again that involved a town square that she thought that she would puke.

"I can't help it." She lowered the camera, turned her head to look at him over her shoulder, and playfully stuck her tongue out in his direction. "I like them," she shrugged and continued to take pictures.

Moments later, when they reached the small veterinarian clinic where Claire worked, Sophia stopped walking and raised her digital camera again. The veterinarian office was located inside of an old house that stood on the other side of the sidewalk, just off the street. The stark whiteness of the house stood out prominently amid the array of red brick buildings and had obviously been built well before those other, more commonly styled businesses. A wheelchair ramp ran up the side of the front porch. A large resin dog and cat sat next to the front door. Each of the animals was painted white. For the weekend celebration, yellow bows were tied around each of their necks. Two rocking chairs sat on the front porch where people could sit and wait while their pets were inside having their checkup completed. The door opened and Levi could hear the ding of the cowbell above the door from where he stood on the sidewalk. A middle aged woman emerged from the interior. She was carrying a small gray kitten that was tucked snuggly into the crook of her arm. Levi could only get a quick glimpse of the inside of the building before the door was shut again.

They passed by the library and the courthouse. Even though it wasn't yet noon, the diner was busy with people going in for lunch. The smell of frying food wafted out onto the street. Like she had done in front of the veterinarian office, Sophia paused to take photos of each of the establishments. As Levi watched her, he was amazed that someone was able to see the enchantment and beauty of the town. He had lived there so long and it seemed to him now that he must be jaded, that he had been taking it all for granted for so many years. He guessed that through the fresh eyes of an outsider like Sophia, the town did seem to be perfectly picturesque.

Jake's Hardware had stood on the square for as long as Levi could remember. Different from the house that held the vet office, the hardware store was within one of those typical, brick and glass fronted store spaces. Standing on the sidewalk, Levi could see the clutter of things on the inside. Rakes stood upright and green water hoses were neatly twined in perfect circles. Several red and green push lawnmowers were in a diagonal row. Screws, nuts, and bolts were all neatly organized in their respectful clear and labeled containers. What Levi had come for though was located on the outside. Wooden pallets had been placed on top of several dinged and scratched and paint spattered wooden saw horses. Various healthy green plants were lined along the makeshift flat surface. The dark potting soil in each of the black trays was moist. The plants had been so recently watered that the sidewalk underneath the pallets was still damp as the water had yet to dissipate from the day's increasing humidity.

Levi picked out several plants from the menagerie that stood before him. He had decided that he would take the real estate agent's advice and try to clean up the yard somewhat. With Sophia's help, he carried the plants inside the store and placed them on the counter. The owner, a woman with frizzy gray hair, was sitting behind the register on a wooden bar stool. She smiled at Levi, recognizing him, and began totaling up his purchase.

"Keegan Atwater said you were in town." The woman's voice was raspy, like she smoked several packs of cigarettes each and every day. "We heard you were selling the place."

Levi nodded. "Keegan Atwater?" he asked, unfamiliar with the name.

"Diesel Atwater's daughter. She works at the grocery store. I saw her the other day. She said you were in there the other night."

"Last night." Levi corrected the woman. He remembered the girl that had rung him up, the girl with the blue hair and the lip piercing. He wondered why she would have even been talking about him to other people, essentially spreading gossip. He was also surprised that the girl was Diesel's daughter. She must've been eighteen years old already. It struck Levi then that he too was old enough to have a child that age. "What did she say?" Levi asked the woman, curious about why the girl would be talking about him.

The woman shrugged her shoulders. "She just said that she saw you; that's all. Twelve fifty, hon." After the woman told Levi the total for his plants, she looked at Sophia and smiled.

Sophia smiled back, but there was no introduction between them.

Levi took his wallet out of his back pocket and paid the

woman. After receiving his change, he and Sophia each picked up two of the generic plastic shopping bags that the woman had placed the plants into.

"Y'all have a good day," the woman said behind them as they were exiting the store.

Outside, the sun was now glaring. Upon exiting the store, Levi paused on the sidewalk, looking around the town that stood before him. Sophia was right. It did seem kind of perfect. On the opposite corner, there was a green pickup. The brake lights were aglow. Levi saw a shift in the driver's side mirror. It was quick, he couldn't tell who it was that sat behind the wheel, but it seemed as if the driver was using the reflective surface to look in his direction. Then, from the corner of his eye, Levi realized that there was movement to his left, somebody walking. When he looked, he saw that it was Mallard. It appeared that the man had been standing on the sidewalk a good distance away, but was now approaching Levi and Sophia. Just like the day before, the man was wearing a black suit and the fedora was sitting on top of his head. The enormous Rottweiler was at his side with the thick chain leading from her collar to the man's clenched hand. Upon spotting the man, Levi quickly turned his back to him and began to walk away. Beside him, Sophia's steps followed his own.

From behind them, the man spoke.

"Levi," he said. "Please, just let me talk to you. I have something of grave importance that I need to tell you."

As they walked, Sophia looked over at Levi, confused about what was going on, not understanding why Levi was ignoring the man.

"Just keep walking," Levi mumbled softly, careful not to let Mallard hear.

A moment later, Sophia looked over her shoulder, confirming that they were out of earshot from the man. "Do you know him?" She asked with a giggle.

"Sort of. He lives next door to my parent's place. I guess he's gone crazy in his old age. Actually though, now that I'm thinking about it, he's always been kind of nuts."

By the time that they got back to the house, there was a missed call on Levi's phone. It was Kathy, the real estate agent.

"Hey Levi, this is Kathy Anderson. Great news! (smiling) I have someone that wants to see the house later today, if that's OK. I know this is short notice and all, but just give me a call back as soon as you can and we can talk about it. Thank you."

Levi placed the phone on the porch step beside where he sat. "It was the real estate agent." He looked at Sophia. "She said someone wants to see the house."

"That's great! When do they want to see it?"

"Later today," Levi said uncertainly.

"I guess we better get these flowers planted then, huh?"

Levi called Kathy back and they agreed on a time of five thirty for the person to see the house. That gave him plenty of time to do some of the sprucing up in the yard that he had already planned on doing that day.

After each of them changed into clothes more suited for yard work, Sophia began digging into the dirt with a garden spade and planting the newly purchased flowers as Levi pushed an old gas lawnmower across the overgrown yard. It was only for a few moments until the spinning blade of the lawnmower hit a thick tree root and caused an alarmingly loud, chopping sound. Levi paused where he was, let the mower shut down, and looked toward the ground, checking to see what it was that he could have run over. After seeing that it had only been the exposed end of a thick root, he started the lawnmower back up. When he lifted his head again was when he saw the back end of the same rusty, green pick up that he had seen on the square. The truck was driving down the road, away from the house.

After all the grass had been cut and Levi's shirt was drenched with sweat, he stood at the edge of the yard and studied the work that he and Sophia had done. He looked at his watch and saw that it was already one in the afternoon. He removed his cap from his head as he looked around at his surroundings. It *did* look better.

White periwinkles bordered the fence. Red geraniums had been planted together in groups of three on each side of the steps. The flower's vibrant color was in harmony with the red stripes on the flag that hung unmoving on the post above them. The overgrown grass and weeds that had been in the yard when he arrived the day before was now cut back and it looked like an actual lawn once again. He had left some of the petunias growing around the perimeter of the house. Several yellow dandelions had been spared from being cut since they had not been high enough to meet the fatal spin of the lawnmower blade. In the corner there was a new basil plant.

He knew that the yard was a long way off from being immaculate, but it looked better nonetheless.

Inside, after getting two cold beers from the refrigerator, one for Sophia and one for himself, Levi picked up his phone and the piece of paper that had Calvin Harris's number written on it in his mother's neat, cursive penmanship. He was planning on calling Mr. Harris for help with the yard. He thought that he would hire him to keep up the property in the coming weeks, just until the house sold. He returned to the porch where Sophia was sitting in the swing. She was reviewing the pictures on her digital camera that she had taken earlier in the day. After stepping in the house for those few minutes and then stepping back outside, it was very noticeable to Levi that the yard smelled of freshly mowed grass. He inhaled deeply. It was a scent that he had always loved. He always thought that the smell carried a hint of watermelon with it. To him, it smelled like summer.

"This one is really good," Sophia said.

Levi sat in the swing by Sophia and looked at the small screen on the back of the camera. It was a low angle shot of the oak tree that stood in the corner of the yard. She was right, the photo was good. In fact, he thought that it was even good enough just the way that it was to frame and hang on the wall.

Sophia lowered the camera and looked out into the yard. "So this is the tree that your great, great, great grandmother planted after she came from Vermont?"

Levi nodded, twisted the top off one of the beers, and handed her the bottle. "And it's where she and Thomas supposedly kissed for the first time. And Weevil, Thomas's dog, is buried underneath it." He twisted the top off his own bottle and took a sip. Together they looked from the digitized photo of the tree on the camera screen to the real thing. "And all out there used to be farmland," he pointed past the tree where there were now houses and paved roads. "It was acres and acres of squash and cotton. Over there was where the plantation house that burnt down was located." He pointed toward the aged brown wood of the house where Mallard lived.

"Did you ever consider getting back in to the farming business?"

"Na," he shook his head. "It's been out of my family for a long time, ever since Constantine sold all the land. And there's also the fact that I don't know *anything* about that type of work."

A moment later, Sophia stood from the swing and stepped down from the porch and into the yard. She began snapping more photos of the tree, the yard, and the house. Levi placed his bottle of beer on the window sill and dialed the phone number that was on the piece of paper.

After a few rings, the man answered. "This is Calvin." His voice was deeply southern.

"Hey, Calvin, this is Levi Stanley, Jill Stanley's son."

"Yeah, can I help you?"

"I know you used to help Mom keep up with the yard work and all. Well, look, I'm selling the place and was wondering if you could take care of the grounds for the next few weeks, just until the house gets sold. With me being in Atlanta and everything I would need somebody to do it."

There was a long pause from Calvin's end until the man finally answered with a sigh of frustration, obviously annoyed with Levi. "Levi, I'll be over there in a little while."

Levi felt a stab of humility. He then realized that the man must have now been too old to work anymore. That he must have already retired. "I'm sorry. I just assumed that you were still working. Really, I don't expect you to -"

"I said that I'll be over there in a little while."

☐

CALVIN'S TRUCK pulled up to the side of the house within the half hour. It was a loud, old red diesel pickup that caused Craven's ears to perk up. To Levi's surprise, there was no lawnmower, rake, or any other yard working tool that had haphazardly been tossed *or* placed neatly in the back.

Levi fretted that he had been correct, that the man really was too old and had already retired.

From the porch, Levi watched the older man as he stepped out of the cab and entered into the yard through the back gate. Calvin wore a pair of blue overalls and a white button down shirt underneath. The older man removed his hat before he began to step up the porch steps. His hair was silver against his pale skin. As he reached the top step, Calvin reached out his hand to Levi.

Levi placed his hand in Calvin's. His hand felt firm and sure with age.

"Nice to meet you, young man," Calvin said.

"Same to you," Levi answered. "And this is Sophia."

"Hey," Sophia said from behind Levi.

"Levi, I'm just going to cut right to the chase. Let me tell you why I came over here." Calvin looked down before he started to speak again. "I don't do yard work." He shook his head. "Well, I used to, but only just helping out your Momma. You see," there was a long pause like he wasn't sure he was ready to tell the next part of what he had to say, "she and I were in love."

Upon the revelation, Levi's jaw nearly hit the once green painted hardwood slats of the porch.

"For a good while," Calvin nodded, reassuring Levi that it was the truth.

Levi stood in silence, taking in everything that he was hearing.

"Don't be mad at me. I promise I didn't mean any harm," Calvin spoke with tears in his eyes. "This all started long after your daddy died."

"Come sit down. Tell me more."

Levi led Calvin to the end of the porch and they sat on the swing.

"Levi, I'm going to step inside, give you two some time to talk," Sophia said and went into the house.

"On the day that she passed away, I didn't just happen to walk up and *discover* her like I led everybody to believe for so long." He looked over at Levi with bloodshot eyes. "I was here with her when it happened."

"I am so sorry to hear that," Levi said. "That must've been traumatic."

"That morning, the day she died, we had breakfast together out here on the porch."

Levi remembered the day that he had come back to the house after it had happened. There had been a butter knife, a plate, and *two* drinking glasses in the sink. It all made sense.

"Afterwards, she was sitting here," Calvin placed his hand on the seat of the swing between himself and Levi, "She was reading one of those romances that she liked so much. I was out there in the yard." He pointed in the direction of the oak tree. "And when I came back up here on the porch it was already too late. You know, I still come here to the house sometimes at night and sit right here in this swing. It was by far her favorite spot of all. I feel like I am the closest to her when I do that."

As Calvin continued to speak, it all became so crystal clear to Levi. He remembered how when he had first seen the swing the day before, it had been obvious to him that someone had been sitting in it and then that night when he had been roused out of the tub by Craven's barking, what he had seen on the porch was that there was a ring of condensation on the windowsill where a cold glass had been sitting and that the swing was rocking gently back and forth as if...

"You were here last night," Levi said. It hadn't been a ghost after all.

Calvin nodded. "I didn't realize that anybody was in there until that loud mouthed dog started barking."

Levi laughed at Calvin's candid description of Craven. "You could've stayed. And really," he shrugged his shoulders, "it'll be OK for you to sit out here anytime you want."

☐

AFTER CALVIN left, Levi sat in the swing and thought about everything that he had been told. As shocking as the revelation had been, it made him happy to know that his mother had been able to fall in love all over again, that she had the courage to do so. At the same time though, it bothered him that for whatever reason she hadn't been able to tell him about the relationship between her and Calvin.

Secrets were like that, Levi thought. Some are *never* revealed and others come to light at the most unexpected times.

When it got close to time for Kathy to show the house, Levi and Sophia headed out to an early dinner.

Possum's Bar was located not too far out of town. It was in an old, brick building that was surrounded by a gravel parking lot. The bar was out on Highway 22 that connected Devlin to the next small town. Between the two towns there wasn't much that was located on that particular stretch of highway. Wide hay fields stood on each side of Possum's and each of the fields were already scattered with tall, round bails of hay. A tractor and bailer had been left in the field on the right, presumably after the worker had finally called it a day.

The inside of the bar was just as Levi remembered it. Throughout his entire life, he had only been in the bar a handful of times, but could easily recall the look and feel of its interior well enough from when he had been younger to know that it hadn't really changed all that much. When he had been there before he had been too young to drink, but had sat with Claire and Diesel in a corner booth, laughing and cutting up with one another after school. Aside from the place serving alcohol, there was also a grill in the back that served up burgers and fries during the lunch and dinner hours. As long as Levi had lived in Devlin, it was the first time that he had been in the bar after 8pm. When the clock hands struck 8 o'clock was when it was clearly stated on the door that Possum's was only for customers that were twenty one and up.

Even though the owners had hung slatted blinds over all the windows, including the glass of the front door, the blinds were usually turned in the open position and anybody that was passing by on the street could see who was seated inside the bar. Of course, this stirred up a lot of gossip and rumors about who had been spotted together. At night, the highway in front of the bar was usually illuminated with a nearly steady red glow from brake lights as drivers slowed down to see who would be inside at that particular hour. Over the years, all of this had led to there being numerous fist fights in the gravel parking lot, but overall the bar was a pretty calm place. Not a lot of bad happened there.

The place got its name because of the owners, the Reynolds family. The business had been in their family for as long as Levi could remember. Each family member really did resemble the bar's namesake animal. Both the Reynolds men and women had dark, beady eyes and long slender noses that almost came to a point at the end. As they had gotten older, the closer the resemblance became and the graying hair on each of their heads only added to the effect.

Possum's was where Levi and Sophia had decided to go while Kathy showed the house. They sat across from one another in one of the corner booths. They had already eaten and the empty baskets that the burgers and fries had come in had already been cleared from the table. Aside from them, there were only five other people in the place, one of the owners (it was Mrs. Reynolds that particular afternoon), a young waitress, a man that Levi did not recognize was seated at the bar, and a man and woman who were younger than Levi, but he thought that they had gone to high school with him, were sitting in another one of the booths.

"Whatever happened to Lucine?" Sophia asked.

"She lived up until I was probably twelve or thirteen. I remember her as being this eccentric old lady. She was in a nursing home by then. She had the whitest hair that I'd ever seen. She didn't keep it short like most of the other old ladies though. The length of her hair was midway down her back. I remember going sometimes with Mom to see her."

"And Constantine?"

Levi shook his head. "I don't remember her at all. She died when I was very little. I *do* know though that she went to New York after selling the house and hardly ever came back to Devlin." Levi stared off into the distance. "But she was buried here, at Mercer Creek, so go figure."

"She never married?"

"I don't think so." Levi shook his head.

The short, heavyset waitress approached the table. "Can I get either of you anything else?"

After each of them declined, the waitress placed the ticket on the table in front of Levi and turned to walk away. Sophia quickly grabbed the ticket out from under him, not even giving him the chance to look at it.

"Sophia - ," he started to ask for the ticket back, but she cut him off.

"I'll pay," Sophia said. "Consider this our first date." She was already reaching into her purse for her wallet.

Levi laughed. "Our first date is at Possums of all places?"

"I'm sure others have done it *before* us."

That evening, the outside of Possum's was just as dead as the inside. Where on most Friday and Saturday nights there would have been a parking lot full of trucks and cars, that night it was nearly empty. There were no people standing outside smoking or talking to one another. The only cars were those that belonged to Sophia, Mrs. Reynolds, the waitress, and the other two customers. The sun was still shining bright in the sky, indicating that there was another good two hours of daylight remaining. As Levi was getting into the passenger seat of Sophia's car was when he noticed that actually there *was* another truck on the far end of the wide parking lot. It was the same rusty, green pickup that he had been seeing around town. There was a bright glare from the sun on the windshield, making it impossible for Levi to see who was seated behind the steering wheel. Levi didn't know who drove what around town, but he wondered if it was in fact Diesel that was seated in the cab of the truck, watching as Levi exited the bar. He wondered again if it was possible for the other man to hold a grudge after so many years. After Sophia started her car, it was only for just a moment longer that the truck lingered where it was before it spun over the yellow curb and onto the road, sending a spray of gravel from underneath its heavy, treaded tires.

After leaving Possum's, Sophia drove the two of them out to Mercer Creek Baptist Church and cemetery. Like she had done in town, she wanted to see it and take some pictures of the structure and the surrounding grounds. She knew that the town's legend of Anna Moore would make its way into her artwork one way or another. She just wasn't yet sure in what capacity that it would be there.

When they got there, the area was quiet. The only sound and movement was from the occasional blackbird or wren that fluttered out of the magnolia trees or chirped happily in the sunlight. Not surprisingly, Sophia and Levi were the only people around. Sophia parked the car in the dusty gravel driveway that led to the cemetery. Together they walked around the perimeter of the wrought iron fence that surrounded the old tombstones. They didn't go inside the gate. Instead, Sophia took pictures from where they stood on the outside. They walked past the reconstructed, brick church building. Behind the church, nestled in the woods was where the original building stood near the edge of Hollyhock Lake. Sophia got a few pictures from the beginning of the narrow dirt road that led into the trees.

They followed the rutted tire tracks in the red clay until they came to the remains. By that point in time, all that was left of the original structure of the church were four support columns made out of brick that had at one time held up the weight of the single room building *and* its congregation. The columns were only nearly waist high. A small, ancient cemetery was located in the corner near the woods. It was not fenced in like the one that stood near the newer of the two churches. A historical marker stood to the right of what was left of the original Mercer Creek Church. The ground surrounding the ruins was tidy and had recently been mowed. Levi and Sophia stepped across the grass and into the center of the four columns. Sunlight broke through the tree branches, causing their shadows to stretch across the scene as they walked. From where they stood, the shimmering water of Hollyhock Lake could be glimpsed through the tree branches. In the distance they could hear the occasional sound of cars passing by and slowing down as they neared the curve on the other side of the water.

Like the grass on the outside of the structure, the inside was well tended. Even though there were no dead leaves or debris on the ground where they stood and the branches overhead were not nearly bare with only a few orange leaves remaining, it was easy to see how the setting could become spooky on a cool, fall night.

"Evidently the kids in town still like to come here and hangout." Levi pointed at a stack of empty beer cans that sat in the corner next to one of the brick columns. A neon green heart had been spray painted on the brick. For as long as he knew of, Devlin's teenagers had come to the ruins of the church in search of the ghost of Anna Moore. He knew that usually they would just drink beer and tell ghost stories while they were there, but there were the occasional punkish delinquents that did things like the graffiti that they saw before them. "Some things never change," he said, shaking his head.

"Did you?" Sophia stepped closer to the corner and snapped a photo of the remains of the adolescent mischief.

Levi looked at her.

She turned to face him. "When you were a teenager, did you ever come here to hang out?"

"One time," Levi told her. "It was on Halloween night and we thought that it would be cool to come out here like all the other kids at school. Like I said, every kid in Devlin goes through that stage. I guess it's kind of a rite of passage around here. The ghost of Anna Moore is a great example of a small town legend that never seems to die. The town council even found a way for Anna to be in the haunted house that they put on every year at Halloween."

He thought back to that particular final night of October. It had been unusually cold that year. He remembered how he had sat against one of the brick columns and watched as Claire and Diesel were sitting on the ground across from him, scrunched close together. All of them had been drinking beer. Each of them was at the age where they no longer dressed in costume. Instead, due to the weather, they wore their heavy winter coats. Earlier that night they had been to the annual haunted house in town. *The House of Nightmares* was put on each year in one of the abandoned buildings that stood along the square. It was an event that the kids around Devlin eagerly anticipated as All Hallows Eve grew near.

Back then, the relationship between Claire and Diesel was brand new and until that night, Levi hadn't even known. They hadn't told him; it had only become evident to him as he saw the way they touched one another.

As they had entered the final room of the haunt, a room that had been constructed to resemble the old church, Claire's arms were by then wrapped tight around Diesel's waist. The room had been done with incredible detail. The wood, the old windows, it felt like the set of a Hollywood movie. Claire screamed when the woman dressed as Anna Moore unexpectedly banged into the room carrying a fake butcher knife. The woman was wearing a time period appropriate dress. Where here heart would have been, the front of the dress was drenched in blood.

By then, Levi was already in love with Claire, and it ripped at his heart to see her clinging onto Diesel like she was. Just as neither of them had told *him* what was going on, he had not spoken about his feelings for Claire to anyone, not even Diesel. But evidently, Diesel had felt the same way. As the night progressed, Levi watched as the two of them barely took their hands off one another. It made Levi wonder how long it had been going on. Why hadn't they told him? It made him realize that he was too late. And that was the problem he thought, Diesel had acted first. It was that Halloween night that Levi first saw the signs of their friendship falling apart, that he realized that when they had been younger they had been wrong; a girl *would* come between them.

"What supposedly happened to Anna anyway?" Sophia stepped closer to Levi. The sound of her voice brought him back from the night where it was believed that the border between the living and the dead was at its thinnest, where the past and the present were closer than ever.

"The story goes that Anna was in love with the preacher of the church. She was crazy. She was so obsessed with him and so determined for his heart to be hers that when he refused to give her the time of day, she came here to the church. The preacher was here by himself and Anna cut out his heart and took it with her. They say that several of the more vengeful members of the church's congregation tracked her down and did the same to her. There's another twist to the story that says that before *she* was buried, they sewed a summer squash in her chest cavity where her heart would have been."

"Why?" Sophia scrunched her nose at the gruesomeness of the tale.

"I'm not sure why." Levi shrugged his shoulders. "That's the story. And they say that because of the evilness that was inside of her, a squash plant that was full of disease blossomed up from her grave. It is from that plant that the disease comes every few years that kills all the town's squash crops. A vengeful Anna supposedly roams around this area of land, searching for the preacher and her heart, harming anybody that gets in her way."

"Spooky," Sophia said with an exaggerated, scared tremble in her voice. "And have *you* ever seen her?"

"I haven't, but there are people around town that supposedly have. I do remember one time though when I was little and there was some sort of blight that struck all the squash crops in Devlin. It killed almost all of them. That scared the crap out of me." He laughed. "I just knew that it was because of Anna that all the plants were dying. And as I was saying, the kids of Devlin love to come here to this place and scare one another."

From the church, they began the short drive back into town. The car crept around the dangerous curve of Hollyhock Lake. That summer, the namesake flowers grew in abundance by the road, some of them taller than the car. The blossoms were various shades of purple, pink, and white. The late afternoon sun tore into the windshield. The sky was the color of fire. From the passenger seat, Levi scanned the landscape that was outside his window. The perimeter of the pond was overgrown. The water was still and reflected the sun with a fierce intensity. The guard rail was dented and scraped from other cars that had had the misfortune of losing control. Black tire marks were on the road where someone had slammed onto their brakes after the severity of the turn had taken them by surprise. It was where Maxwell and Violet, among many others had crashed. Of course the marred guardrail wasn't the same that Maxwell's car had crashed into that long ago, fateful night. That one had been replaced many years earlier. The curve was so sharp that Sophia, not used to the road, slowed to a near crawl.

They had a brief stop at the house where they retrieved Craven. Together the three of them walked past Mallard's house. From the other side of the chain link fence of Mallard's back yard, the Rottweiler barked at them. The large dog stood on his hind legs and propped his front feet on the fence in an intimidating gesture. Levi and Sophia walked down the short stretch of road until they came to the path that led to the acre of land that they had set out for.

They stepped off the road and through the tall weeds. Levi pushed a low hanging branch to the side, letting Sophia through. Just as he had the day before, Levi followed the meandering footpath that led through the brush. The narrow creek ran along the ground at their side. There was brackish rainwater still standing in the bottom of the creek.

"This is Mercer Creek, but I don't know if it is technically big enough to be a creek," Levi told her.

"So you think size matters?" Sophia looked at him.

Levi laughed at her question. "What?"

"Men always worry about size," she said matter-of-factly, shrugging her shoulders. "If it's supposed to be a creek then let it be a creek," she said.

"OK, you're right. It's a creek. So let me get this straight." Levi pondered his next words, trying not to sound *too* sexual. "If size *isn't* important, then it is what you do with it that matters?" He laughed at his own, age old, lame, juvenile joke.

"Well, actually yes," Sophia answered honestly

"Oh, really?" Levi stopped walking and faced her with a raised eyebrow. He was smiling, enjoying the erotically tinged words.

"That's the way it is about everything. This creek," she pointed to her side, "memories, the past, the present, life in general. It *is* what we do with it that matters."

"OK, then," Levi nodded. "Understood," he said.

By then they had reached the clearing. He watched as Sophia immediately raised her camera and began snapping photos.

"So this is *the unclaimed acre*," she said as she twirled around, taking it all in.

"Yep, this is it." Levi looked around at his surroundings. "I think I might change that title, though," referring to the story he had written.

Sophia lowered the camera from where she was trying to get a shot of the tree house at just the perfect angle. It appeared to Levi that the way she was shooting it would allow the garden shed to be seen in the background. It was like she wasn't trying to hide the monstrosity's existence, but showing its relevance. It made him proud to feel like he was beginning to understand the whole art thing.

"Why?" Sophia looked at him. "I think it's good."

Levi sighed. "I don't think I even mention that phrase in the entire thing. I think I could rewrite and rework the story *forever* and not be able come up with a scene or something that really makes the title work. I don't know if people would see the significance of it. I agree that it's a good title, but do you think it's kind of forced?"

"Maybe the problem that you're seeing is in the structure of the story," she suggested.

Levi looked at her, wearing a confused expression on his face.

"If it was a romantic movie, there would probably be one more pivotal scene that takes place here. It would be where the main character's story arc would lead him to one more time. It would be where he would come to the realization that what he wanted had been right in front of him all along. It's where he would make amends with the past and accept it for what it was. It would be a scene where he realized just how important of a role the unclaimed acre had played in his life, and how he wouldn't change any of it. Anyway, I think I like the title. And really, does the significance have to be spelled out for everyone?"

As they began walking back, the sky had already turned to the color of dark washed jeans. Levi thought about what Sophia had said. He realized that *he* was beginning to accept the past for what it was. He knew that he was in love with Sophia and that everything that had happened on that piece of land, the good *and* the bad, had in one way or another led him to where he was now. And he wouldn't change any of it. He did wonder though, if the acre of land *hadn't* been unclaimed, if instead it had belonged to someone, would any of it ever had happened. Would he and his friends even have built the tree house in the first place? Would Sarah have fallen in love with Thomas way back in the 1800's?

By the time that they got back to the house, the sky was an even deeper blue, an almost black. Levi was just coming back outside through the front door with two beers in hand. He sat down beside Sophia where she was already sitting on the porch swing. Craven was underneath the seat. Several empty bottles were already neatly lined along the floor boards against the wall. The porch light was off. The only light came from the stars and moon that were now fully visible and shining through the trees. A cardboard box was on the porch near the swing where it had been placed an hour earlier. The top flaps were splayed open. Sophia had been looking at the objects inside: the sea shell, the photo of Maxwell, the flyer featuring Bonnie dressed as a mermaid, the almanac, and the package of seeds.

"So I don't think you've told me yet, where did the pack of seeds come from?" She asked him as she held the paper package in her hand.

"Lucine." Levi told her how his grandmother had given the seed pack to her own daughter, Jill. "She told her that if she ever needed to know the truth, then all she had to do was rip it open and all would be revealed."

They sat that way a little while longer, drinking beer, and talking.

"I've got it," Sophia said excitedly. "You like beer, so why don't you start a brewery?"

"Really?" He looked at her across the width that separated them. "How do you come up with these ideas?" First it had been writing a book and now it was starting a brewery.

"People do it," she said. "It's *not* that far fetched of an idea. Have you ever tried home brewing?"

"Actually, I bought a kit one time, but it never even made it out of the packaging," he told her with a chuckle and then sipped from his bottle.

Sophia laughed.

It was true. Several years earlier, he had bought the home brewing kit simply because it had been on clearance at the department store. At the time, he had been genuinely interested in trying it, but work and other things had gotten in the way and so it had remained in the box, at the back of his closet ever since. Actually, it was currently at the back of *Paige's* closet.

Now with what Sophia had mentioned, he imagined owning a brewery. In the vision, he wasn't the least bit surprised to see Sophia standing among the tall, silver tanks and equipment.

When it came time to go inside, Levi held out his hand to Sophia. She placed her hand in his and he pulled her up. They stood that way, with their hands together, for only a brief moment before their lips met for the first time in eighteen years. It didn't take long for the soft kiss to turn more needful for each of them.

"Let's go inside," Sophia whispered as she finally pulled herself away.

Levi led the way and Craven followed behind them. Just moments after the door was closed, they began undressing each other in the living room. Levi eased Sophia back onto the couch. It was something that each of them had been craving so hungrily that the act only lasted a few minutes before Levi collapsed on top of her.

"I've been looking forward to that," Sophia said.

"You have?"

"Don't sound so surprised. You haven't?"

"Yeah, I have."

"That's what I thought."

IV

Saturday…

YELLOW. IT is a color of hope and happiness.
    Another connotation of the color is one of danger.
    When Levi woke up the next morning the world seemed to be full of yellow; the sunlight that reflected against the hardwood floor, the hair of the woman who still slept peacefully beside him; outside, even without seeing a single glimpse of it, he knew that the town square was swathed in the color, anticipating the start of the day's festival.
    Levi looked at Sophia. They had fallen asleep on the couch and that was where they had remained all night with their limbs intertwined with one another's. It was still hard for him to comprehend how everything that had happened in the past had led him to be with her. It had been nearly eighteen years since they had met for the first time. Over those years they had not spoken once, yet there they were.
    Like most mornings at about that time, Craven whimpered at the door, wanting to be let out. Levi stood from the couch and began pulling on his pair of jeans that had been left in a rumpled pile on the floor.
    "Good morning," Sophia's voice came from behind him as he was fastening the button.
    "Good morning," he said and when he turned around she was already sitting up on the couch. The thin, white blanket was draped over her bare flesh. He walked over to her and kissed her on the forehead.
    After throwing on his t-shirt and cap from the day before, Levi stepped outside with Craven. The morning air was surprisingly cool and dew was on the ground. In the distance, there was the

sound of the high school marching band as the kids were warming up, preparing for their big moment in the parade. Levi was standing on the porch, waiting on Craven to pee, when his cell phone came to life. Sophia was inside making coffee.

"Levi," (with a smile), "this is Kathy Anderson. Good news! The person that I showed the house to yesterday is interested in buying, but he seems to think that something may be wrong with the air conditioning unit. We can negotiate the repairs in the closing costs if you want."

It was too early in the morning for Levi to comprehend all that the real estate agent was saying. Interested, something wrong, and closing costs. It all made him feel anxious. "OK," he said. "How does that work?"

"Tell you what, (smiling again), why don't I send somebody out there, just to check things out. Are you going out to the festival today?"

"I was planning on it." Through the front door, Sophia stepped onto the porch and handed Levi a steaming mug of coffee. "Thanks," he whispered to her. Sophia leaned against the porch rail, holding her own cup of coffee in her hands. Both of the mugs were adorned with flowers.

"That's what I assumed," Kathy continued. "Let's see, he can probably be there this afternoon, but you probably won't even have to be there for him to check it. How does that sound?"

"That sounds great." After hanging up with Kathy, Levi looked at Sophia. "Somebody's interested in buying," he told her.

Sophia was quiet for a moment and then, "what do you think?"

Levi could hear the apprehensive tone of her voice. "What other choice do I have?"

☐

THE FESTIVAL was packed with throngs of people that had parked down all the streets that surrounded the square, including the narrow road that ran in front of the Stanley house. Levi and Sophia walked to the festivities and by the time that they reached the square, the parade was just beginning. As always, the high school's marching band led the parade. Cymbals, drums, saxophones, and trumpets beat and clanged down the street. Flags twirled, cheerleaders cheered, the town beauty queen smiled and waved to the crowd. Fire trucks, police cars, and ambulances drove slowly through the procession, each of them occasionally sounding their sirens. Local businesses had floats constructed on flatbed trucks and trailers that were pulled by green tractors. The people on the floats jostled about as they waved and threw candy to the kids. Most of the floats were festooned in yellow. Yellow drapes and ribbon, glitter, paint and paper decorated all four sides. The library, the funeral home, Jake's Hardware, Possum's, various farms, Mercer Creek Baptist Church, all and many others were represented. The veterinarian office had a float that featured patrons *and* their pets. Men and women held on to their beloved animals as they rode in the back of a pickup. Other people walked their dogs on leashes on each side of and behind the truck, they too a part of the show. The parade ended with the grand marshal. That year Levi was surprised to see that it was Mallard, *THE OLDEST RESIDENT OF DEVLIN*, the banner on the side of the car proclaimed. Mallard was riding in the back seat of a red convertible that had its top let back.

"Is that the man from yesterday?" Sophia asked, referring to the incident on the sidewalk the day before as she and Levi had been leaving the hardware store from where they had purchased plants, how Mallard had followed behind them insisting to talk to Levi.

"That's him," Levi answered.

As the car slowly crept past where Levi and Sophia were standing, Mallard's attention was drawn toward Levi. From the back seat the old man seemed to study him and Levi tried not to let his eyes meet with Mallard's.

All of Devlin was enamored with the sounds of the hoopla as the parade slowly made its way through the heart of the town. Around the square, people perused through the arts and crafts that had been made by the local talent. Crocheted blankets, jewelry, various knick knacks, baked goods, canned fruit and vegetables were just a handful of the items that were up for sale on each of the tables that lined the grassy block.

The food vendors seemed to feature squash that had been cooked every way imaginable. Fried, steamed, baked, grilled, casserole, soufflé, they had it all. For the more adventuresome, there were the more unusual options as well, such as fried squash blossoms and one truck even proudly advertised squash ice cream. Patty pan, straight neck, butternut, spaghetti; all those varieties of the vegetable were represented in some way or another, but it was the crooknecks that Devlin was known for. The line for *Mrs. Coleman's Famous Squash Casserole* was already wrapped around the corner. Mrs. Coleman was an old lady who had been cooking and selling the casserole in small containers at the festival for as long as Levi could remember. She always donated all her earnings to a good cause. No one ever discovered the secret to how she made it, and of course she refused to tell, but it was by far the most popular and sought after item at the festival year after year.

After waiting in line, Levi and Sophia finally reached the table. The tabletop was covered in a sky blue cloth that had a repeated pattern of yellow squash blossoms and green leaves printed all over it. Mrs. Coleman's daughter, who was also well up in years, was taking the money while Mrs. Coleman herself was happily handing the container of casserole, plastic fork, and paper napkin to each person, thanking them with a smile. It was the first time that Levi had been in that spot, taking the small bowl from Mrs. Coleman in a very long time, since he had been a kid. And as he took his and Sophia's from the lady's hand, the simple, long forgotten act filled him with comfort. Even though it had been so long, it was so familiar. He didn't quite understand why he did it, but Levi made sure that the tips of his fingers brushed against Mrs. Coleman's as the casserole was handed to him. It was something that even though he didn't exactly remember having happened before, he was sure that it *must've* happened at least one time in just that very same way.

☐

EVER SINCE the night two years earlier when he had had gone to the tree house in a drunken daze, the night that he had scratched through the sketched picture of Levi, Diesel had begun the upward climb toward sobriety. That night had been bad, *really* bad. In fact it had been one of his worst, *and* most embarrassing. After Claire had driven him home that night, that was after she had pushed him onto the ground, he had insisted that he wasn't leaving her car until she gave him what he wanted. Even though he knew now that the ultimatum had been out of line, at the time he hadn't meant it in a *crude* way, he had simply meant that he wanted for them to be together as a couple once again. But being drunk and not being able to put the appropriate words together, it had come out all wrong.

With his refusal to leave the car, Claire had called the police, and Cooper, who was the sheriff by then, was the one that had shown up. Cooper had to pull Diesel from the car by his arm and practically carry him into the house where he eased him onto the already unmade bed. It was only a brief moment before Diesel was out cold, lying on top of the blanket.

When he finally woke the next day, it was mid afternoon and the sun was shining vehemently through the window blinds at Diesel's bedside. He squinted his eyelids against the brightness. He realized that he had passed out while still wearing all of his clothes, including his boots. His head throbbed. His stomach was weak and sick; it nauseously sloshed with the hops, yeast, and fermented grain of all the beer and liquor that he had drunk the night before. The inside of his mouth felt clammy. What he had done had left an incredibly bad taste in his mouth. He carefully stood and began his way to the bathroom. He needed to pee and brush his teeth. The floor was cluttered with discarded clothes and shoes. He carefully stepped around the mess. By the time that he reached the toilet he had lost the battle with his stomach and he heaved over the porcelain bowl, eventually falling to his knees where he stayed for what seemed like an eternity.

After that day, he started rehab and hadn't had a single drink since. It was a victory that he was incredibly proud of. He wished that he could be the type of person that was able to enjoy the occasional drink here and there, and maybe one day he could, but he knew that for the time being he wasn't. Since that last night of drinking, he had gotten his life back in order and was better off than he had been in a long, long time. He felt healthy, his shop was doing good business again, and one of the things that he was *most* proud of was his daughter. Keegan had just turned eighteen. She had been living with Diesel for the past year. It had been Keegan's idea to move to Devlin. Her mother Julie, or *Jewels* as she was more commonly known, had moved away from the town shortly after becoming pregnant. The single night that he had spent with Julie had been a stupid mistake, one of many. It was the summer before he and Claire had become a couple, and it had been just once, and as dumb as the hook up had been, something good *had* come from it, Keegan. Over the years, Julie didn't let Diesel have much to do with their daughter, but as soon as she was able to, Keegan had made her opinion very clear. She wanted to live with her father. That fact alone made Diesel happy, that even though he had his own problems he was still more of a parental figure than the girl's schizophrenic, drug addicted, stripper of a mother. Then there was Keegan herself. She was enrolled at the local college, majoring in Media Arts. She had a job working at the grocery store. She was trying to make something out of her life and Diesel was profoundly proud of her.

And actually, Keegan was a big contributing factor in Diesel finding the ability to turn his own life around. He watched as she pushed herself to be something, even though many kids her age would have found it easier to fall into the same abyss as what she had grown up seeing. It made Diesel realize that he had to put his own past behind him and to not let it dictate what he did with the rest of his life. He knew that he couldn't keep beating himself up over it. And he had done just that, he had beat himself up for so long that he knew that it would eventually get the best of him and that it could one day even kill him. Over time he had reconciled with Claire and they had found a way to remain friends. He had watched from afar as Claire and Cooper started dating and eventually got married. And he was OK with it too. He realized that he and Claire were not meant for one another in a romantic way. He had even started dating someone new, a woman by the name of Susie that he had met at one of his AA meetings. He was even thinking about proposing to her soon.

For the past couple of days, from behind the steering wheel of his pickup, he had been seeing Levi all around town. Once at Possum's, once on the town square, and even once in the front yard of his house. Each time he had thought about stopping to talk, but had ultimately decided against it. He hadn't been sure how Levi would react to seeing him face to face. He had, after all, threatened Levi's life at one time and the way that he had acted way back then now filled him with humiliation.

Rumor had it that Levi was in town to settle things with the house and put it up for sale and Diesel knew that once the house was sold there was a good chance that Levi would probably never return Devlin. There was something that he needed to tell him, something that had been kept secret for way too long. He knew who had bashed his head in with the metal pipe all those years ago and he *had* known all along. He felt bad about keeping the truth hidden. Of course he could one day look up Levi's phone number and call him, or write it in an email or a letter, but he wanted to tell him in person.

It would be more appropriate. He needed to tell both of them, Levi *and* Claire. Diesel had put the truth on the back burner for a long time and he knew that it had been *too* long. He had always assumed that both Levi and Claire would always be around, but now it was evident that they wouldn't be. He also knew that with each day that passed it was becoming more important for him to get the weight off his shoulders once and for all.

As Diesel pulled up to the house, he saw that two cars were parked in the driveway. He knew that one of them was Levi's and the other belonged to the woman that was there with him. Diesel walked into the backyard just as he had done so many times before when he had been younger. Everything looked tidy. It was obvious that Levi had been sprucing the place up in an effort to sell. It was nearing dusk and the house's windows were illuminated with a warm yellow glow. From inside the house he could hear Levi's dog barking. Diesel was nervous with what he was doing, so nervous that his hands were trembling. Would Levi assume the worst? That he was there to finish what he had promised eighteen years earlier? Or would he discover that somewhere over the elapsed years that Levi, like him, had found a way to put all that behind him. But one of them needed to be the one to make take the first action at restarting their friendship.

And so Diesel hesitantly walked up the steps and knocked on the door.

☐

SURPRISINGLY, IT didn't take much convincing from Diesel for Levi to agree to the meeting.

Levi had been on the phone at the time, talking to Kathy Anderson.

"The AC guy found a problem. The duct work under the house is messed up. He said that one room isn't getting any air at all," she was saying.

That was why it was so hot in his old bedroom, Levi thought. It wasn't a residual haunting caused by him and Claire kissing after all.

"But like I said, we can work something out in the closing costs for the repairs," Kathy added.

That was when there had been a knock on the door. Once

again, Craven spun himself into a frenzy of barking and scampering feet. This time though there was no coffee mug on the table for him to knock over.

After getting off the phone with Kathy, Levi opened the door. He was more than surprised to see Diesel standing on the other side. But like he had always assumed there would be if the two ever saw each other again, there was no tension between them, instead Levi could tell by the other man's appearance and demeanor that all was OK, that he had moved past those days. It was impossible to explain, but just the simple fact of finally being face to face, Levi knew.

Diesel was wearing a nice pair of jeans and a collared shirt that had been tucked in. He wasn't wearing a cap. Instead, the jagged scar was clearly visible. It was as if he didn't feel like he needed to hide it any longer. It felt good to see him. Diesel hadn't stayed long, only long enough to fill Levi in on a few things, that over the past couple of years he and Claire had gotten divorced, that Claire had married Cooper. Since Levi no longer had any connection to Devlin, he hadn't known any of it until then. Diesel told him that there was something that he needed to get off his chest and he thought that while Levi was in town would be the best time. He wanted to tell him and Claire at the same time. As Diesel told Levi all of this, Levi thought that he had heard a tone in his voice that indicated a sense of urgency, that he felt that he needed to do it before it was too late. And so they agreed that they would meet at the hospital, in Claire's room.

The small, county hospital was located just outside of the town limits, nestled amid the surrounding woods. The seclusion made the hospital seem cozy. As Levi pulled into the parking lot he saw that there were not a lot of cars there. He parked his own car several spaces over from Diesel's truck. The sky was just becoming dark and the old fashioned lamp posts on the property had recently come on. After stepping out of the car, Levi and Sophia walked across the black asphalt and up the cement path that ascended the slight incline of grass and led to the hospital's sliding glass doors.

As the hospital doors slid shut behind them, Levi and Sophia stepped across the lobby. The inside smelled the way hospitals always do. Trying to describe the smell would be pointless as it was one that everyone already knew. A round reception desk stood in the middle of the white and gray tiled floor. Rubbery, elephant ear plants were growing healthily in planters all the way around the base of the desk.

After checking in, Levi and Sophia walked to the elevator that was located behind the desk area. When the door opened, a middle aged man wearing hospital scrubs emerged. He was pushing a wheelchair that carried an old man. Both the nurse and the man in the wheelchair smiled at Levi and Sophia. Levi's apprehension and anxiety worsened as the elevator went up. The range of possibilities of what Diesel needed to confess was staggering. Levi assumed that it had something to do with when they had been younger, but Diesel had given no indication of what it might have been. In fact, those days hadn't even been mentioned when Diesel was on the porch earlier in the evening. It had seemed to be a silent understanding between the two men that Diesel had put it all to rest. When the doors finally opened again, a starkly white hallway stood in front of Levi. Serene, framed prints of flowers and scenic beauty lined the walls. Aside from the occasional nurse, Levi and Sophia were the only ones walking the length of the hallway that night. Their steps echoed off the walls. From a door at the far end of the hall, Cooper emerged. He was wearing a pair of jeans and a red polo shirt. From the distance, Levi could see the silver badge that was clipped to his belt. A pistol in a leather holster was on the other side. Cooper didn't look in their direction. Instead, he turned and walked the opposite way and around the corner.

When they reached the door that was not pulled all the way shut, Levi could hear voices from the other side. He tapped against the door with his knuckles, careful not to push it inward.

"Come in," a surprised sounding, older female voice that Levi did not immediately recognize came from the other side.

Levi pushed the door open. There was the steady, rhythmic beep of machines. Inside the room, Diesel was the first person that he saw. He was sitting in a chair across from the bed. Claire's mother and stepfather were sitting in the other two chairs that were pulled close to the bed where Claire lay underneath the bleach white cotton blanket. After stepping inside, Levi eased the door shut behind him and Sophia.

From the bed, Claire was looking at Levi. She was smiling. Her hair was pulled back in a ponytail. "Hey," she said.

"Hey," Levi told her and stepped closer.

"This is Blythe," Claire said proudly.

The baby was tiny. She was snoozing against her mother who held her tight. Her unimaginably small hands and fingers were as pink as Craven's tongue. Levi smiled at the baby. "Hey there, Blythe," he said and gently touched her hand. "It's nice to meet you. My name's Levi. I'm an old friend of your mom's."

"Cooper just stepped out for a cup of coffee. He should be right back," Claire told them.

When Cooper returned, he looked as proud as he must've felt with being a brand new father. He walked to his wife and daughter. To Levi, the three of them looked like the picture of happiness.

All of them stayed right there and chitchatted for a while. There was no tension in the room. The past was never spoken of, but Levi still felt the silent understanding that everything was OK when Diesel and Claire looked at him.

"Well, Diesel had something that he wanted to tell us," Claire announced a moment later.

On cue, Cooper, Mr. and Mrs. Watkins, and Sophia all stepped out of the room, closing the door behind them, leaving Levi, Diesel, Claire, and Blythe alone in the room. Of course the baby was way too young to one day remember the upcoming revelation, but one day in the future, people would tell Blythe that she had been there on the day that Diesel had revealed the truth.

Diesel was still sitting in the chair across from the bed. Levi sat down in one of the others. "I did it to myself," Diesel said without much hesitation. "That night, with the pipe, it was me."

Levi couldn't help but to look at the scar. It was prominent in the horrible fluorescent lighting. It made him feel sick to imagine how hard and quick and how many times Diesel must've hit himself to cause enough blood loss to black out.

"I was so torn up over everything that happened that I did it to frame Levi." Diesel looked at Levi when he said it. Levi could see the sorrow in his eyes. "I did it to make it look like he had beat me up," he was looking a Claire now, "but afterwards, I couldn't go through with my plan." He clasped his hands together. "That's why I swore that it wasn't him that did it and made up the story about it being a woman. I realized how stupid it was, and for all these years I've just let it go." He sighed and looked from Diesel to Claire again. "I'm sorry for everything that I've put y'all through."

Years later, Blythe would tell her own grandchildren how long ago the actions of the desperate, love struck teenager had led to her parents, Claire and Cooper, meeting for the first time. She would tell them that she had only been one day old and still in the hospital, held tightly in her mother's arms, when the truth had been revealed.

Not much later, outside in the parking lot, Levi saw Diesel standing against the side of his green pickup. Levi wondered if Diesel was waiting on him.

"I need to go talk to him for minute, I'll be right there," Levi told Sophia as he handed her the keys to his car. Sophia walked to the car, unlocked the door, and sat down in the passenger seat.

Levi walked across the pavement to Diesel. Diesel stood up straight. Behind him there was a flash of distant lightning, the beginning of a summer storm.

"I'm sorry," Levi said, "for everything that I did." Soon after Diesel's revelation, it became agonizingly clear to Levi that he had yet to apologize to Diesel for what he had done way back then. And he needed to. He knew that it had been a brave thing for Diesel to bring the three of them together and make the confession the way that he had. Being in the room with Diesel and Claire had brought forth a new perspective. It was obvious to Levi that the two of them had moved on, and that *he* was the one that had been hung up on the past. All along he was the one holding the grudge, afraid to see Diesel or Claire.

Now he knew that he didn't want those friendships to slip out of his grasp.

Diesel smirked. "You know, all of that's in the past. It took me a long time to get over everything, but I did," he nodded. "I figured it all out. And I mean, it looks like everything turned out to be OK. We're all happy in the end."

Levi nodded in understanding.

"And I know the last time you saw me," Diesel continued, "I was a different person back then, but people change, Levi. I'm proof of that. To be honest with you, even just a couple of years ago, I thought I hated you. I was ready to kill you," he stated matter-of-factly, shrugging his shoulders.

Levi laughed. "I was the bad guy, Diesel." It was true. Levi *had been* the bad guy during the whole ordeal. Claire had been Diesel's girlfriend. Levi knew that it had all been instigated by him, by what he and Claire had done behind Diesel's back. "You had reason to hate me."

"But like I said, all of that stuff is behind me now," Diesel said.

"Sometimes, do you think that you wouldn't change any of it even if you could?" Levi asked. "Do you wonder if all that *hadn't* happened then we wouldn't be where we are now? Like you said, we're all happy."

"Yeah, sometimes I do," Diesel admitted.

Just a second after they parted ways, Diesel called Levi's name. Levi turned back around.

"Let's keep in touch, OK?" Diesel asked. "I would like to be friends."

Levi nodded. "I'd like that too." It surprised him how much things *had* changed, how just earlier that same day he had thought that he never wanted to see Diesel *or* Claire again.

"I'll talk to you later then," Diesel said and got into his truck.

From behind the steering wheel of his own car as he was driving away, Levi looked in the rearview mirror at Diesel's truck. It was idling in the parking lot. Diesel was on his cell phone.

"You know, it's weird how I was the one that went away and tried to escape all of this, but they stayed here in Devlin and it appears that they are the ones that made peace with everything first," Levi told Sophia.

From beside him in the passenger seat, Sophia said, "maybe being here is what you needed."

Before pulling onto the highway, Levi looked in the mirror one more time. Diesel's truck was still sitting in the same spot. The cab light was on and Levi could see that he was still on his phone. Whoever it was that he was talking to, he was smiling.

The first rain drops began falling from the sky. On the radio there was an announcement of a severe thunderstorm warning for the entire listening area.

☐

BY THE time that they got back to the house the brief rain shower had already ended, but according to the weather reports more was on the way. There was a manila envelope that was standing upright on the porch, propped against the door. The glow from the porch light illuminated the delivery. A length of binding twine had been tied around the slim package in a bow similar to the way that shoe laces are tied. Underneath the twine there was a yellow square of paper that had been stuck to the envelope at a catawampus angle. Levi's first name was all that was printed on the paper.

After opening the door and letting Craven out, Levi sat on the swing with the envelope in hand. Sophia stepped inside. In the black, starless sky there was the occasional flash of lightning and rumble of thunder. Levi untied the twine and lifted the flap that was folded over the back side of the envelope. Inside the package was a stack of white paper that had been clipped together. He fanned through the pages and recognized pretty quickly that what he was looking at was the story that he had written about his family. He was confused about what he was seeing. How had someone gotten a copy? Or did they break into his house and take *his*? Why and who would place it on his porch? He flipped back to the front page and saw that it was not the first page of the manuscript. It was a letter. The words had obviously been printed from an old fashioned typewriter.

Levi,

I read your story. The end is all wrong. I've been trying to tell you, but every time that I've tried, you've run away. It is evident that you've always thought that Lucine gave Maxwell the ultimatum of choosing her or Violet. That is not true. Lucine went there that night to end things with Maxwell and to tell him that she was pregnant with someone else's baby. After Maxwell and Violet died in the car crash, Bonnie and John fell into a deep depression over the death of their only son. When Lucine finally saw Bonnie face to face for the first time, she told her a lie, she told her that she was pregnant with Maxwell's baby, knowing that it would comfort the older woman. Sure enough, Bonnie said that it filled her with a new sense of hope because she knew that part of her son would live on. Bonnie was looking forward to the baby's arrival so much that Lucine kept putting off telling the truth, that the baby that she carried was not Maxwell's, that it wasn't Bonnie's grandbaby that she would deliver; that instead, the baby belonged to me. Lucine and I had been seeing each other behind Maxwell's back. We never married out of fear that someone would count backward and figure it all out, crushing Bonnie and John in the process. Lucine said that on the day when she saw John show the baby the farmer's almanac and tell her that it had belonged to her father, she knew then that she would never be able to tell. I, too, saw how much they loved that baby so I harbored this lie to protect them, to make them happy. I've kept this secret long enough and it is time for you to know that I am Jill's father, your grandfather.

With All Sincerity,
Mallard

P.S. If there is any doubt remaining about what I've told you, don't forget that you have the package of seeds, the ones that are able to reveal the truth

Could it really be true? Or was it simply that the man was crazy like he had assumed all along? Secondly, Levi wondered again about when and how the man had gotten the manuscript from inside the house. Before then Levi had been so caught up in everything else that had been going on that he hadn't even realized that it was missing. It was disturbing to think that Mallard had broken into the house and taken it with him. Levi wondered if he had been sleeping at the time of the intrusion. It made his skin crawl to think that someone, *anyone*, not just Mallard, may have been creeping around the house while he was dreaming. Regardless of whether or not any of it was true, the man *was* nuts, Levi reasoned. As he looked at the pages in his hand one more time, he imagined the man sitting all alone in his house late at night, surrounded by taxidermy animals, tapping his fingers away on an old black typewriter.

Levi placed the paper back into the envelope. He was in disbelief about all of it. This along with Diesel's revelation, and the one from Calvin from the day before was just too much for one weekend. According to what he had just read, most of everything that he had ever thought about his family was not true. This meant that genetically he wouldn't even be part of the family that moved to South Carolina from Vermont. He looked across the yard to Mallard's house. Aside from the soothing yellow glow of one lamp in one window the house was dark.

Levi wondered again, was Mallard really his grandfather?

But in a way it *did* make sense. Levi thought about all the stories that he had always heard about his family. He thought about how the older ones were more detailed, how he knew more about events dating all the way back to the 1800s than he did about the years surrounding his own mother. It was the recent decades that were vague, those dealing with Lucine, Constantine, Maxwell and Jill. All of this became very evident to him when he had been in the lake house and had written the narrative. He now knew the reason why: it was because everything that he had been told about the recent years was all based on a fib, a lie to comfort someone that had been hurt beyond repair. No one had even known the truth, no one except Mallard and Lucine.

"What did it say?" Sophia asked. She had come back

outside and was standing over him.

"A lot," Levi said and handed the envelope to her.

Sophia sat on the swing beside him. The first fireworks from the town square exploded in the dark, indicating the conclusion of that year's festival. The sky was filled with showers of red, blue, and yellow. Craven took a moment from where he had been lying on the porch to sit up on his haunches, hold his head high and howl into the night. Aside from the multicolored fireworks, lightning was now flashing in a closer proximity than it had been before.

As Sophia read, Levi stood from the swing and went inside. He didn't say where he was going or what he was doing. A moment later, he returned to the porch with the pack of squash seeds in his hand.

Sophia's mouth was hanging open, shocked at what all she had just read. She looked at Levi. "Do you think it's true?"

Levi held up the seed packet, "We're about to find out," he said.

He gently peeled back the sealed flap on the top of the pack, careful not to rip the entire thing in the process. Inside were the decades old seeds. He leaned closer to the porch light that was over his shoulder. He gently pressed the sides of the pack together so that interior was wider open, tilted his head, and peered inside. He could see that one side of the interior was blank and that on the other there was neat, cursive writing. It was the formal type of penmanship that had seemed to fall out of fashion over the years. Not wanting to rip the pack all the way open, it took him a moment of leaning toward the light at just the right angle, but he was eventually able to decipher every word of it. Mallard is the father, it said.

☐

THAT NIGHT, after snuggling up on the sofa once again, Sophia told Levi that Mallard's revelation wouldn't change anything about his past, that it would only add a new layer to his future.

When he finally fell asleep, Levi dreamed of being on a dirt road. It was night. Tall trees loomed on each side of him. He was alone except for the figure of the blonde woman dressed in a long white gown. She stood a good distance in front of him. Her back was turned. She looked over her shoulder in his direction. It was Sophia. She motioned for him to follow. This time his feet *were* able to move. He walked to her and clasped his hand around hers. Together they walked away, forward, toward the future.

☐

IT HAPPENED fast. It was a nerve wracking, heart thumping few minutes between Levi jolting awake from the loud noise that came from somewhere in the dark house and seeing the undecipherable, black clad figure that was rushing toward him. There was a scary blur of sounds. Craven was barking defensively. Sophia was screaming. There was a metal pipe and then nothing.

☐

WHEN LEVI first regained consciousness he had no idea where he was. In fact, there were only a few things that he knew for certain.
 One, the building that he was in was dark.
 Two, underneath the smell of old timber there was another. It was one of grimy auto parts. It was the kind of odor that sticks to the hands and the clothes of mechanics.
 And three, his head pulsated with agony.
 As his vision adjusted to the darkness he began to look around at his surroundings and realized that he was lying on a hardwood floor. From what he could tell through the resonating pain that shot from his cranium and throughout the entirety of the rest of his body, the confinement seemed to be that of a single room structure. He could see that on the other side of the windows, the sky was pitch-black. There was the occasional flash of distant lightning. The lightning was the first thing that caused him to begin to remember.
 Hadn't there been severe storm warnings for the area? Levi twisted his head to the side and winced with agony. Even though he tried, he wasn't able to stand. His wrists and ankles had been tied. The length of old binding twine itched where it touched his skin. Was he in some type of convention center? He looked up at the ceiling and saw that there was a simple x shaped wooden light fixture that held a single, flickering candle on each of its four arms. He thought that it was the type of thing that would've been used during colonial times. The fixture was hung by a much thicker piece of rope than what tied his wrists and ankles.

Even though the sight of the lighting fixture stirred on the fringes of familiarity, it wasn't Levi's current location that was brought to mind. Somewhere in his memory, a long time ago, the light was somehow associated with the small town where he grew up. That was it, the realization. He was in Devlin. Then bit by bit other pieces of *before* began to slam to the surface.

The last thing that he remembered before blacking out was being in his family's house. He had come back to sell the property. He could recall someone being in the house with him. It had been his assailant. The person had arrived unannounced. Levi could remember being surprised and terrified of the sudden entrance. It had only been a moment before he was attacked. He had not been able to see the face. All he could remember was seeing a dark clad figure approach him just before he was thwacked on the side of his head.

The impact had left a lasting impression. Even though he couldn't reach his hand up to feel the injury, he could tell that a huge knot had come up where the instrument had made contact with him. He could feel the blood and the heat radiating from the spot as it throbbed with his every pulse. Had it been a piece of wood that he had been struck with? It seemed more solid, a metal pipe maybe?

The increasing wind caused tree limbs to scratch at the outside of the structure. Levi wondered how far away from another person he was. He wondered if there were any houses nearby. He thought about screaming for help. His eyes scanned around the room. It seemed that he was indeed alone.

Where the hell am I? Levi thought about his surroundings and then it hit him. He had been there before. It was only a few short miles from where he grew up. Of course the last time that he had been there it had been on Halloween night many years earlier. He had been in high school at the time. He was in Mercer Creek Baptist Church. It was an abandoned building that had been rumored to be haunted for as long as he could remember. It was the place that all the kids dared one another to venture to late at night.

But who had brought him there now? And why?

At the opposite end of the building, one of the two doors swung open and a silhouetted figure stood in the entranceway. Levi could feel the other's glare on him. He could sense the hatred from across the width. He knew that it was the same person who had already knocked him unconscious and was now coming back to finish the intentions. Levi closed his eyes and wished for help. When he reopened his eyelids the figure was already standing over him.

Then he remembered that all that was left of Mercer Creek Church was nothing more than four brick columns. Levi remembered that he had actually been there earlier that same day. The building that he was in was one that had been constructed to resemble the original church. It was the set that was used year after year as the final room to *The House of Nightmares*, Devlin's annual Halloween haunted house. He remembered that he had been to the festival. He recalled seeing Diesel and Claire. He knew that the last thing that he remembered before falling asleep was lying down next to Sophia and wrapping his arm around her. He realized that he was only wearing his boxers and the white t-shirt that he had fallen asleep in.

As the figure standing over him became clear, he realized that it was a woman. She was dressed in a long, rustling petticoat and stockings. Her leather boots were laced up knee high. She had long, black hair that was as dark as raven wings. There was a dripping crimson splotch of gore on her left breast. It was where her heart *would've* been if she had one. But he knew that this woman didn't have a heart; it had been cut out many years earlier. It was Anna Moore that stood looking down at him. Levi looked to her face. The features were cast in shadow, but every once in a while the candlelight glimmered in the blackness of her eyes. Then there was the shimmer of silver near her mouth. The woman had a silver hoop that was looped around her bottom lip. It was a startlingly weird contrast to the period clothing. The piece of jewelry was also a jolt of recollection. Levi knew that he had seen her somewhere before. He realized then that the black hair wasn't real. The wig was slightly askew atop her head. Underneath the long, synthetic hair he could see the edge of the real hair color. It was bright blue.

Keegan Atwater.

part three
a tale of madness

I

"WHAT DO you get when you cross a teenage alcoholic with a future stripper? Me!"

It was a horrible, off color joke about herself that Keegan had come up with a couple of years earlier. It was a statement that she would tell anyone that would even halfway listen. Back then she had still been living in Columbia with her mother. Back in those days Keegan had helplessly watched as Jewels' life was ruled by methamphetamines. Most nights Keegan sat in her room and listened to her mother's heavy platform shoes clomping through the small apartment at all hours of the night. Day by day, through the thin walls she could hear the seemingly endless rotation of men.

Back then, Keegan hated her life. But as much as she hated it, she knew that she was not going to allow herself to fall down the same rabbit hole that her mother had so willingly swan dived into when she herself had been around Keegan's age. She would do whatever it took to escape that fate. As soon as she was of legal age to make her own decisions, Keegan moved to Devlin to live with her father. She knew that Diesel, like Jewels, had experienced his own struggles in the past. His was with alcohol instead of drugs. But he had recently made great strides in putting his life in order.

On the morning that she finally moved away, Keegan had stood in the tiny kitchen facing her mother. A large duffel bag was thrown over Keegan's shoulder. She was wearing a black tank top, a cut off pair of jeans, and a tall pair of scuffed combat boots; her hair was purple at the time and was tied up into two girlish pigtails. Jewels was sitting at the table. A steaming cup of coffee was in front of her. A twirl of smoke drifted up from the cigarette in her right hand. Her pink nails were nearly neon. The kitchen smelled of grease, coffee, and cigarette smoke. Jewels' bleach blonde hair was a frizzy mess of just waking. She still had on the previous night's way overly done makeup. Her eyes were painted in black. Her lips were red. Silver glitter covered her flesh. She was wearing a too large plain white t-shirt. Her feet were pulled up into the chair's seat and Keegan could see that she was wearing a lacy, pink pair of underwear. It was a scene that looked like early morning, but it was already after three in the afternoon.

"Keegan, what are you going to do?" Jewels asked her daughter and took a long drag from the cigarette. She flicked the ashes into the nearly overflowing ashtray that was centerpiece on the table. "I already told you I can get you a good job at the club." She took another hit from the cigarette.

Keegan had just graduated high school the day before. The idea of her own mother suggesting for her to work at a strip club *would've* made her feel sick to the stomach, but the idea had been talked about and hinted at for so long that it no longer had that effect.

"I'm not going to be like you," Keegan said. Months later, Jewels' reaction to this statement would be one of the things that would bother Keegan the most. She never knew what her mother's reaction would be to anything. One minute she could be happy and the very next she could be screaming bloody murder. It would upset Keegan to think back on that day and realize that there had not been a single iota of hurt on her mother's face as a result of what she had told her. Instead, Jewels just rolled her eyes at the statement.

"Keegan, don't be ridiculous," Jewels said.

A man walked into the kitchen. He was not wearing a shirt, only a baggy pair of jeans. He stopped in the doorway and studied Keegan. At her age she was no stranger to the hunger of men's eyes and could tell that he was contemplating what he was looking at.

"Jewels, you didn't tell me that your daughter was so smoking hot," he said.

Not saying another word, Keegan walked out the door.

Of course she had been to Devlin before. She had been there on various occasions to visit her dad, but it was something that her mother hadn't let her do very often, regardless of the fact that out of the two parents, it was Jewels that had proven to be the most unfit.

"Your father was a mistake that I made, simple as that. I hope you never do something so stupid," Jewels had told her daughter one time.

Devlin seemed like an OK kind of place. The town itself was small and not a lot seemed to happen, but there was a local college that she could attend and that was exactly what she intended on doing.

    Her father had been more than welcoming for her to begin living with him. He had already told her over the phone that she would have her own room in the small house and by the time of her arrival he had already cleared it out for her. When she walked into the room for the first time she placed her bag on the floor and marveled at what she saw. Like her future, it was a blank slate that she could do anything with. It didn't take long for her to decorate the walls with posters and magazine covers. The house was the same that Claire, her ex stepmother had once shared with Diesel. Keegan had liked Claire, she had grown up knowing her, but the relationship hadn't worked out. Keegan didn't know the details of what happened, but she had seen so many different men with her mother over the years that she thought that it was nothing out of the ordinary for her to see the relationships of adults crumble into nothing.

    One day she found a necklace in the bottom of an old cardboard box that was crammed full of memories. The length of black twine was underneath several high school yearbooks, photos of her father together with two of his friends from when they had been teenagers, an old wrench, a handwritten play, a glass jar that was full of beer caps, and the yellow page from a carbon copied receipt that had been written and signed in Diesel's father's handwriting.

    Her father told her that the necklace had once belonged to Claire and that he had made it for her himself. A tiny glass bottle was tied onto the twine. In the bottle there was a floating insect, a mosquito. Diesel told her that she could have it, that he was sure Claire wouldn't mind. Sometimes she would lie on her bed at night and twirl the bottle around between the tips of her fingers, studying it, admiring the way the overhead light sparkled through the glass. She imagined that it had been made just for her.

    She started college in the fall semester. She was a Media Arts major with the intention of working on movies one day. She found a part time job working as a cashier at the town's only grocery store. She didn't particularly like the work, but the job would help pay for school and give her a little spending money.

    At the grocery store was where she met Jason. He worked in the produce department. It didn't take long for each of them to realize that they had a shared interest in horror movies. It was

Jason's idea to make a short video about Devlin's legend of Anna Moore. Over the years Keegan had heard bits and pieces of the ghost story, but together the two of them immersed themselves into the tale. They went to the ruins of the church. They checked out books from the library and researched both the legend and the time period on the internet.

Many people said that the woman's life was a tale of madness. It was stated that Anna's own mother had been mentally ill. Many people thought that Anna had inherited the sickness from her mother. Reading these things made Keegan afraid; it made her pulse race. Would it be possible that she would one day succumb to the same psychotic mental state as *her* own mother, Jewels? That it would all be out of her control?

Over the years, Jewels had shown many symptoms: the drugs, the promiscuity, the sleeplessness, the mood swings, and the hallucinations. One time Keegan had walked into the kitchen to discover Jewels carrying on a conversation with someone that wasn't even there.

It was after becoming sick with malaria that Keegan began having hallucinations. The disease was extremely rare for South Carolina, but occasionally it did happen. The recent rainfall had caused an overly abundant mosquito population that year. It was so bad that you couldn't walk outside as dusk neared and not get attacked by the tiny winged vampires. It was through one of these bites that Keegan contracted the disease. At night, her fever was sky high. It caused her dreams to be extremely vivid. Sometimes when she awoke she wasn't sure what was real or what had only been in a dream. In one dream, she was lying on the bed and a mosquito that was the size of a housecat was perched on her chest. The insect plunged its abnormally long stinger into Keegan's chest. The pain was unbearable. She knew a little bit about piercings and recognized the circumference of the stinger to be close to a fourteen gauge barbell commonly placed in the tongue. In the dream she knew that the mosquito wasn't drinking her blood; it was infecting her with the same mental sickness of her mother.

When she woke up, the dream lingered. Due in part to the fever she began to become more and more concerned that she was losing touch with reality. Her thought process and rationale began to become random. She became increasingly paranoid that she would one day end up crazy. She started thinking that everybody was out to get her.

    She didn't know that the drugs that she was taking for the malaria could cause an onset of psychosis in people that were already susceptible to the mental state. Over the weeks that followed she seemed to be on the brink of losing it every moment of every day. Even though the symptoms of malaria slowly went away, the drugs crashed her mind. If before she had been immersed in the legend of Anna Moore, now she was living in that world a good portion of the time. She began to understand Anna's reason. What the woman had done had been out of love. She wanted the man's heart and so she did what any strong woman *should* do, she took it. In Keegan's delirium, it all made sense.

    She had remained on that delicate brink between this and that until the night that she finally lost the battle. She and Jason were shooting their video. Keegan's own grandfather, Diesel's dad, had the haunted house set, the one of Mercer Creek Church, stored in the shop behind his house. One afternoon, she and Jason had put the four walls together. Because of the way that it had originally been built the construction had been easy for them. The frame just simply had to be bolted together. They placed the ceiling across the top of the four upright panels and hung the light. They placed the lightweight, pressboard podium at the far end. The floor was several wooden panels that had hardwood slats nailed onto them.

    Keegan had found the Anna costume right away. It was hanging on a wire hanger from a metal pipe in the corner of the shop. The dress was covered in plastic. As soon as she put it on for the first time, she felt at home. She stood in front of a full length mirror and studied her reflection. The dress was blue. The bottom section had layers of crinoline underneath, causing it to poof out at the hips. The top was laced tight. It had long sleeves that covered her arms. Frills were around the neckline and wrists. There was a splotch of red paint on the left breast. The "blood" trickled down the front of the fabric. Keegan loved the shoes, a pair of knee high black leather boots that laced all the way up to her thighs. She pulled her own blue hair back and placed the black wig on top of her head. The transformation was complete and she hardly felt like herself anymore. Instead, she felt like she was on the outside looking in on someone else.

    After shooting a scene inside of the set of the church, she and Jason were on the road by Hollyhock Lake, one of the infamous areas that Anna's ghost was believed to linger. As apposed to Keegan's period costume, Jason was wearing a pair of jeans and a black t-shirt. Across the road from where Keegan stood, he had a video camera set up on a tripod. They had done a few test shots and each of them had loved the way that it looked. Behind Anna there was the occasional flash of distant lightning in the black sky. There had been a brief rain shower, the first of a band of storms that was supposed to come through the area, and the asphalt and ground were wet. The water glistened in the moonlight. When it was finally time to shoot, it was to be a simple shot of Anna walking along the water's edge, there was an approaching pair of headlights in the distance.

"A car!" Jason yelled from across the road. "We need to wait for this car to pass!"

As the car got closer, Keegan could see that it was not a car, it was truck. She watched from the side of the road as the trees behind the truck were lit in red. The person's foot was on the brake. She knew that where they were was considered to be a dangerous curve. It was only a brief moment before the entire world went crazy. There was the loud screech of the car's tires on the wet asphalt. The sound ripped across Keegan's heart. The driver must've applied the brakes too heavy. The truck spun on the black top. Keegan darted out of the way. There was the loud crash and scrape of metal against metal as the vehicle's side careened into the guard rail and bounced back off as if it were a ball in a pinball machine. Keegan had fallen to the ground and watched as the truck spun away from her, toward Jason. It all happened so fast. There was a crash of metal and shattering glass as the truck met its end against the trunk of a large tree.

Keegan stood from the wet earth and ran across the road. The truck was totaled. The back end was off the ground. The tire was still spinning. The scene was lit by the truck's still glaring headlights and brake lights. Smoke was coming out from the bent hood. Keegan recognized the truck. It was her father's. Her heart was pounding as she ran around to the passenger side. She didn't see Jason and realized just a moment later that he had been pinned between the truck and the tree. When she looked into the cab of the truck she saw that her father was slumped over. There was a lot of blood, too much blood.

That was when she lost it. She screamed into the night. Both of the people, the *only* two people that she truly loved had been taken away from her at one time. She had been on the fence of sanity and something else for so long, but at that precise moment she fell headfirst into the world of madness.

II

SOPHIA! LEVI knew that he had to find her. As more pieces of memory came back to him he recalled how he had been sleeping at her side earlier in the night, just before this crazy, looming girl that was dressed as Anna Moore had attacked him, and presumably both of them, him *and* Sophia. He knew that he *couldn't* let anything happen to Sophia. He hoped that it wouldn't be too late, that something unthinkable hadn't already happened to her. He knew that he had to fight back.

Keegan stood over him. He saw that she held a metal pipe in her hand. He wondered if it was the same pipe that she had already used to hit him with. She was the picture of insanity. The costume that she wore was not only covered in what he knew to be theatrical blood, but also dry, cakey mud. Her makeup was streaked down her face where she had been crying. For the first time he noticed the loose black twine around her neck and knew without a doubt that the preserved mosquito that the small glass bottle held was the same one that Diesel had put there when they had been kids, the one that *he* had shown Diesel how to do properly by using glycerin instead of mouthwash.

"All of it is your fault," she said and began pacing the floor in front of him. She repeatedly swung the pipe against the open palm of her free hand, making a sickening slap of flesh in the otherwise quiet setting. "When he saw me he must've thought that he was actually seeing *her*, the ghost of Anna. That must be why he crashed."

"Who? What are you talking about? Who crashed?"

She quit swinging the pipe and held her hands out to the sides. "My father you idiot!" She stepped closer to Levi again. "He and my boyfriend are both dead because of you."

Was it true? Was Diesel really dead? Levi twisted his hands, still trying to loosen the twine that tied them together behind his back. He wiggled his feet, attempting the same with *that* piece of binding. "How is it my fault?" He asked through the grunts of attempting to free himself.

Keegan sighed in frustration. "This whole chain of events is because of you."

Levi looked at her in disbelief.

"I don't know the details, but I do know that the scar on his head was caused by something you did when y'all had been kids. He told me that," she nodded her head. It was true. Diesel had told his daughter that the scar was a result of an incident from when he and Levi had been younger. He didn't tell her why, just that it had happened because of a girl. Keegan didn't even know that the girl in the story was Claire. "I got a phone call from him earlier tonight."

Levi remembered driving off and seeing Diesel talking on the phone as he sat behind the steering wheel of the idling truck in the hospital's parking lot. He had been talking to Keegan.

Keegan began pacing the floor again. She was slapping the metal pipe against her other hand like before, but this time it was more forceful, louder. Thwack...thwack....thwack. "He said," thwack, "that he was in," thwack, "the hospital parking," thwack, "lot and that," thwack, "he had set," thwack, "things right," thwack, "with you." She turned to face him, holding the pipe at her side. "He wouldn't even have gone to the hospital; he wouldn't have even been out on that damn road if it wouldn't have been because of YOU!" She lifted the pipe over her head.

Levi hoisted himself up by his elbows and swung his entire body around. His untied legs met Keegan's, tripping her. She fell to the floor. The metal pipe clattered to the hardwood. Levi got to his feet and kicked at Keegan. His foot met her stomach and she twisted her body in pain. Levi, with his hands still tied behind his back, ran. He went through the doors of the constructed set only to realize that he was in another, much larger building. The floor was concrete. There was another door directly in front of him. The door was propped open. He ran and when he crossed the threshold he was outside. The damp nighttime air felt pleasantly cool against his sweaty flesh. Still not recognizing where he was, he spun around to look at the building that he had emerged from. It was Mr. Atwater's shop. The unclaimed acre was straight ahead. It was the quickest way to cut through to his house. Lightning flashed. There was a loud rumble of thunder. He ran, ducking underneath vines and tree limbs. In the dark he couldn't see exactly where he was going. Thorns pierced and scratched at his flesh. Sand spurs and rocks jabbed at the tender flesh of his bare feet. By the time that he reached the clearing he looked like he had been in a fight with a feral cat. He heard a soft thump from within the garden shed. He looked and saw that the doors were closed. He noticed that there was an open padlock through the hinged latch. He glanced over his shoulder to make sure that Keegan wasn't in sight.

She must still be on the floor, he thought.

He leaned close to the door of the shed.

"Sophia?" he whispered, not wanting Keegan to hear him. "Sophia, are you in there?"

From within the structure he heard her voice. "Levi, it's me," she said.

"Open the door. My hands are tied," he told her through the thick plastic.

The door eased open and Sophia stood on the other side. She was wearing a pair of gray pajama pants and black tank top. She didn't have her glasses. The expression on her face was one of dread. Levi slipped into the shed. "Shut the door," he told her quietly. She pulled the door to. With the door shut, the interior was dark. It took a moment for Levi's eyes to adjust enough to be able to see. "Untie my hands," he said.

Sophia's fingers began working at the twine that was wrapped around his wrists. "She brought me to the tree house," Sophia whispered. "She said that she was going to burn the castle to the ground, just like you had written it."

Levi remembered the play that he had written when he had been a kid. In the story, an evil king trapped the princess in her castle and set it ablaze. The tree house had served as the castle.

"But first she said," Sophia continued, "that she was going finish with you. That was when she left. I don't know how, but I managed to untie myself. I didn't know where to go so I hid in here."

The twine fell from Levi's wrists and he wrapped his arms around Sophia. On the other side of the plastic walls there was a sound. Levi knew that what he was hearing was the sound of Keegan's long, dragging dress as it rustled against the tall weeds.

"Levi - ," Sophia started.

"Shh-shh-shh," he held his finger to her lips, hushing her.

Levi knew that he needed a weapon. He scanned his surroundings and all he saw were beer cans and the girly posters that had been taped to the wall. He could throw empty cans at Keegan and slap her with a glossy paper of some woman's tits. *That* should do the trick. Then he remembered that just next door in the tree house there was that old garden hoe that had been used as prop in the play.

Just then there was a thud against the side of the building. Sophia screamed. Just like he had been positive that he was hearing Keegan's dress dragging through the weeds earlier, Levi knew that what he was now hearing was Keegan hitting the plastic siding with the metal pipe.

Levi knew what he had to do. He kissed Sophia on the lips. "I love you," he said and hurled himself against the door. The weight of his body flung the door outward, ramming into his target. Keegan fell to the ground. Levi fell beside her. He scrambled to his feet and slammed the door shut. He slapped the latch over and closed the padlock.

Keegan was scrambling on the ground, still trying to get to her feet. Her hand clasped around Levi's ankle.

He kicked himself free and ran the short distance to the tree house. He saw that a red gasoline can was sitting on the ground at the tree's trunk. He reached in through the tree house's door, scanned the interior and saw what he was looking for.

The hoe was lying flat on the floor against the wall. He grasped his hand around the tool and when he emerged with the weapon, he spun himself around and saw that Keegan was standing across from him. She had an unusually large box of matches in her hand. The size of the box was so exaggerated that it looked like it too could've been used as a prop in a play.

Keegan fumbled with her fingers and pulled one of the long matches free. She ran the tip across the flint on the side of the box and a small flame popped to life. She looked at Levi and smiled deviously before tossing the match his way. Just a second later, orange flames shot up all around Levi, making it evident that she had already drenched the ground with the gasoline.

Levi held the hoe firmly in his hands and readied himself for what he was about to do. He looked at the weapon and saw that the sharp end was pointing upward. He knew that if he hit her against the head it would surely kill her. He wondered how he could do what he was contemplating to another person. He didn't even know what her full intentions had been. Was she going to kill them? Or in some sick way was she trying to teach him a lesson?

He spun the handle around in his hands so that it would be the blunt end that he used. From within the circle of flame he looked up at Keegan. It was the first time that he had gotten a really good look at her since lying helplessly tied on the floor. The wig that had been askew was now nearly falling off. Her blue hair was visible and falling out from underneath the black in crazy strands. Her face was streaked with tears and mud. The dress was filthy. The orange flames gave her an appropriately sinister look. The fire shimmered against the silver hoop around her lip. She wobbled on her feet, presumably from both pain and mental hurt. She moved the arm that was holding the pipe and looked toward the closed door of the garden shed. Levi raised the hoe and ran forward through the fire. He swung the garden tool toward his target. The sickening thump was like hitting a watermelon. Keegan immediately dropped the pipe and fell to the ground.

He didn't have the key to the lock on the garden shed door, but Levi could see that if he didn't find a way to get Sophia out that it was likely that she would succumb to the fire as the flames were inching closer every moment. With the sharp end of the hoe, he swung and hit at the padlock and the clasp. The blade scraped against the plastic of the door and dinged against the other metal. From the other side of the wall he could hear Sophia scream.

"It's me," he said. "I'm going to get you out."

Finally, the entire clasp finally fell loose. Levi threw the hoe to the ground and swung the door open. Sophia ran into his arms.

By then the fire had spread across the ground. The flames had caught on the bottom of Keegan's dress. The girl still lay unconscious on the ground. Levi knelt down and grabbed onto her arms. He pulled her safely away from the fire and stomped out the flame that had caught on her clothing. He walked back to Sophia and wrapped his arm around her waist. As they began walking, just as it seemed that there were no coincidences, that every event was caused by another, the sky opened up, drenching both them *and* the fire. And by the time that they made it to the road, all of the flames had already been extinguished and there was only thin smoke drifting upward. The tree house, the land, and Keegan had all been saved.

LOST DOG.

It was something that Levi had hoped that he would never have to print on a flyer, but when he and Sophia made it back to the house he discovered that during the home invasion both the gate to the yard and the front door had been left standing wide open.

Craven was nowhere to be seen.

Levi walked into the house and picked up his phone from where he had left it on the coffee table. As he called the police, Sophia found her glasses. There were several officers that responded to the call, Cooper was among them. They questioned both Levi and Sophia about the night's outlandish events. From where they sat at the kitchen table they heard the siren of the ambulance as it was rushing away and knew that Keegan was in the back. The flashing red lights shone through the windows. By the time that all was settled, the sun was already rising. All the commotion had caused several residents of Devlin to emerge from their homes early that morning and stand on the sidewalk, observing. From the porch, Levi and Sophia watched as the men and women pointed and whispered to one another, knowing that gossip would be spreading as soon as alarm clocks began to blare. He spotted Mallard standing among the small crowd. The old man was dressed as usual in a black suit and tie. The fedora was on his head. His Rottweiler was at his side. When Levi looked closer, he saw that the man's other hand, the one not holding the large dog's metal chain, held a leash that led to the collar of a basset hound, Craven.

Mallard walked away from the crowd and into the yard. Craven scampered along at his side, running toward Levi.

"He was sleeping against my fence when I got up this morning," Mallard said. "He was on one side and she was on the other," he motioned toward the Rottweiler. "She was lying right up against the fence by him." He handed the leash to Levi.

The fact that Craven was safe and sound made Levi happy beyond words. He took the leash from Mallard and knelt down by Craven. He patted the dog on top of the head. When Levi stood back up, Sophia was standing beside him. She placed her hand on his lower back. Levi was eye to eye with Mallard.

"Thank you," Levi said. "I really do appreciate it."

Mallard nodded, knowing that it wasn't only the safe return

of his dog that Levi was thanking him for.
It was also for telling the truth.

epilogue

Five years later…

AN EXCERPT from a local business magazine…

    Unclaimed Acre Brewing Company is owned and operated by Mr. and Mrs. Levi Stanley of Devlin, South Carolina.
    "It was my wife's idea. Sophia insisted that I finally use the home brewing kit that I had purchased a long time ago," Levi said with a laugh. "I don't know if she just got tired of seeing it around the house or what, but she convinced me to finally try it and since brewing that first batch, the rest his history. I just fell in love with the process. What I'm doing now just stems from that. It's just on a much larger scale now."
    Levi and his wife, the artist Sophia Forrest Stanley, moved to Devlin three years ago. The couple is expecting their first child in the spring. When we spoke to Sophia, she only had great things to say about the small town.
    "I love it here. It's where Levi is originally from, so as a family we have a lot of ties to the area. We actually live in the house where Levi grew up. We have great friends. And it's right by the brewery. He definitely doesn't have a long commute."
    The brewery is located in a turn of the century home. The bottom floor is where the brewery is operated and the top floor has been transformed into a bar/tasting room that is open to the public Thursday thru Saturday from 3pm to 7pm.
    "It's actually the house that belonged to my grandfather," Levi told us about the building that the brewery is located in. "It was a strange turn of events. I didn't even know until the past few years that he was related to me, but five years ago he had bought the house that Sophia and I live in now. He bought it from me, actually. A couple of years later he passed away and left both this house *and*

his house to me. From there it didn't take much deliberating. I talked to Sophia and we both agreed that moving to Devlin seemed like the right thing to do. And so she and I, along with Craven, that's our basset hound, packed up and relocated here."

Changing subjects a bit, we asked Levi about the heavily publicized attack on him and Sophia. Five years ago a young woman by the name of Keegan Atwater was arrested for breaking into their home and violently assaulting both of them.

"You know, it was an unfortunate and scary situation. She's clearly unstable. I feel like she's getting the punishment deserved, but at the same time you kind of wonder about what makes someone do something like that. It's the whole nature vs. nurture question."

When asked about his relationship with Keegan's deceased father, Levi said that he had no comment.

Unclaimed Acre has been named as one of the top ten craft beer breweries of the South and the beer has won several prestigious awards.

"You know, I could've never predicted that it would be as successful as it is. We're just happy to be where we are," Levi told us. "I feel like I have finally found my place in the world."

discussion questions

☐   *Frankenstein* is mentioned several times throughout the novel. What are the various ways that misunderstood "monsters", some of which have been created by others, are represented within the book?

☐☐After reading what Levi had written, Sophia mentions that she sees a lot of Levi's own life mirrored within the text. What do you think she means by this and what ways to you see that the two are similar?

☐☐Various hereditary traits are brought up within the book; alcoholism and mental sickness among them. Do you think that the fates of the characters that were affected by these things were any more or less inescapable than those of the other characters?

☐☐Which of the characters do you think changes the most throughout the novel? The least?

☐☐Storms are mentioned several times as a driving force in the novel, pushing the characters forward. In what other ways did you notice that nature progresses the story?

☐☐Near the end of the book, Keegan discovers a cardboard box of her father's "memories". How does Diesel's box differ from that of Levi's? What do the contents of each box tell about the two characters?

☐☐How do you think the three big secrets within the book (Calvin's, Mallard's, and Diesel's) will alter Levi's future?

☐☐In the novel what are some of the ways that the knowledge of stories and lore plays a pivotal role?

☐☐The way that the past influences the present and future is important to the book. Within the novel, what do you think are the biggest events from the past that led to the eventual outcome of the various characters and the novel itself?

☐☐Do you think that Levi will put forth an effort to learn more about the past of the newly discovered side to his family? Would you want to know more?

Made in the USA
Middletown, DE
17 March 2017